I0721838

WITHOUT TRACE

WITHOUT TRACE

A GLYN JONES AND GRANDMA WILLIE MYSTERY

RAE RICHEN

Without Trace

Copyright@ 2024, by Rae Richen All rights reserved.
Published in the United States of America by
Back Beat Publications
an imprint of Lloyd Court Press

3034 N.E. 32nd Avenue Portland, Oregon, 97212
www.lloydcourtpress.org
Cover design by Diana Kolsky
Book Design by Amit Dey

Paper   ISBN: 978-1-943640-22-5
E-book ISBN: 978-1-943640-21-8

While inspired by actual societal situations, this is a work of fiction.
All characters and incidents in this book are fictionalized by the author.
Other than Willie, perceived resemblance to people, living or dead,
business establishments, events or locales is purely coincidental.

Publisher's Cataloging-In-Publication Data
(Prepared by The Donohue Group, Inc.) Names: Richen, Rae, author.

Title:	Without Trace / Rae Richen.
Description:	Portland, Oregon : Back Beat Publications, an imprint of Lloyd Court Press, [2024] | Series: A Glyn Jones and Grandma Willie mystery ; [1]
Identifiers:	ISBN 9781943640225 (paperback) | ISBN 9781943640218 (ebook)
Subjects:	LCSH: Young Adults, Drummers (Musicians)--Crimes against--Pacific States--Fiction. | Kidnapping--Pacific States-- Fiction. | Rescues--Pacific States--Fiction. | Organized crime-- Pacific States--Fiction. | Grandmothers and Grandsons --Pacific States--Fiction. | LCGFT: Detective and mystery fiction.
Classification:	LCC PS3618.I3455 W58 2024 (print) | LCC PS3618.I3455 (ebook) | DDC 813/.6--dc23

DEDICATION

To Clifford and Wilhalmena Williams for showing us how to create a life of infinite interests and of care for all who surround us. Thank you for leading the way.

CHAPTER ONE

THE YEAR 1997

TRACE AND TACO BELL

Sixteen-year-old Glyn Jones swerved the Camry over to the curb at the corner of Interstate Avenue and Killingsworth Street, Portland, Oregon. His passenger, Trace Gowen yanked open the door.

"Thanks, Man," Trace mumbled.

"You on something again?" Glyn asked.

Trace laughed the high laugh that Glyn knew too well. The laugh alone made a lie of anything Trace said.

"Go home and clean up." Glyn put the Camry back in drive.

Trace took the hint, climbed out, not too smoothly. He caught one long dread lock on the window handle, yanked it out, and missed the door handle twice before he got the car door closed.

Glyn glanced at the trash Trace had left on the floor of the car, a sack of Taco Bell wadded and crushed, an empty paper cup, rolling around on the floor mat. He decided not to get Trace to clean it up. Getting him out of the car became more important. Lately, Trace seemed to be on one drug or another and Glyn wanted the smell of it out.

Glyn hoped the pop container was empty. This was Mom's car.

He signaled a turn, pulled into the lane, and headed toward home.

He passed the corner on Fremont and Fifteenth where he'd picked Trace up and wondered why Trace had been in such a swivet. Five miles down Fremont Street, he heard his cell. He pulled it out of his pocket, swiped the face and answered, "Lo?"

He punched the speaker phone button and dropped it on the seat. "What up?"

"Bring me my stuff." Trace shouted.

"What stuff?"

"They'll kill me, Man."

"What stuff? Where?"

"In the Taco Bell. Hurry." Trace's voice cut off.

Trace's fear invaded Glyn's cocoon. He flipped around the next corner to the right, roared around the block and came out at a traffic light on Twenty-Fourth Avenue. At this hour, no one drove on Fremont, and he sat first in line, so he ignored the red, and angled into Fremont going back toward Trace. He felt the sweat on his hands as he smacked on his horn, urging the slow Volvo in front of him to regulation speed. Finally, he passed the old geezer and roared down the street hoping to make the green at Fifteenth.

He glanced down at the crushed bag. He didn't even want to know what was in it. Clearly, Trace had been sampling.

Another problem the guy would face.

Last week's effort by the fellows in the rap group had failed to get Trace to leave the drugs alone. Trace had heard nothing, cared less, and now he'd pay for it, big time.

Glyn and the Camry flew through the yellow at Fifteenth Avenue. At Eighth, he heard the siren.

"Hot damn." Glyn pulled to the right and parked. His mother's voice whispered in his head.

"Be polite, but don't over-do it. People suspect too polite."

How did Mom know that? He'd never asked, too embarrassed that she guessed he needed the advice.

He rolled down his window and waited. The policeman sat in his car, lights blinking, so anyone who passed would know he was in trouble. Lots of people in this neighborhood would know this car. Mom designed and installed nearly all the good- looking yards nearby.

Please don't be looking up State of Washington records, Glyn prayed.

The cop was taking an awful long time there. Glyn worried about Trace. What cut him off so fast? Where could he hide from anybody on that corner?

Finally, the cop opened his car door and approached the Camry.

"May I see your license?"

"Sure. It's in my back pocket." Glyn knew the police were always looking for kids to reach for guns. He heard enough stories from the band. That was how Markus's cousin ended up on a respirator. Glyn had the advantage of being white, but he also was under twenty, so who knew what ideas ran in this cop's head.

"Well, get it out," the officer said.

Glyn left his right hand on the steering wheel, rolled his butt up and reached into his left back pocket for his wallet. He handed it to the officer and tried hard not to glance at the Taco Bell. The officer flipped open the wallet and examined the photo ID.

"Cut your hair?"

"Yeah. Shaggy."

"So, you had some trouble like this in Washington State, right?"

"Yes, sir."

"Didn't learn much, I see."

"Not enough," Glyn said. *Come on. Come on!* He thought.

Trace was standing on that corner with nothing.

The cop glanced at the right-hand floor of the car. "A little early in the day for fast food, don't you think?"

Glyn finally took a moment to survey the sack on the floor. "I love grease," he said. "No grease in Mom's oatmeal."

"Don't I know. You ran a red and then a yellow and I clocked you at fifty-five in this thirty zone."

"Yeah, suppose I did all that."

"Ticket for that is expensive, my friend." And the patrolman ripped an already written ticket off his pad. Then he seemed to think better of handing it over. "Should I search your car?"

Glyn swallowed hard around the word "Sure. Shall I get out?"

"Nope. Want to hand me your keys?"

Glyn pulled them from the shaft and held them up to the window.

The man took them and went to the trunk, opened it and found what Glyn knew was in there – a short root pruning shovel, a pair of loppers, hand pruners, Windex and a roll of paper towels, plus a weed identification manual and a notebook list of invasive plants.

He came back around. "You a landscaper or something?"

"No. Mom. Those are her tools." Glyn kept his attention on the policeman's face and off the Taco Bell. He hoped the sweat wasn't evident.

The man handed him the keys.

"Jones, eh?" the officer said, staring once more at the ID. "Why the funny spelling for Glyn?"

"Those Welsh. They love the letter Y."

"Yeah, well drive the speed limit. You're pushing this old Camry beyond its capacity."

"Yes, sir."

The officer stared at him for an extra-long time. "You know," he said, "If this were your first, I'd have given you a warning."

"Yes, sir."

"You mean, Yes, sir, I won't do it again."

"Yes, sir, I won't be speeding anymore."

"Huh! Better not, cause next time is the charm." The man turned about and returned to his car, plopped inside, slammed his door and appeared to be making notes. Glyn waited a couple of seconds, to make sure he was dismissed. He imagined Trace standing on the corner of Interstate and Killingsworth, imagined all the cars in and out of the local Chevron, where they often met to use the back room for recording their hip-hop beats.

He imagined Trace waiting while the MAX, Portland's light-rail trains, hunkered north and south, stopping, rolling, stopping, rolling. He imagined the thugs Trace feared. In his mind, they pulled to the curb and Trace stood alone, without product.

He held the Camry to thirty until out of police sight, and then gunned it.

At Interstate and Killingsworth, Trace was not standing on the corner, none of the corners, nor the MAX platform, nor in the filling station.

Felipe Perez, manager of the filling station, said, "I ain't seen him. Nothing."

But Felipe surveyed the other attendants as he said this, and never looked at Glyn. The other guys and the one gal glanced away and wouldn't make eye contact either. They all knew Trace, drummer of the Ancient Nation rappers. And they knew Glyn and his computer-generated beats for the group. The guys and Anita looked tense, scared.

Glyn decided to let Felipe off the hook, and said, "Must have gone home. Can you give me a ten's worth of regular?" He handed Felipe a five, and five ones.

Felipe nodded and let air out of his tight body. As Felipe stuffed the hose into the Camry, Glyn called Trace's phone and got the forwarding message. Not even on. Then he checked his own phone. Trace had left a text.

"There commin."

He knew it was Trace. The guy never bothered with spelling distinctions. Glyn grabbed the trash from the floor and climbed out of the car. He started to toss the sack into the garbage can, but Felipe reached out.

"We recycle paper here," he said.

"Okay," Glyn couldn't figure. Felipe Perez seemed to be aware of what was in the bag. "You sure you want this? It's trouble."

"I'm just gonna say, "The kid left this on the ground when he drove in here.""

Glyn shook his head. "I don't know, Mr. Perez. Seems risky."

"Not as risky as having nothing. And it might save the kid."

"True. Has Trace used Taco Bell bags before? That how you know?"

"He's come to practice with his hand in such a bag and he's always a little loopy when he does."

"I hope this is the right thing," Glyn said.

"I send the guys and Anita down the block the back way if I see that car again. Meanwhile, I'll recycle that bag."

"Well, I hope you know what you're doin'," Glyn said, and he handed him the bag, well-aware that old food bags were not recycled in Portland. He said, "Trace needs your help, Felipe."

"Not seen Trace, I tell you. And that's what you tell anybody else."

"All right. Not seen him."

Felipe clicked off the gas nozzle. "That's a ten's worth of Gas."

"See you at rehearsal time. Maybe Trace'll show."

"Can't have you rehearsing here this afternoon."

Glyn studied Felipe and the others. "I'm outta here then. Be careful."

CHAPTER TWO

None of the guys had seen Trace since the Taco Bell situation the day before. Twenty-four hours and the Ancient Nation members had pressed all their connections. They'd come up blank. The guy was gone. They feared gone, as floating in the river, but none of them said it.

Leneld came closest to it. "Wish he'd just stepped into Darrell's Bar on the corner."

"Darrell wouldn't stand up to guys like that," Glyn said. "Yeah. Not for some strung-out black kid who was scared,"

Leneld added.

The guys were all afraid. Afraid for Trace and afraid to push the wrong buttons on the wrong people who might explode on them and on the people they loved.

The other consequence of Trace's disappearance was the loss of practice space, so the guys met now in Glyn's basement.

Which was good because that's where Glyn's computer sat, and if they were practicing, he could be writing beats for them at the same time. Easier to do on this computer than the laptop he took to the filling station garage.

Of course, today, there was no music happening. They were trying to figure out how to get Trace back safely.

With Dad off being a mathematician for an insurance company, and Mom designing gardens from her office on the second floor, they could talk pretty freely, as long as they stuffed the laundry chute with old sheets and fabric from Mom's quilting stash. Glyn knew she never used the grayed-down fabric other quilters gave her, so they stuffed in those old-looking fabrics. They'd decided they would un-stuff the chute at the end of this meeting and hide the stuffing material in a bag in the furnace room for future meetings.

Mom's office was in the room at the top of the chute, and she had good ears. Susan Stamps Jones was that rare designer who never listened to music while drawing gardens and deck- building details. So, her office had all the acoustic possibilities the band didn't need during serious talks.

Glyn studied the guys. Leneld, who always called it like it was. Lonny, always eager to please, because a white wanna-be. Markus, tall, flamboyant, sure, great with the artwork for posters and album covers.

Missing was Jon Wood, who hadn't shown up since the Taco Bell incident and was probably lying low for reasons only others could guess.

"Lonny," Glyn said, "From now on, can you help me un- stuff the chute when we desist? Easier for two."

"Desist? Where do you get these words? You're a twit, Glyn."

"Twit or not, you got a job."

"Maybe," Lonny said.

Leneld said, "You got a job, Lon." Lon slumped. " 'kay."

"We gotta figure Trace's last movements again," Markus said.

Leneld went over it. "His mom says you picked him up at their house, Glyn. You say he came out with the Taco Bell and actually ate the burritos in your car, so why do you think he had product in there?"

"It weighed."

"What? Ounces?" Markus asked, twiddling his drawing pen.

"I got no idea what it weighed," Glyn said. "You see a druggie scale down here?"

"Okay, weighed something," Leneld went on. "And you dropped him at the corner because . . .?"

"He asked. Assumed he was fiddling with his drum set before rehearsal."

"But, later, when you tried to toss the Taco Bell, Felipe wanted it," Markus said. "Why'd you hand it over?"

"Yeah, so we talked. I figured he knew, and had a way of getting it to Trace."

"Maybe he just wanted it for himself," Lonny said. "Felipe's not the druggie type," Glyn said. The others nodded.

"He's afraid of the stuff," said Leneld, "and for good reason."

"Did you ask about the drum set?" Markus asked.

Tall, gangly Leneld said, "Felipe unloaded those into my car this morning. Couldn't get rid of them fast enough."

"We can help unload later," Markus said.

Glyn said, "I got the speakers and the other crud yesterday afternoon. But the weirdest thing . . . Felipe, Anita and the guys had them all packaged up and hidden behind the tire sales area. It was like they were hiding them for us."

Leneld said, "Whoever got Trace woulda sold that stuff if they knew. Felipe saved our asses."

"How's your Mom gonna be about all this noise?" Markus asked.

"She's down with it," Glyn said.

"Yeah," said Lonny. "She's off digging in people's gardens half the day, anyway. No skin off her teeth."

Glyn stared at Lonny and said, "She did say there were rules."

"Rules? Shit, Man!"

"Rule one: Don't use words your grandmother wouldn't approve of, and she knows your grandmothers."

"Not mine," Lonny said, "She's in the Pen."

"Actually," Glyn said, "my grandmother knows your grandmother. Grandma Willie teaches writing for corrections."

"My grandma don't write."

Glyn raised his eyebrows at Lonny. Lonny "No way. Writing about me?"

"Remains to be seen. Anthology coming out next spring."

"Jeeezus."

Markus asked, "What's the second rule?"

Glyn nodded. "Rule two: Don't eat anything that has a 'don't eat me' sign on it."

"That's sort of weird." Leneld said. "You'd think it'd be easier to mark the 'do eat me' stuff."

"Way my mom thinks," Glyn said. "She figures we'll eat anything, so just labels the really don't- eat-me stuff. She stores seeds in the fridge, you know."

"Why?"

"No clue. Calls it scarifying them."

Leneld laughed. "Scarifying us, for starters."

*   *

Over the next hour, the guys tried to come up with sources of possible information about Trace: where he might have been before he stuffed product in the Taco Bell bag; who he might have gotten it from – a list that Lonny was able to provide, a very iffy list, but Leneld and Markus were willing to look into his supposed street connections. They thought maybe some of those sources could tip them off to Trace's supply guy.

"Supply guy or maybe woman," Glyn said. "Yeah, yeah," Markus said.

But Leneld emphasized the idea. "Guy or gal. Watch your prejudices, Markus."

Markus snorted, and held up a drawing of Trace. It was perfect, right down to the long and short dread locks. "Let's find him."

They duplicated the drawing, turned it into a flyer and each took copies to post around town. "Missing person. If you see him, call 555 0451".

Leneld had the burner phone with that number and kept it in his pocket.

*   *

The more iffy meeting for Glyn, was that afternoon. He signed into the visitors' desk at Holly Hills Retirement Center and took the elevator to the eighth floor. He stood a moment outside the door of eight-fourteen, the door with the aromatic wreathe of dried eucalyptus leaves and the name, 'Wilhalmena Stamps' on the door. He straightened his shirt, hitched up the draggy pants and knocked.

Inside the door, he heard his grandmother shuffling, imagined her laying down whatever book she read, and pushing her walker around the coffee table filled with magazines and Readers' Digest contest entries. Moments later, her door opened.

"Ah. My favorite recalcitrant," she said. "Explain to me about this three-hundred-dollar speeding ticket." She stepped back to let him in.

Glyn knew not to say anything about Trace, the Taco Bell or the extra stuffing in the burrito bag. Grandma talked to police. She taught writing at the main community college where policemen got their training. She taught at the corrections facilities. She recognized bullshit at five miles. At five-foot-two leaning on a walker, Grandma Willie was not to be messed with.

"Barely sixteen," she said, "and in debt to the state for having a lead foot."

"Yeah," Glyn said, "Not too bright."

"Oh, you're bright enough. Just not wise. What was the hurry?"

"Had to fill up Mom's car and get it back to her on time."

"Well, you got to pay that fine, and I'll be switched before I let you stiff your parents for it. So, sit down here and fill out this application."

"Loan application?" Glyn asked. "Job application."

CHAPTER THREE

HOLLY HILL DINING HALL

Fried chicken or baked salmon were the choices for the evening meal at Holly Hill Dining Hall. Easy choice for Wilhalmena Stamps. In her Texas youth, she'd had fried chicken enough to have grown half as wide as she was tall. Now, she preferred Northwest fare, and baked salmon rated top of that list.

But, she couldn't order until her neighbor, Geneva Oppenheim showed up. Not polite. Not done. Willie still had her southern manners, no matter that she'd lived in Oregon these forty or more years.

Geneva was her guest at the table tonight. As a result, no other residents signed up for this table. Bunch of old, stuffy ladies.

Sure, Geneva had a few problems. It was sometimes hard to understand what she talked about, but Willie was certain that with a show of understanding, Geneva could calm down, feel accepted, even learn to ask questions and listen to others. She just had not had enough security and love in her life, so Willie grew determined to fill that gap.

And, while providing empathy for Geneva, Willie could keep an eye on Glyn Dower Jones, her grandson. Glyn's first night working in the dining hall was this one.

He was a handsome young devil, she thought, big bright eyes, curly blond hair and already taller even than his father. He seemed to have inherited none of her family's short genes and certainly not her family's dark hair, but he inherited her daughter's curiosity, and the empathy for the hurts of others that was a Stamps trait – much to generations of Stamps' detriment. Empathy had made Willie's father a poor man, losing one grocery store to the debt of his depression customers, and another to the debt of his dry-land neighbors during the dust-bowl days.

Willie knew her own wealth had more to do with the wisdom and investing capacities of her late husband, Clifford, than with her own ability to make money grow. Clifford had taught her to laugh. She had taught him how to support worthy causes.

And today, Geneva and Glyn were her causes.

Grandson Glyn had applied, and despite his driving ticket, with Willie's negotiating in the development office, he had the job.

Gordon Cartier, the development manager had looked at the application and asked her, 'What's with the name?"

"What do you mean?" she knew the name would intrigue him.

"Glyn Dower Jones?"

"His father, my son-in-law, is Merlyn Jones, a Welshman. I suggested that every Merlyn should have his Arthur, but that wasn't acceptable. No greater Welshman than Owain Glyn Dower according to Merlyn. Thus, no better name."

"Kid's a speeder, huh?" Cartier said. "That's the kind of teenager pushes the old ladies' wheelchairs too fast and can't take the time to remember orders correctly."

"I assure you, Glyn is very thoughtful of old ladies. He understands me quite clearly."

"So do we, Wilhalmena Stamps. You have no trouble making yourself understood in the development office."

"Then you will convey your approval to human resources?"

"Provisionally." Mr. Cartier stacked the application on top of her unsigned annuity form.

"They will love him," she said. "Provisionally."

"No. Whole heartedly."

*　*

So, across the room, she watched Glyn help seat old ladies at another table. Willie realized she was going to be very glad to have him nearby. Sharp kid. Knew how to spar with his grandmother, and would add the spice of youth and adventure to the bland politeness that passed for friendship in an old folks' high rise.

Ah, here came Geneva. Willie stood and waved her over. Geneva seemed disoriented and disheveled. Her hair, in fact, stood on end, and not the way some youngsters like it, with mouse and sparkle and spikes. Geneva's hair looked as though it had been hurricaned, each strand blown inland as the wind made for shore.

"Come sit down, Geneva. Are you feeling quite well?" Willie asked.

As Geneva sat, one of the student servers, started to settle two gentlemen at a table in mid-dining room, then, at some whispers from the balding younger man, the server swerved and brought the men to the table behind Geneva and at the edges of the dining room. One seemed old enough to be a Holly Hill resident, the other, the balding one, a tall, slightly pudgy young relative. Probably checking out the food before deciding to move dad in.

Geneva plopped into her chair and smacked a fist on the white tablecloth, then grabbed at her linen napkin. "They're doing it again," she said. "Slavery, that's what it is. They'll starve them and work them till their fingers freeze, and then just replace them with more."

"Who is doing it, Geneva?"

"The Nazis, of course. They haven't given up. They're still out there, waiting for me to let my guard down."

Willie nodded, "I know you are frightened sometimes by those old memories."

"You don't understand. They are here. Now. Taking those poor children to the work camp."

Willie knew that Geneva had lived through the death camps of the Second World War. She'd been six when Mittlebau-Dora Concentration Camp and its factory, Mittlewerk, had been liberated – Mittlewerk, where children with small hands were prized workers in munitions, especially the development of the dreaded V2 rockets.

Peenemünde and then Mittlewerk, Willie thought, the wartime work places of Wernher Von Braun. Von Braun was now dead, but for many years after the war, he'd been a famous rocket scientist for the United States. Yet, he'd been head of a rocket research team at Mittlewerk when Geneva was there. No wonder Geneva couldn't let go of the idea the Nazis followed her here.

"Geneva, dear, let's order our dinner." Willie waved over her grandson.

Willie thought Glyn Dower Jones looked ever-so-much better in a button shirt and slacks. Those draggy jeans and messaging t-shirts of his were plain ugly.

He arrived at the table, slung a white napkin over his arm like a British butler, in what Willie thought was sarcasm aimed at her.

"Lose the butler's napkin, and take our order, young man," she said.

Glyn clicked his heels, together, performing a mid-century European bow, kept the napkin and said, "Yes, Ma'am, what may I get for you two ladies."

"What a nice young man," Geneva said.

"A little officious," Willie said, aiming her remark at Glyn. "Anything to please," he said. "Our evening choices are frayed chicken and balked salmon."

Willie ignored him, "I will have the baked salmon, with the Caesar salad and the green beans, thank you."

Geneva said, "Frayed chicken? Is that something like that pulled pork?"

"No, ma'am," Glyn said, "Frayed chicken is dipped in condensed milk and then in spiced flour and then deep-frayed to a crispy golden brown."

Willie looked at Glyn over her half glasses. His overly- enthusiastic vowels were aimed to poke fun at her rarely- evident accent. She raised her left eyebrow and whispered, "Please leave my home state out of your English."

Geneva said, "I believe I'll have the frayed chicken and the house salad."

"Right away, ladies."

Willie glared at Glyn's back and almost missed the next thing Geneva said. When her attention picked up Geneva in mid-sentence, what she got was:

"And they have them ready to ship out to the concentration camp. Held in that warehouse and starving."

Behind Geneva, Glyn greeted the visiting gentleman and his young relative. "Good evening, Mr. Corrigan and Mr. Rylant," Glyn said, picking up their guest name tags for accounting. "Have you decided what to order for dinner?"

"Yes," the older man said, "We'll have the fried chicken, potatoes and Caesar salad."

Willie yanked her attention back to her own table and answered Geneva. "What warehouse, Geneva?"

Geneva glanced around and then whispered, "The warehouse by the railroad tracks, you know, just like in Peenemünde. Right by the railroad tracks. Shipping cattle."

"Oh, Geneva, I'm sorry to hear that."

Geneva whispered, "The Nazis have invaded with their ideas about purity and using lessor human beings for the workhouse. The damned German workhouse."

"I believe that was England, dear," Willie said, thinking of all the Dickens novels she had read.

Geneva stared at her. "I thought you were my friend," she said, loudly.

"I hope that I am your friend," Willie said, quietly. "I'm just sorry that these memories keep intruding into your present life."

"Did you not hear me? Are you trying to make me seem crazy and paranoid?" Her voice rose. Her hands scrabbled with the cloth napkin in her lap.

"Geneva, tell me more about the railroad tracks," Willie said calmly, but thinking that paranoid must have been a word used by Geneva's psychologist. Geneva had visits with the Holly Hill psychologist ever since she'd begun thinking that the house across Seventeenth Street was beaming X-rays and laser rays into her balcony windows.

Geneva said, "The tracks run right behind the whole company, because, of course, they use it for shipping to Mittlewerk, and to Stuttgart for Daimler-Benz warehouses. But this one building is full of pesticides and herbicides and no one is supposed to go into them, and I just know that's where they keep the children."

Willie remembered that Mittlewerk factory had been set up underground in the Harz Mountains after the Allies bombed Peenemünde. Geneva had been found in Mittlewerk in 1945. By that time, her family and many friends in the nearby Mittlebau-Dora concentration camp had died. Floggings, hangings, starvation, no wonder Geneva's mind was flailing back to those times.

"Geneva, dear, have you taken your vitamins this morning?" Willie knew that Geneva had been told her anti-depression medicine was a vitamin – a lie Willie did not approve of. Be honest and let the patient decide, she believed. But that didn't seem to be the easiest way for the retirement center nursing facility. What was easy was Nurse Robinson's way.

During the sudden silence from Geneva, Glyn delivered their dinner plates.

"No, young man," Willie said. "Mine is the salmon. Miss Oppenheim will have the fried chicken."

Glyn switched plates and murmured, "Sorry, ladies." Then he concentrated a stare at his grandmother, and said, "I am new to the job, and a very short-term employee here."

"Provisional and poor, or so I hear," Willie said, smiling up at him. Then she raised her eyebrows toward him. "You've got to decide how to fix the poor part and be less provisional."

She returned her attention to Geneva while Glyn swooped a plate of fried chicken onto the visiting neighbor's table.

"Here you go, Mr. Corrigan and Mr. Rylant."

Willie was glad to see Glyn had already memorized the names of guests in Holly Hill.

"I ordered the baked salmon," Mr. Corrigan said.

"I'm sorry, sir. I have written fried chicken, potatoes and house salad for you, sir."

"Yes, uncle, it was the fried chicken," the tall relative said. "You are just not remembering."

"Not so, Christopher," Mr. Corrigan pouted. "Uncle, you have merely forgotten."

The older man seemed to deflate, then rally and look at Glyn with renewed stiffness. "Fried chicken, then, young man," the man said.

Headed to the Alzheimer's unit, Willie decided and then forked into her salmon as Geneva stared at her chicken.

"Willie, Wilhalmena. That's a German name, isn't it?" Geneva asked.

"Dutch, actually, and not even the usual Dutch spelling."

"Might as well be German."

"I think the Dutch would object."

"They didn't much object when my family was moved to Buchenwald."

"You were in Holland before the war?"

"Tried to escape into Holland. Those Dutch fools let Germany walk all over them and we were taken away on trains, trains, trains."

"I don't believe the Dutch had much power to tell the Germans to stay out, or to keep their hands off most of the Jews of Holland."

"You are like all the others. You don't listen to me, and you apologize for the ones who let it happen."

"Geneva, I am trying to listen. You say it is happening again, here and now, but then you tell me about the tracks being used for places in Germany. You haven't been to Germany since 1946. What I hear is you thinking in the past."

"You see?" Geneva threw down her fork. "It's you, mixing me up. It is here, I tell you. They are here."

Geneva stood and pointed at Willie. "You are part of them, trying to make me look stupid, just like they did back then. I know what I know, and you aren't going to stop me."

Willie saw Glyn pick up on the strife. He hustled toward her, but she waved him to stop. People at other tables turned to watch. Willie said, quietly, "Geneva, tell me where it is happening. Stay in the present and in the United States and tell me what you are worried about."

"Nazi spy," Geneva shouted at Willie. "I knew you were the one. You have the laser that flashes into my windows. It was you, all along."

Geneva strode from the dining room. Willie stood, trying to catch up with her, but she tripped over the chair at the next table and reached out to catch at anything solid.

In that moment, Glyn had his arm around her shoulders, pulling her upright again. She blinked up at him.

"Sorry," Mr. Corrigan said, drawing in his chair.

"Uncle Don!" the younger man, Mr. Rylant, said, and then glanced at Willie. "I'm so sorry, ma'am. My uncle isn't quite himself these days."

Willie glanced at Geneva's disappearing back, decided to give up and merely said, "It is no trouble."

Glyn said, "Need the walker?"

"No, thank you. You really are fast."

"Speed is useful," he said.

"Just not in a car," she said.

He smiled, "Even there, sometimes."

"I believe I should finish my salmon. What is for dessert?"

"Grandma," he said, after she'd been seated, "Should I catch up with your neighbor?"

"No. She'll calm down by the time she's climbed eight flights"

"Climb?"

"Won't get in an elevator since the war."

"Since Mittle-bau – that place she yelled about?"

"By eight flights, she might forget that I've been added to her list of suspects."

"A list?"

"Certainly. She's accused several here of having been in Cologne, or Amsterdam before the war, or of working in the Mittlebau-Dora Concentration Camp. Eventually, I expect she will accuse every one of us of something."

"Paranoid," Glyn said. "Strong old memories."

CHAPTER FOUR

Glyn felt his interest in work at Holly Hill perk up when he saw the young lady who served the tables in the private dining room which was off the north end of the main dining hall. He realized that room often was reserved for small parties, or for business interests who needed a quiet space. The expectations for service in that dining room were a step above what happened in the main dining room.

He knew that fact by watching the young lady, who served always from the right, never rushed, but also never left people with dishes they didn't need at the table.

Her movements seemed slow, almost what grandma would call 'languid'. But the truth was, he saw, that she did not ruffle the awareness of her clients, yet everything she did was efficient. She was small, but elegant – a dark-haired beauty with a dimple in her right cheek that he kept hoping to see as she walked toward his observation point.

Glyn stood close enough to the door to hear one of the other lady servers call her Violeta. And then, he noticed the embroidered flower on the right shoulder of her blouse – a flower sort of like the pansies that his mom loved, but simpler and violet colored –Violeta.

Over the next days, partly because he watched and imitated the calming efficiency of Violeta, Glyn found that work at Holly Hill gave relief from his deep fear for Trace.

Among his band members, a lot of sweat and work went into searching for Trace. Leneld and Markus tested Lonny's theories about sources of Trace's drugs. They found that most of what Lonny had to say about street life came from Lonny's imagination.

"As real as his dreadlocks," Leneld said, "And as old as his hair gel. The guy couldn't buy a joint on his own."

So, to find out what other members of the band knew, here Glyn was, knocking on Jon's door, hoping to pry a little info from the guy who missed most of their meetings and seemed most scared by Trace's disappearance.

Jon opened the door and said, "Come in, quick." Behind him, his terrier huddled in the background.

Glyn stepped in. Jon closed the door and then he said, "They know he was in your car. They think you still have the stuff, but they couldn't find you."

"Who's they?" Glyn said.

"The guys that sold him the Happy Powder."

"You mean he's been using coke? What the hell is Trace thinking?"

Jon snorted. "Why'd you imagine that Trace thinks?"

"What did these guys look like?"

"Just guys. Older than us. White."

"Yeah? And you gonna tell me all white guys look alike?" Jon nodded. "Mostly. The difference is hair color and zits."

"And these guys?"

"Brown hair on one, black on the other and Brown has zits right up into his hair line."

"Tall? Fat?"

"Skinny. Like they both been using a long time."

Glyn didn't want to imagine the bad guys looking for Trace – and him. And he didn't want to finger Felipe to get himself out of a spot. This was serious.

"How'd they know it was my car?" *The car that's really my Mom's car. Damn.*

"He texted you."

"All right. They have his phone, so they have him and they have my phone number and name. Who are they?"

Jon said, "I don't know, I just heard from Ray Burt what the stuff was and where he got it." Jon fidgeted, and then said, "Ray said he heard it down at the Taco Bell."

"That where these guys hang out? That why he had the stuff in a Taco Bell bag?

"I don't know. Ray works there after school. Trace always eats there. Got no other idea where and who. I just heard this stuff."

"Jon, how come you are hiding out?"

"They know you and Trace are Ancient Nation. Ray said if they see me with you, they might come here looking for you. We can't be meeting."

"Not near me, eh?"

"Yeah. Nothin' against you. Just, you were his wheels that day."

* *

An hour later, Glyn had Mom's Camry parked in a lot on Forty-Eighth and Fremont, the location of Mom's friend and car mechanic. Glyn and Jon had jimmied some wires and Ron, from the car shop, had arranged to tow it in for a fix. It was sitting behind his shop, waiting for a part, the part that now sat on the floor of Ron's garage.

Glyn didn't want Mom in that car until he got this figured out. He also didn't want his sister, Arwain, to happen to borrow the car to go to a college class, so he told Ron the truth.

"All right," Ron said. "I'm tenting the Camry, and I'm recommending that Susan . . . that your mom, rent."

"She's always renting to deliver plants to customers," Glyn said. "Big garden designs are a U-Haul project."

"What about the police?" Ron asked.

"The guy that's missing was carrying product."

"Did you fellows ever think maybe jail would stop him from using? Might be safer, even for him?"

"You know anybody comes out of jail to a better life?"

"Got a point there, Glyn."

"If I find him, I'm hoping his mom will put him in rehab."

"That only works when the kid wants it to work," Ron said. "So I hear," Glyn said.

"Best thing might be to take him out to that tree farm your family inherited. Leave him there 'til he's desperate."

"Even a tree farm has neighbors. And my aunts take the dogs out there to hunt the wild mushroom."

"Not the wilderness then. Got no more ideas for you, but we'll keep mom's car under wraps."

With Mom safe, or at least safer, Glyn asked Ron to drop him off at the family home. Dad was practicing the piano when he came in. The Schumann stopped in mid-phrase.

"How come Ron brought you home?"

"The Camry's toast."

"You speeding again?"

"No. Ron says the alternator is gone and the thing's old enough it will take a while to find parts. He called Mom and recommended renting while he looks for a better used car deal."

Dad studied Glyn a moment and then started playing, exactly where he'd left off. Merlyn the Mathematician had that kind of mind. It always gave Glyn a laugh that Dad was so rational and so focused. Even out at the farm, you could see him measuring trees with his mental calculator – so many board feet, so many inches growth on the leader branch.

As Dad played, he asked, "So, the basement has now become The Beat Kitchen, I hear. Explain, please."

"Felipe needs the space in the filling station for storage."

"Kind of sudden."

"Uh, yeah. Pressure from Chevron National, I guess."

"That all that's going on, Glyn?"

Damn. Dad wasn't dropping a note, but he was into this interrogation with laser ears for fog facts.

"Can't think of anything else," he said, and went into the kitchen as if to find a snack.

Dad continued practicing.

Glyn hated lying to Dad. He hoped they could find Trace and get him into rehab instead of jail, but this sneaking around the people who trust you wore pretty fast. Dad, Mom, and certainly Grandma had a trust in the police and the justice system.

That system worked for white folks, mostly, but Glyn had come to realize it was a trap for his black friends. He was glad his adopted older brother, John Phillip, was away in the Marines. At home, because J.P. was black, he'd been stopped for minor traffic violations Glyn could have gotten away with easily, stopped in the stores and frisked, stopped in the mall and questioned because someone thought he looked like the black man who did something somewhere. White witnesses and white policeman were notorious for not recognizing the differences that made black people individuals.

Glyn didn't want Trace to be part of that system just because at sixteen he'd been a fool for a few months.

Had it been only months? He thought back to their freshman year. Trace had started blowing smoke over his mind pretty soon after the first assignments were handed out. He'd felt out of his element, couldn't read as fast as the curriculum moved forward, and didn't have a computer to write on, so didn't have any kind of speed built up to get out the assignments.

Even after Leneld had given Trace an old computer and wrenched him into the chair to learn how to type, Trace felt behind, out of it, and in need of some kind of high to make him part of life.

Reading, Glyn thought. It all went back to their grade school days and some kind of trouble with reading. During those years, no one had paid a lot of attention, except the few teachers who gave Trace extra lessons in phonics. When they were little kids, volunteers came and read to kids like Trace, trying to help fill in gaps left by whatever made reading difficult.

Trace's own mom came and read to others, while someone read to Trace. It wasn't like the teachers and family didn't work at helping, but nobody seemed to have the key to unlock his abilities. Each year, Trace was farther behind, until it all crashed on him in high school where seven different teachers could hardly find time to communicate with each other. They had no time for goof-offs who found weed an entertaining relief from real life.

Glyn took some potato chips up to his room and called Trace's mom, Alice Gowen.

"No. No sign," Mrs. Gowen said. "Leneld and Markus have been all over the neighborhood and into Darrell's Bar at the corner where you let him off."

"Church? Would he hide out with Reverend Jackson?"

"I tried that," Mrs. Gowen said. "The whole congregation is on the look-out for my boy."

* *

Figuring that Felipe and his guys were the only real source of information, Glyn decided to skip Thursday classes. He put on his helmet, hopped his bike and took off uphill toward Emerson Street. Half an hour later, he rolled in and pretended to pump air into his tires.

After a moment, Felipe came over, saying loudly, "You want some help with that?"

Felipe bent down, took the air hose and said, "They look for you."

"Didn't you give them the Taco Bell?"

"Yeah, but not enough. See those new bullet holes in the wall?"

Glyn squinted at the white wall and the new pock marks. "Any of the guys get hit?" he asked.

"No. Showing off that they could. They wanted info. They think you used some. Or sold it."

Glyn's neck stiffened. Choice: throw Trace to the drug guys or become the target. "Where's Trace?"

"Fat guy with curly hair took him. Right off the corner by Darrell's Bar. Don't know where.'"

"What did they look like?"

"One guy's got a big gut. The other two seem like walking death."

Glyn thought of Jon's description. *Like they been using a long time.*

"Thanks, Felipe."

"Please go."

He hopped his bike and took off down Emerson toward the Adidas buildings and the park where he could think.

So, Glyn thought, they know Trace used some. He was flying when I left him here. They've just decided to drag me into this because they can.

He crossed the park and the Adidas campus to let himself down into the Greeley Avenue bike lane. As he rode next to the railroad tracks and the train repair yards of north Portland, his back sweat with alert prickles.

If the seller – the fat guy – didn't spot him, he could get to Holly Hills Retirement Center in time to take Grandma Willie for a walk around the roof garden before work. Of course, she'd ask about school, but she didn't have the calendar, and since the voters of Oregon had decided to cut funding to schools, there were plenty of furlough days to fob off on Grandma as an excuse.

CHAPTER FIVE

Up in apartment eight-fourteen, Glyn failed to fob his lie off on Grandma Willie.

"Goodness," Grandma said. "You are the only student who has a furlough day. Are you in some high school not related to the Portland Public Schools?"

He breathed deep and plunged toward truth. "Sorry, Grandma. I just can't be at school today. Too much goin' on."

"So much going on that hiding out with your Grandma is an improvement? Give with the information, young man."

He thought a moment, fiddled with the magazines on her coffee table and finally said, "Grandma, you gotta promise you won't talk to the police."

"Can't promise, but I can promise I will consider the wisest direction to move. I know that isn't always to the police, since they are human and embedded in a less than perfect system."

Glyn gawked. His assumptions were blown. Grandma knew more than an eighty-year-old might, and maybe it was *because* she taught policemen how to write.

He reminded her about his friend Trace. She'd known Trace since he was kindergarten through fifth grade, so she had the picture. Fact was, she'd read to him once a week in fourth and fifth grade and helped him learn phonics rules to be able to read more easily.

So, Glyn brought her up to date on the whole situation.

"First thing," she said. "We are being honest with your mom and dad. Situation like this, they need to be aware and alert.

Call them now."

He called Mom, who worked at home.

* *

"Ah," Mom said, "So that's what this is about. A kid came to the door looking for you. I'm glad I smelled a rat when he came. His handshake was slime. So, I pretended you'd moved out. Angry. Gone. No contact."

"I'm sorry, Mom."

"The car is not dead, right?"

"Also a lie."

"Ron is in on this lie?"

"Trying to keep you safe."

"Okay. I'll discuss that with him. I need new wheels anyway, so this time we're looking for a plant-mobile. Next, after your call to dad, you have to live somewhere else for a time. May I speak to my mom?"

Grandma Willie took the phone. Grandma listened, then she said, "Remember when you tried to talk me out of a two bedroom, saying I'd only fill it with books? Aren't we glad I vetoed that edict from the Queen of Sheba?"

Mom said, "Who's going to move all those books?"

"Guess," Grandma said, smiling at Glyn.

Later, Dad enlisted his company's lawyer in the search for someone to take on Trace when he was found. Dad said, "That kid has the best rap lines in Ancient Nation. Sometimes, I think he sees people more clearly than any of us. Let's save him if we can."

During the phone calls, Grandma had disappeared into the second bedroom. When Glyn stood in the doorway, stacks of books were still on the bed, but Grandma had clear off some and created pilons of literature under the windowsill.

"Well, your mother was correct, but everybody needs a bedroom plus a library. Her library is in the basement, you'll notice."

"Yeah," Glyn laughed. "I counted eight bookcases when Dad and I planned the new Beat Kitchen sound studio. Half her library will be moving into her sewing room."

"Now, young man, you call, using my phone, and don't text. Tell the guys not to come to your house. We'll find a space in the retirement center. The development department in this venerable community is panting after my stock portfolio, so, I've got a crowbar to pry open spaces and attitudes for your group."

"Thank you, Grandma."

"Three rules, however." Glyn peered at her.

"No words your grandma wouldn't approve of. Don't raid the kitchen at all. And those fellows must leave off the shit- kicker boots. Those heavy-metal toe bands make big marks on the floors. Old ladies with walkers have to look at floors a lot."

"I'll tell the guys."

*   *

In a small bungalow on Northeast Twelfth Avenue, Violeta Aguirre sat on her sister's bed while her Rosaria packed her suitcase.

"Vi," Rosaria said, "don't look so blue. You'll be coming to college in a year and a half."

Violeta shrugged. "It won't be the same, Rosie. We've had all this time to share and then – poof – all things change. I'm going to miss our late-night secrets and our talks."

"And," Rose laughed, "the pranks we play on Papá and Mamá. That mouse was a good one."

"And the spider down from the ceiling …" Violeta laughed behind her fingers.

"And Papá yells the loudest while Mamá uses the broom on them."

Violeta rolled over on her stomach, laughing, but also working not to cry. "What will I do without you?" she asked.

Rosie studied her. "You will do fine. I have to go for this summer term because my math scores were not as good as my English, but your math is great."

"This summer is just to brush up on math?" Violeta asked. "Aren't you taking some pre-med classes this summer, too."

"Sure. Intro to Biology and an anatomy class."

"The shin bone's connected to the … to the what?"

Rose plopped her red plaid skirt into the suitcase. "I'll tell you in my next letter where the shin bone connects."

"The shin bone is way below the level of that skirt, Rosie. Don't you think you should leave that for your little sister?"

Rose studied it. Held it up and looked in the mirror. "Where does it hit you?" she asked Violeta.

"Right at the knee."

Rose pulled it out. "Yes. I guess it better stay with you. But if you get taller, watch out. That skirt is guy bling."

"What do you mean."

"It flips at the edges because of the pleats – makes the guys look twice." Rose wiggled her eyebrows. "And you are never into making guys look twice."

Violeta held the skirt to her chest. "Maybe not, but I've got a guy who does it anyway."

"What?" Rose sat down on the bed. "You mean there is a guy you noticed looking twice? That's not like you to notice. They all do it. You are a looker, sister."

Violeta felt the heat in her cheeks.

Rose leaned toward her. "Who is this guy?"

Violeta smiled shyly at her sister. "He works at Holly Hill since last week. He's cute in a messy sort of way. Curly blond hair, tall, stands near the doorway to the private dining room, looking more than twice, really. And then when he is working, he does everything exactly the way I do it."

"What? He's making fun of you?"

"No. At least I don't think so. He just uses the motions I use and then when he glances at me, he seems embarrassed to have been doing it."

"That's weird," Rosie said. "Watch out for weird."

Violeta smiled. "I will definitely watch out for weird. What time is your bus tomorrow?"

"Ten o'clock in the morning. I think I get to George Fox University by one or one-thirty."

Do you have a class tomorrow?"

"No. They start the next day."

"Great. You'll have time to explore the town."

Rosie shrugged. "Of course, I had to promise Papá that I wouldn't explore the town by myself, but I won't know anyone on the first day."

"How about Liza? Won't she be your roommate?"

"Liza is living off campus."

"Geez! Her dad let her do that?"

"I'm not sure how she got to do that, but Papá would have a cow if I even asked to live in an apartment."

"Papá plus Mamá."

Rose laughed. "Maybe by the time I'm a nurse or a doctor, I won't have so many rules."

"Yeah," Violeta laughed, "by the time you are forty."

Rosie tossed the red plaid skirt at her. "Off my bed, little sister. I have to get up in the morning and get to college."

*   *

Back in Holly Hill Retirement Center, Grandma Willie waited for Geneva to appear for lunch. Later she hoped she would appear for dinner. But Geneva didn't come to the dining hall at all.

The center's social worker checked on her. Geneva told the social worker to go eat something shaped like bratwurst.

So, Geneva was alive, angry, and articulate.

Willie had talked Glyn into going to school in the afternoon, at least to pick up homework. During school hours, Susan, Glyn's mom and Willie's daughter, brought some pajamas, changes of clothes and Glyn's computer. They looked at and reserved two large empty storage spaces in the basement where the hip-hop band could practice. These were spaces left by recent deaths of people in the center's care facility, so availability would only last until the vacated apartments were rented.

Glyn's dad, Merlyn Jones, came for dinner with Susan and Grandma, partly, Dad said, to watch his son wait on others.

Yeah, great, Glyn thought.

Glyn's sister, Arwain, had called him. She said she wanted to come witness the same thing, but, thank God, she had a presentation in her U.S. history class at University of Portland that evening.

"Waiting tables is a mighty switch for the well-catered kid," Papa Merlyn said.

Glyn thought, *Dad, you wouldn't know what catered looks like unless you looked up from your integral theory book when Mom brings you a latte.*

But he didn't say such things, because he liked to watch Mom and Dad take care of each other. He knew lots of friends who would give their golf club membership to have such luck in the parent department.

At the end of serving desserts, Glyn sat down and the three of them brainstormed how to keep the family safe while some drug lord seemed to be hunting for Glyn, for Susan's car and possibly for other people.

"What about Arwain?" Mom asked. Glyn's sister lived at home and attended the University of Portland, working toward a masters-in-teaching.

"We should move her into a friend's home for a while," Glyn suggested. "How about if she lives temporarily with Claudia Ash?" Claudia lived in a high rise near U. of Portland., and often had Arwain over after late classes.

Mom texted Arwain not to come home after her six to nine evening class, and then texted Claudia asking if Arwain might live with her for a while, explanations to follow.

Glyn was relieved his brother, John Philip, aka Phip or J.P., was not at home. His Marine instincts would have had him out shaking down guys for info about Trace. J.P. could be effective, but in town, his methods were not backed up by the corps. The Marine motto, Semper Fi, might work in the corps and during a battle, but in the streets, drug lords were loyal only to money and fear.

Barney, their security friend had come by today to upgrade their home system with outdoor lights and alarms triggered by motion. He'd also put his call staff on high alert for the home address.

"Now," Grandma said, "how do we keep Glyn in school, but safe? That's where they'll get at him, or any of the other boys."

And there, the adult planning fell down entirely.

*   *

That evening the Ancient Nation met in the new rehearsal space. First, they worked on the school problem. Lonny kept interjecting ideas that came from west of Alpha-Centauri, then pouted when ignored. His fantasy street life wasn't going to help them.

They figured they could work with some teachers to pick up homework assignments. The chem teacher, would be a problem.

"Chem Ventura, claims he makes no exceptions for students on the road," Markus said.

"Well," Leneld said, "We're not actually on the road, just on the lam."

Jon braved his fears. "I'll go to Chem class for Markus, Glyn, and me."

In the end, those in Ventura's class agreed to take turns showing up. They'd avoid opening and closing hours, when Trace's people would most likely be looking for them.

"Okay, we got school taken care of," Leneld said. "And now for Trace."

They outlined what Glyn, Leneld and Jon knew about rumors of Trace. Decided to stay away from Felipe's gas station, on the theory that Felipe was in enough hot water from being connected with them. And they decided to go in twos to the hideouts under Portland's many bridges and in the parks hoping he was lying low instead of kidnapped.

Without more information, they couldn't unravel his disappearance. They hoped something would pop up soon. Living scared, even for Glyn in a locked retirement center, didn't appeal. Nobody knew how many members of the rap group were watched by the people who might have taken Trace. Glyn and Jon for sure, but who else was in danger?

Glyn had to go up to the kitchen and work on late night dishwashing. The rest of the crew split up to visit the bridges, and they worked two by two.

Glyn climbed the back stairs from the storage practice area and turned a corner to enter the kitchen. He recognized the girl at the other end of the room, the girl with the violets embroidered on her blouse.

Violeta Aguirre.

She seemed to be leaning her head in her hands. Hearing the squeak of Glyn's shoes, she straightened abruptly, kept her back to him, and pretended to have been straightening a shelf of pans that didn't need straightening.

"Violeta," he said. "¿Cómo está esa noche?" Glyn spoke slowly, trying to remember the little Spanish he'd learned in his freshman class.

"Muy bien. Y usted?." She answered as if she knew he needed all the talk to be very slow."

"Más o menos," he said. She missed his elegant gallic shrug because she didn't turn to face him. All his watching as Grandma taught acting was wasted on this little one.

Glyn guessed she was maybe a sophomore, but dinky, not like she didn't eat, but like she moved swiftly everywhere she went. He knew she normally did move pretty fast. He'd been watching her clean tables after dinner for the last two weeks. He always hoped to catch a glimpse of her dimple and those big brown eyes, but she rarely looked at anything but her work.

She turned toward him at last. Her eyes were rimmed in red and a tear hung at the edge of her lid.

"Why are you crying, Violeta?"

She shrugged, and then said, "Oh, I am being silly."

"No, in English the word is sad. Why are you sad?"

She glanced at him as if he were a sooth-sayer. "You are right, sad, for a silly reason. My sister, my best friend, left for the university this morning. I should be glad for her. She has a scholarship to become a doctor."

Glyn nodded. He knew this feeling. "Yes, glad for her, but sad for the change in your lives together. I have a brother and a sister. They are both away and that makes me sad, so I understand."

She looked at him with surprise. "Where are they?"

"My brother is in Iraq, so in danger. That scares me for him, so I just write a lot of letters and hope. My sister goes to school here at the University of Portland, and she actually lives at home, but I am almost never home when she is there."

Violeta sat down near the sink. "I'm sorry to worry you with my little problem."

"Your sadness is no little problem."

She sat there, looking at him solemnly. Finally, she said, "Thank you."

He had a sudden idea. "¿Puede enseñarme un poquito español?" He hoped she could teach him Spanish. That way, he'd get to see those eyes more often.

"¿Está triste, amiga?" he asked. She looked about as sad as he could imagine.

"No. Hay una cebolla en el refrigerador."

He thought fast to figure out she teased him now, by blaming her sadness on an onion. Thank goodness for some memory from that class.

"¿Puedo luchar con esta cebolla? Can I beat up your onion?"

Finally, she laughed, a shy laugh that she tried to hide behind her hand. "¿Porque quiere aprender el español?" she asked.

Did he have a reason for learning Spanish? Might as well be honest. "Para hablar con usted, Violeta. ¿Es este una razón suficiente?"

She seemed to be surprised by the idea that talking to her might be sufficient reason to learn a language.

She said, "Me gustaría te lo enseñar el español. I would be glad to teach you Spanish."

He smiled, and finally she smiled, showing him the best view of the day. "Thanks," he whispered. "I mean muchas gracias."

By the time Glyn finished his kitchen detail, he'd learned how to buy a bus ticket (puedo comprar un billette?), and shop for onions and beef in a Spanish tienda (donde estan los cebollos y bif-tec?). He learned to say good night and then saw Violeta out to her father's car where he was able to say "Mucho gusto de conocerlo, Señor Aguirre."

After Violeta and her father left, he climbed up to Grandma Willie's place. She met him at the door and handed him a key. "Be quiet when you come and go. Geneva's still torqued at me, and her room is just the other side of your bedroom wall."

Glyn fell into bed without changing.

CHAPTER SIX

In the morning, a banging on his bedroom wall brought Glyn straight up.

"You stop that, you Nazi Jew hater."

He recognized Geneva's high voice just as Grandma Willie opened the door and motioned for him to say nothing.

Waving him into the living room, Grandma backed up into her walker, grabbed the handlebars and whipped around. Glyn didn't even have a chance to stand up and stop her. She stopped her own potential fall, righted herself and then whispered.

"She heard you snoring. I see you're already dressed for school."

"Just didn't change last night. But we worked it out." At her quizzical raise of eyebrows, he explained. "Ancient Nation.

Each of us goes one day, gets homework for the band. That way, we only expose one person at a time to the ones looking for us. My turn is Thursday.

"And this is okay with the teachers?"

"Leneld is taking a message today. We'll see."

"While you're here, then, there are some things I've been asking maintenance to do. I hope you can do them."

Glyn grew wary. "Such as."

"Set up my new bird feeders on the balcony."

"Grandma, birds shit."

"And I've got a tarp for underneath them."

He snorted. "A tarp which you will wash where?"

"We'll take it to the Laundromat at Twenty-Eighth and Sandy."

"We?"

"It's big," she explained.

A few minutes later, they left the apartment for breakfast in the dining hall. Today, Glyn was Willie's guest for breakfast and lunch, he worked the dinner and cleanup shift. As they trudged down the hall for the elevator, a door behind them opened.

"I thought you had that boy sneaking around, getting into my things."

Glyn pivoted. "Good morning, Miss Oppenheim. Want to go to breakfast with us?"

"And have you pick my brain? You stay out of my rooms, boy!"

Grandma Willie put her hand on his arm. "Geneva, this is my grandson, Glyn. He's here to visit for a time."

"I saw him last night. Sneaking into the basement with those boys," she shouted. "I know they want in my storage space, but I got that locked so Houdini can't break in."

Around them, other doors opened. Heads poked from corners. The people waiting at the elevator held the door, so they could hear what might happen next.

The door across the hall opened and her neighbor, Henry Crick poked his head out. "Hello, ladies and gentlemen. May I offer my assistance?"

Grandma said, "We are working things out, Henry. Thank you."

Miss Oppenheim glared at Henry. He smiled at her. "Ma'am," he said, as if tipping an imaginary cap to her.

Henry then glanced at Glyn and said, "Nice to see you, Glyn." Then he poked his head back inside his room.

Grandma spoke to Geneva. "We'll see you at breakfast, dear."

"Leave me alone, Wilhalmena."

Grandma ignored Geneva's anger and trudged down the hall toward the elevator.

Glyn whispered, "Is she for real? Or is this a put-on so she can get committed?"

"Don't be mean," his grandmother whispered. "This is what post-traumatic stress sometimes looks like."

"Stress from when she was five?"

"You don't get rid of that early trauma. You just live around it, until sometime when it attacks you again."

"Yeah, well she's been attacked by something, that's for sure."

"Glyn!"

"Okay, Grandma. But for three years you and Miss Oppenheim have been friends. I've been here to visit, and she welcomed me. Now, she doesn't even seem to remember me."

"Yes. The whole thing is very disturbing. I don't understand what has triggered this relapse for her."

"What's she accusing you of?"

"She's not giving up on the idea that I'm German. There is nothing we can do once she gets that firmly in mind."

The first breakfast crowd entered the elevator while Glyn and Grandma were still twenty feet away. The door closed.

"What was she saying the other night," Glyn asked as they waited for the next elevator. "I mean just before she got angry with you?"

"She was remembering her days as slave labor in the camp that built the V2 rockets in Germany."

"But you and she used to go to the Art Museum together. What happened?"

"She thought I wasn't taking her seriously."

"What were you doing?"

"Trying to sympathize. It didn't work."

Glyn shook his head and poked at the elevator buttons.

*   *

Later that morning, Grandma went off to read to the people in the Alzheimer's unit, one of her many jobs in Holly Hill.

Glyn began bolting her bird feeder stanchions to the rails of her balcony. The feeders would hang on wrought-iron stakes. The top of each stake had a shepherd's crook for hanging the feeders. Above the crook, the stake was topped by a sharp point, like a medieval soldier's pike.

"Perfect," Grandma had said. "an infantry weapon for birds to sit on and poop."

He'd convinced Grandma to cut the heavy painters' tarp into three pieces and put one under each feeder.

As he drilled the third bolt hole, Geneva came out on her adjoining balcony. She stretched out, and around the wall between them.

"Boy, you take those things down, or I will turn you in to the manager here."

"Hello, Miss Oppenheim. I'm sorry about the drilling noise. These hold Grandma's bird feeders, and they are permitted."

"Don't try to fool me, Glyn Jones. Those are signals to satellites."

"Ma'am, Grandma has no way to send signals anywhere. She doesn't even have Wi-Fi in her apartment."

"She's got a cell phone, doesn't she?"

"Yes, I gave her one for Christmas." Glyn realized Geneva could be very with it and present sometimes, aware that Grandma had a cell phone, but she went to some other place and time during other parts of a conversation.

"Cell phone," she said. "Thought so. Take those down, now."

He grabbed up one of the bird feeders and hung it on the shepherd's crook. "See? This is what they're for."

"That's camouflage. Like the V2. Paint it like a forest and dirt and make everyone believe it isn't what it is."

Glyn stood up. "Tell me about that V2. How did you work on it?"

"You're young. You couldn't have known. Why are you working for her?"

Glyn thinks about her accusation, and thinks they should be more open with Geneva. But he also noticed a change in her voice, a rhythm that made her seem more foreign when she talked about those times. He wanted to help her be more rational about Grandma and others.

"Grandma lived in Colorado, in the U.S. while you lived over there. My grandpa worked for the United States Air Force."

"She cooked in the camp," Geneva insisted. "That porridge-making, watery soup creator. I know what she did there."

"Miss Oppenheim, my Grandma is not German. She's a pacifist."

"See?" she pointed a long finger at him. "More camouflage."

"What didn't she understand the other night?"

Her face hardened. "You just want me to reveal my sources. You're part of the plan."

"Plan to . . .?"

She slumped on her balcony rail. "All those children. They will starve, or the commandant will find some reason to hang them."

"I'm sorry," he said. "Those times scared everyone." Geneva straightened. "It's coming again. Watch your back."

She pulled herself back to her side of the wall, but he could still hear her. "They'll move them out of the warehouse soon, and we'll never again see them."

Glyn stood on his side of the wall, thinking how weird the woman seemed. Her voice changed, her whole manner changed back and forth from fearful child to grown, but angry woman. The last thing she said, she sounded more like the woman who had lived in the United States for almost sixty years. He didn't get it.

*   *

In the Alzheimer's Unit of Holly Hill Retirement Center, on the fourth floor, Willie read aloud for everyone. She'd been a drama major in college and helped out with many amateur drama presentations in her children's school days and at the Methodist Church, so she'd maintained her ability to hold an audience with her voice.

For the next few weeks, she'd chosen *Little Britches* by Ralph Moody, a great book for kids and adults. It dealt with the difficulties of the ranching life in Colorado, the Great Depression, which many of her audience remembered better than the events of yesterday. Ralph Moody wrote from his life as a little boy who wished to be a great horseman like the ranch hands who worked on ranches near his family.

She wondered how soon her neighbor, Geneva, might be moving into this unit with the ten who already lived here. Some of these people had been her neighbors in earlier years, the friend they no longer remembered. But she knew from watching, that forgotten sons and daughters suffered much more greatly at the loss of the parent who still lived.

She wondered about the newest inhabitant, Don Corrigan. His nephew had helped him get settled on the morning after Geneva's blow up, but several days later, Don still didn't participate in the readings. He hung around on the edges of everything. The nephew had been back once, but didn't seem that close to Don, just a hovering pressure for Don to stick with some program the nephew had planned out for him.

So, Don Corrigan sat in the living room, but not in the circle of those who listened. Still, Wilhalmena was certain he listened.

Maybe he remembered the Great Depression, as well. Some memories lurked yet within her old friends, so she tried to find books that would relate to those memories.

As she wrapped up, Willie noticed that Glyn had entered the room. While he hovered near the doorway, a small and very tidy lady came up to Willie and asked. "Why are you reading this book to us? You know that Little Britches' dad is going to die in the end."

Willie smiled. She had anticipated this feeling but assumed it would not be asked out-loud. "Well Pauline, Dad may die, but what is happening for the whole family in the meantime?"

"They're just hard scrabbling to create a ranch. That's no life."

By this time, one or two others hovered nearby, curious. "Does Little Britches have any advantages in his life?"

Willie asked.

"He's got nothing," Pauline said. "That boy is from the lowest of the lowest."

Others nodded their heads. But one asked, "What boy are they talking about?"

"Our book kid. That Britches kid," someone answered. "How are you measuring low and high, Pauline?" Willie asked.

"He doesn't have enough food. His dad is sick. His mom has to work all the time, and his sisters are pests."

Willie took out a sheet of pink paper and began writing in big letters.

"Here is what I'd like you to do for us all, Pauline," and Willie turned to the others, "Any of you can think about this with us. My question is, 'What does Little Britches have that we all need?' Tomorrow, let's talk about the answers you think of."

A couple of people started to answer her, but she stood from her reading chair, and said, "I'm leaving the question on your bulletin board here. If you want, you can write your answers on the sheet with the question. Let's talk before we read tomorrow."

She shoved her walker toward the bulletin board near the coffee urn and pinned her pink question at about head height. The friends in the area followed her there and began re-reading the question.

"I'll see you all tomorrow at 11 a.m."

Willie pushed her walker toward Glyn and the doorway. "Getting hungry?"

"No. Well, yes. Always. But I wanted to tell you that Geneva has been in your apartment."

"Well, that's not a total surprise. She comes in to water my plants when I'm away on a trip. Maybe she thinks I'm gone."

"Come see what I have seen," he said.

As Willie started out the door, she noticed that Don Corrigan followed her. "Mr. Corrigan, what can I do for you?"

He stopped, looked at his shoes, and said, "I'm just going downstairs."

"Don't you live in this floor?" Willie asked. She knew that Alzheimer's residents were not supposed to leave their floor for fear they might get lost.

"No, I live on the eighth floor, but I'm going down to the dining room and library floor."

Glyn frowned at his Grandma, and started to hurry her to the elevator, but she went on talking to Don. "Mr. Corrigan, I need to stop by the desk here, you go on and use the elevator. I'll be along in a few minutes."

Don Corrigan fiddled with his pocket change for a moment and then moved on down the hall.

"Grandma . . ."

"Young man, I think it is best if you call me Mrs. Stamps while we are at Holly Hill. That way no one can accuse you of getting your job by nepotism and they won't look too closely into where you presently live."

"Sure, okay, but we ought to catch the elevator, so I can show you what she's been up to."

"We will not catch the elevator with other people and talk about Geneva. She has enough detractors."

Glyn started toward the stairs, saying, "By the way Grandma, nepotism has everything to do with my presence here, and you know it. In fact, everybody knows it. Let's be up front about that."

"Hmphh. Everybody guesses that is true, but we'll let them continue in suspense. I'll see you on the eighth floor," she said.

*   *

Willie had discovered from the Alzheimer's Unit attendant that Don Corrigan really did live on the eighth floor. She wondered why he came to the Alzheimer unit and flattered herself with the idea that he liked the story she had picked out.

When the elevator came back, she entered the elevator, and found Rolly Goforth already inside, and, as is the way of big men, he took up the whole middle of the space.

"Rolly," she said, and pushed her walker against the front of his big shoes, forcing him to step back.

"Wilhalmena," he said, hulking over as much space as he still could, "I understand Mrs. Oppenheim has finally gotten around to accusing you of being a spy."

"Yes. I seem to have joined the club."

"That woman is nuts."

Willie didn't want to talk about her neighbor, who once had been her friend, so she asked, "Rolly, I know you used to be an accountant. Are you volunteering with Tax Aide this year?"

"I'm retired. I don't do accounting anymore."

Willie let that statement drift into silence. She had expected the answer, but also wanted him to squirm. She knew he had tried to set up shop in Holly Hill as a cheap alternative to H&R Block, but after the first year, he had no takers. He'd shown himself to be a very careless accountant who didn't pay attention to the annual changes in the rules.

He'd certainly never volunteer for a free service that would give him a test before they accepted his assistance. Thank goodness for the IRS free tax preparations program.

The elevator came to her floor, and Willie pushed out her walker, but as she shoved out, Rolly stuck his hand in the elevator door and said, "If I were you, I'd complain about The Oppenheim to the manager. She's getting to be a danger."

Willie turned to him and said, "Geneva is not The Anything.

Don't be talking about others as if they were things. It makes you look crass."

She slid her walker beyond the doors and down the hall, hearing him punch the 'Close Door' button six frantic times. Willie shook her head. Some folks were hard for her to like, so she decided to let God love them while she merely tolerated.

And she had liked Geneva, who in her prime read good books and loved depth in music and movies. Geneva Oppenheim once had been a good companion at dinner and played a mean game of Scrabble. Geneva was one of the few inhabitants who still worked when she moved in. She had said she wanted the companionship of others. But she'd continued to work for the next few years as the secretary of the chief financial officer for a garden tool and chemical company.

And then, she had abruptly quit her job, or been fired from her job. Afterward, there had been her slow slide into what appeared to be paranoia and then accusations.

As Willie walked down the hall, she approached the open doorway of her neighbor, Henry Crick. She heard his daughter's rather raucous voice inside his apartment, and could tell this was the same argument she had every visit. "Just sign that paper, Dad. I'll take care of your taxi, quick as a wink, and you won't have any insurance or tax worries."

Passing the door, she heard Henry's normally calm voice rise. "Brenda, you're on about the taxi, but you are the only one worrying about it."

Brenda glanced out, saw traffic in the hall and slammed Henry's door.

Willie arrived at her apartment to find Glyn waiting outside. "Mrs. Stamps," he said. "The office said you needed help with a shade cord in one of your windows."

Willie realized he was speaking for any nosey neighbors. "Young man, I think you are the right height to fix it. Come on in."

As soon as they entered, Willie knew Glyn had assessed the situation correctly. The magazines on her gold and white coffee table were neatly stacked instead of slewed about as she normally left them. Her most recent teacup had been washed.

These neatness actions Geneva used to do without thought whenever she visited. Mess caused her discomfort. Clean became her automatic response.

Further into the room, they found that Willie's small desktop had been straightened and the two drawers had been closed completely, instead of as Willie always left them – closed as far as the first kitty-wampus file folder. Not one file folder interfered with the smooth running of the drawer.

Geneva had been here.

Willie said, "She and I exchanged keys, back before she became so fearful. I took care of her plants, and she took care of mine when we went on vacation."

"What could she be searching for?" Glyn asked. "Probably proof that I'm German."

"Does she know about your Grandmother Malka Silverberg?"

"Malka, the Jewess whose daughter became a Baptist? I don't think that would be a good recommendation as far as Geneva is concerned, especially in her present state."

"Besides," Glyn observed, "Living in Arkansas as a Jew may have been hard, but not anywhere close to as frightening as living in Germany in the 30s and 40s."

"So, she believes I am German."

"Malka's family came from Holland, didn't they?"

"At this point, that holds no water for Geneva, either. She thinks the Dutch gave in too easily."

"Let's change the lock on your door," Glyn said. "I'll get the stuff from Atlasta Lock on Grand and take care of it tomorrow evening after work."

"Meanwhile," Willie said, "Tell me more about the hunt for Trace."

"We've divided up the nine Bridges and the zillion overpasses in Portland and are hunting among the homeless."

"But Felipe told you they took him from the corner."

"True, but we don't know who took him and have no idea where that 'who' may own a building or a house."

"You haven't called in the police because…"

"Because the guys' experience is that the police will chalk it up to gang and drug stuff and not take it any farther until a body turns up."

"How will you know if a body turns up?"

"Beats me," Glyn said, "but that's the guys' call. They don't …"

Willie held up her palms. "I know. They don't trust the police. Some of the stuff I hear at the police academy tells me there are some they shouldn't trust, and some that won't confront the noisy ones, and a few who call the noise for the bigotry it is."

"If you know who to trust, tell my guys."

"When does the rap group practice next?"

"Tonight."

CHAPTER SEVEN

That afternoon after painting class, Willie tossed her cleaned brushes and watercolors in her locker in the recreation area of the Holly Hills Retirement Center. She studied her canvas.

There, laughing at some joke they once shared, stood her deceased husband, Clifford, his head thrown back, hands on his hips, mouth open, eyes shining with fun. She laughed with him, sighed, and then set the painting in the upright rack of drying paintings along the wall of the art room. If only, she thought, if only he had never taken up smoking.

Damned addiction!

But his addiction was legal and made money for large companies with a lobby in Washington D.C.. Trace's addiction? A product from outside that made no money for U.S. growers.

In fact, in some states, incarcerating users had become the big money maker. The drug war offered an excuse to create a new class of slaves. Thank goodness Oregon wasn't using private prisons.

Yet.

She walked around the empty classroom, admired the landscape filled with fairies that her sixth-floor friend, Elisa Nadelstein worked on. Next to the fairies stood the large oil painting of Valkyrie maidens that was clearly part of a long 'series' by Leah Müller. Leah's Valkyrie were famous among the residents as a depiction of racial angst, and an over-reaction to something, but no one seemed quite certain what.

Side-by-side, fairies and Valkyrie seemed to nudge Willie toward poetry, but she knew if she advertised the poem, it would be seen as a slight at the deeply held beliefs of both women. So, she went into the Holly Hill library. She wrote her poem on a grocery receipt unearthed from her purse, and hid it in what once had been her own book, *Nine Plays of Eugene O'Neill*.

No one would bother to look there. O'Neill was unheard of and un-read in this establishment. He looked nice on the shelf but was never checked out.

On Reconciling Two Visions

Wagner's Valkyrie,
Mere fairies writ large,
Ride Down from Valhalla,
With hope to destroy
Shakespeare's Royal Opposition,
The Queen and King.

Titania, Oberon, cover your ears.
Hunting horns of the Rhine
May tatter your Wings.
But you own a weapon.
Send broonie Puck to whisper
Self-doubt in Valkyrie minds.

Puck, sow existential posers,
Questions of eroding power.
Mention your fairie indifference
To fictions of Racial Purity.
Blow Fairie laughter

Through self-important egos.
Destroy vestiges of pompous Myth.
Then disappear in Fairie mists.

*   *

Wilhalmena Stamps never much cared if her little poetic jokes went anywhere beyond her mind. She wrote and was done. She placed her poems where they might be found, one hundred years on.

In her imagination, by that time, the library would be dismantled and the need for retirement homes no longer felt. In a century, either all aging processes would be stopped by science, or (more likely) tribal life that resulted from incessant war meant that the old were put out to die in winter's cold.

"So much for thinking positively," she chided herself.

She worried about Glyn and his friends. They really should bring the police in on this Trace situation, she thought. But she knew why they did not. The police have a reputation – an earned reputation amongst some cadres of policemen – for making negative assumptions about Black men and boys. And then acting on them with violence.

Add to that Trace's addiction and the so-called War on Drugs.

No, the Ancient Nation kids were right not to involve the police in finding Trace. But that gave advantage to the drug sellers who had kidnapped him off the street corner.

What advantage do we have? She wondered.

We have numbers, and we care enough to persist.

What advantage do I add to this effort? As long as those storage areas aren't rented, I can house the band while they work, and keep them hidden from harm. But they go out at night looking in dangerous places.

I can go out looking in the daytime. No one suspects a little old lady pushing a walker to be searching for a missing kid.

Of course, I won't get far. Susan won't help me do such a thing, and neither would Glyn.

I guess I have to resign myself to listening, analyzing and sifting information that the boys bring back to me. And going out only as far as a walker can take me.

She headed back out of the library, and nearly became squashed by the swinging of the door.

In rushed Valkyrie lover, Leah Müller.

"Oh!" Leah said. "Why are you standing right there? Don't you know the door swings?"

Willie righted herself and said, "It swings both ways. I was just leaving."

"Well, that's fine. But you must expect people to come in, so don't just stand there."

Willie gritted her teeth and said, "How about if you hold the door open so that I may shuffle out?"

Leah put a hand to push open the door. After practicing patience for upwards of five seconds, she said, "You know, if you moved faster, these things wouldn't happen."

"If I could move faster, I'd have swung first, and you'd be on the floor."

As Leah puzzled that out, Willie pushed the door open, held it with the front of her walker and moved into the hall.

Leah followed her and hung a sign on the door that said, **Library Reserved.**

"Are you giving a reading this morning?" Willie asked. She knew better, but the question gave her a warm feeling.

Leah lifted her Teutonic chin, brushed back her blond bowl cut and said, "The Rhine Maidens Rowing Team is having a meeting," Leah shut the door.

Willie smiled to herself and spoke to the air. "Reserve the whole library so the Rhine Maidens won't be distracted by the Adonis-like Siegrieds who live in a retirement home."

No surprise that Geneva long ago accused Leah of being a Nazi. Leah was too young to have been alive during Geneva's war times, but she had the attitude.

Then Willie pondered why Leah had come to live here at all.

Willie had often seen Leah and one or two other Rhine-like Maidens, or Maiden-like Rhines race-climbing the stairs, passing her door and continuing their twelve-flight ascent. Had they come here to have access to stairs? To have access to continuing care as they slowed? Or was it to have access to people who might help them feel superior in their athletic old age?

"The view is also nice," Willie reminded herself. From her balcony, she could see both Mount Hood and Mount Saint Helens.

That reminded her to go into the main dining hall kitchen and retrieve a package she had stored in the refrigerator – suet for her birds.

She headed for the kitchen.

But before she arrived, she passed the front desk and the Holly Hill receptionist called her over.

Willie saw who the receptionist talked to and groaned inwardly.

"Hello, Officer Bailey," Willie said. "May I help you?"

Bailey yanked in his stomach muscles and looked as imposing as habitual laziness can seem.

Willie straightened from her walker, adopting her teacher pose as Bailey turned to face her.

"We've had a report that you steal food," Bailey said. "Really. Would you like to have a key to the larder?" Willie said.

"Steal food in a camp."

She lifted her walker. "I'm unlikely to go camping."

"Some place called Dora."

Now, Willie began to understand. Officer Bailey had taken a call from Geneva and, because he had disgruntled feelings toward herself, he had decided to harass.

"Can you tell me where this camp is?" she asked.

He looked uncomfortable. "Doesn't matter where it is. What have you to say to this accusation?"

Willie shrugged. "I think you might want to come back when you have the facts. I believe your informant thinks I was the cook in a concentration camp in that closed in 1945."

"So, are you the cook?"

"At that time, I lived with my husband and two babies in Colorado."

"Is that where this Dora camp is?"

"No. At the time, we had Japanese internment camps. But I was not the cook in any of those."

"We could have camps now," Bailey said. "Yes, we do have. At the border. We have these abominations whenever we elect someone who sells fear, in the manner of Joseph McCarthy, Colonel Karl Bendetsen, or Hermann Goering. Have we done that?"

Bailey looked confused. "Who are they?"

"People who accuse others without proof. Dead now," she said, letting Bailey think they died because they accused.

Bailey huffled a moment and then said, "You're the focus of an investigation. I'll be back."

He turned as fast as awkward weight would allow, and left for his parked police-mobile.

The receptionist stared at Grandma Willie, who noticed the woman engaged in a search of the internet.

"That's Karl with a K and Bendetsen. Designed and sold Executive Order 9066 sending the Japanese to concentration camps in the United States."

Willie left for the kitchen to check the larder for snacks for birds and for the Ancient Nation.

*   *

In the kitchen, she saw the back of the young lady that she knew had been hired to serve in the private dining room. She also filled and emptied the dishwasher each evening and on Saturdays. At the moment, she washed the lunch pans and cried.

Someone had embroidered flowers on her blouse. That helped Willie dredge up her name.

"Violeta," she said. "Has someone hurt your feelings?"

Violeta jumped, wiped her eyes with soapy hands and then regretted the move. Willie grabbed a towel, pushed it into her hand and said, "Let this absorb the soap. Then rinse the rest out."

Violeta did as directed.

Willie pulled her to a chair. "Now tell me, what is this crying all about?"

Violeta gestured toward the pan of soapy water, but Willie said, "Not the soapy water. Before the soap. Has someone been mean? Is there some way I can help you?"

Violeta looked carefully at Willie, then at her hands, then at Willie again. Willie waited silently, letting her assess and debate.

At last, Violeta said, "Mi Rosaria, my sister is missing." Willie hurt with understanding. "How long?"

"A week. She left on the bus for college and never arrived."

Willie's heart jumped in her chest. How afraid her mother must be, and how helpless. "Where is the college?"

"In Newberg."

"Ah! So, the Quaker College, what is it called?"

"George Fox University."

Willie hesitated for a moment, then asked, "Was she going to be a DACA student?"

"Yes, Childhood Arrivals."

"Has the college helped you look for her?"

"They want to call the police."

"And your family fears the police?"

"Si, mucho temor."

"May I help?"

Violeta looked at Willie's walker.

Willie said, "The walker is a disguise. People don't know that I'm actually an action hero."

Violeta glanced up, realized something about her new friend's face and laughed. "You are The Secret Walker."

"Yup, Willie the Wanderer."

Violeta wiped her face again with the towel and said. "I don't want you in danger also."

"You think your sister was stolen off the bus?"

"Si, Papá put her on the bus. There was not supposed to be a transfer, but the bus arrived at Newberg, the counselor for DACA was there, but there was no Rosaria."

"I will do what I can without being in danger, but I must tell you that I teach writing at the training center for policemen and also at the jail. There may be information I could glean by listening."

"And reading their writing," Violeta added.

Willie nodded, glad to have met so smart a young lady. "Exactly. Now let's get some facts. Your sister is Rosaria."

"Rosaria Aguirre."

"How old?"

"Eighteen."

"We're you born here, Violeta?"

"Yes, my father and myself, but not my mother and my sister."

"What bus company did she use to get to Newberg."

"The Leapfrog – the intercity transport."

"Was she traveling with a friend, another student?"

"Papá said she didn't know anyone on the bus."

"Forgive me for asking, but is it possible she did know someone and didn't want to tell your papa – someone she may have thought he wouldn't approve of?"

Violeta straightened and declared, "Rosaria is a good girl."

"Parents are often very protective. It wouldn't take much – someone who often stayed out late, who didn't go to the same church, maybe …"

Covering her mouth with her hand, Violeta glanced at her shoes. A moment later, she said, "Rosaria had a friend who also will go to George Fox. She offered Rosaria a ride, but the driver was a boyfriend, so Papá said 'No'."

"What was this friend's name?"

"Liza Cramer."

"And the boyfriend?"

"I didn't know him. I don't think Rosaria knew him either – someone Liza had met at a party."

"And was he a student at George Fox?"

"I don't think so, but I don't know for sure."

"Did Liza arrive at George Fox?"

Violeta stared at Willie. "I don't know. I hardly know her, but I think I know where she lives."

"How about if you show me where, and I find out if she is safe. It may be important."

"I will walk by there and get the address for you. Thank you for asking these questions, too. I'm afraid for Rosaria."

"Violeta, let me make inquiries. I think it is safer and less threatening for an older person to be asking questions about things than it is for you. We don't want you missing as well."

Violeta nodded. "I will just walk there, not knock on the door."

"Do you know the name of the counselor who was to meet Rosaria?"

"No, but I think my Papá has that name. I will ask him."

"Good," Willie grabbed a paper towel and wrote on it. "I live here, on the eighth floor, but if you need to send me a message, here is my cell phone number, as well."

CHAPTER EIGHT

Glyn slipped into the kitchen that evening after dinner. He grabbed a towel and began drying a plate.

"Este es un plato, ¿no?" Violeta smiled, slightly.

Still sad that her sister is gone to college, he thought.

She said, "Si, es verdad. Un plato." She held up a glass. "Y este es un vaso."

"Un vaso para agua," Glyn said. "A glass for water."

"Si. ¿Que es este?" She held up a cup. "What is this?"

He took the cup and held her hand, "Este es un mano hermoso, a beautiful hand."

She let him hold it a second, and then pulled away. "Señor Jones …"

"Glyn."

"Señor Glyn, no tengo paciencia con un hombre que hace chistes y lisonjas."

He asked, "You don't have patience for guys who make what? Chistes?"

"Jokes and flattery."

"No jokes, but yes, I like to flatter you. I enjoy your company. Is it un chiste to say that?"

She looked at him, solemnly, and he saw a sudden tear fill her eye. She swiped at it and turned back to emptying the dishwasher.

He leaned down and said to her, "I hope you will tell me what is wrong. Has someone been mean to you?"

She stood up quickly. "You sound like . . ." and then she stopped.

"Like who?"

"It doesn't matter. You just reminded me of a friend."

"A friend. That's good. I hope you will see I can be your friend as well."

"You are very good, but I cannot have the easy time right now to enjoy friends. I have things I must take care of."

"May I help you?"

She sniffed. "I must be careful. Someday, maybe I can ask you for help, but not yet."

"Well, I can vouch for the fact that you don't need help with English. And that you will become a great teacher, if that is what you want to do. Anything else I can help with, you let me know."

She almost laughed, "I will ask you when I need letters of recommendation to get into coll . . . college." At that moment, she banged a pan into the sink and began to scrub it.

"Violeta, I want to help you now. You check me out. People will tell you I'm mostly a good guy."

"Mostly?"

"Well, I'm not perfect, but I'm working at it. I drive too fast, but I work hard and have good grades."

"Drive too fast? Is that your only failing?"

"My most costly one, at any rate."

"Aha!" she said, "Drive fast, plus get caught, eh?"

"Si, señorita. La policía y mi abuela saben que tengo un pie de plomo. Grandma and the police know I drive too fast."

"The lead foot? Un pie de plomo? Is that why you came here to work? To pay a fine for driving?"

He stepped back, completely surprised by her intuition. "Well, that's why I came, but now that I'm here, I like this place. Interesting people with interesting pasts, and stories, and lots of dishes to wash and dry with you."

She looked at him and said, "Could you walk with me to get an address?"

"Sure. Where are we headed?"

"Not tonight, but tomorrow morning?"

"Sure, I can come by your house . . ."

"No. Please meet me before school at Broadway and Fifteenth. Seven in the morning?"

"Wait, don't you have to go to school?"

"Yes. I catch the bus to Saint Mary's at seven thirty."

"Seven it is. Broadway – how about if you wait inside the Peet's coffee shop? Safer."

"I will."

The kitchen door to the basement swung open. There stood Lonny Dement. He stared at Violeta and then grinned at Glyn. "Hey man. Making time?"

Glyn said, "What do you want, Lon?"

"It's our turn for the Burnside detail."

"I'll meet you in the practice room in fifteen minutes."

Lonny wiggled his eyebrows, trying, unsuccessfully, to look lewd.

"Go on," Glyn said. Lon withdrew slowly.

"Burnside detail?" she asked.

Glyn said, "Is your dad picking you up?"

"Burnside?"

Glyn sighed, "I've got a friend who is missing since three days ago. The guys in the band, we're looking for him on the streets. Tonight, Burnside Street."

"Under the bridge? That's dangerous."

"We'll be fine. I don't bother people, just look."

"Find any girls?"

"Mostly guys and older women."

"You find any girls, you get them out of there."

"They'd have to want to get out," Glyn said. "Maybe they want, but can't say so."

"True. You got a friend down there?"

She looked off at the refrigerator and said, "Glyn, my sister is missing."

"Your Rosaria?"

CHAPTER NINE

Fifteen minutes later, Glyn had helped Violeta finish the dishes, learned all he could about where Rosaria might have been, found out what her parents were doing in order to find her, and pledged to search for her, as well.

He ran downstairs rousting Lonny from sleep.

Glyn had no idea how to look for either Trace or Rosaria Aguirre, Violeta's sister. The story of each one's disappearance was extremely different, but he knew they had to start looking somewhere and the somewhere tonight was under the Burnside Bridge.

"Let's start with the skate park," Glyn said.

Lonny wiped his eyes, and yawned. "Bunch of little kids at the skate park."

"Young maybe, but they see things."

"That place is a dump," Lonny said.

"Do you expect to find Trace in a McMansion?"

"Yeah, sitting next to the guy that sold him the stuff."

"I wish. Let's go."

Glyn decided not to tell Lonny they searched for Rosaria as well. Lonny's mind leapt about, hard to corral on the best of days. His fantasy life as a street hoodlum interfered with his grasp on what should and shouldn't be said.

Glyn knew Leneld had paired them up because usually Glyn could stuff Lonny's words down his throat just by a hard look, but lately, Lonny wanted more recognition as a cool dude. He'd blat out just about anything he'd heard or thought he'd heard on television. Plus, the guy started fights he couldn't finish.

*   *

The Burnside skate park had been built over time, started by a several young fellows, now grown up. Some of them still designed skate parks all over the world. They had liked the bridge location, even though the street tent dwellers were people with lots of problems. The leavings of a tough life became all too easy to see and smell.

But the designers had used left over concrete and discarded materials, plus the frame of the bridge pillars to help them build. Other kids had come. The area got cleaned up, some. The kids added to the curves, and they all learned how to make do. They also learned how to convince the city that kids needed a skate park to keep occupied and moving in the right direction.

Glyn liked the story of the park, but he only skated to and from work and school. He didn't pretend to be a trick skater.

Lonny skated everywhere and often chose to test garden walls along the way. So, they arrived on their boards.

They got there after dark. The place didn't smell of car fumes, as you would guess. Those fumes went up into the clouds. It smelled more of the people who had only tents and cardboard for homes.

But the noise of cars and trucks created a constant irregular beat overhead. The Burnside Bridge itself had been designed in the previous century by an architect – early Portland city fathers searching for beauty back in the 1900s. So, the pillars underneath had a sturdy but elegant look to them, which you could still find if you looked around the tents.

The area between Second Avenue and the river stretched to about three blocks at this point. Close to the river under the bridge was very dark. Close to Second Avenue enjoyed streetlights. The building next door had a logo on the top that read, "Long Live the Wildcards, Misfits and Dabblers."

Seemed like the right place for a skate park and a store outside the norm.

Bridge lights and the moon provided enough illumination to see the five kids who were still out. Two were older, more like out of high school – sturdy-built guys who might have heavy- lifting jobs, but still practiced their moves in the evenings.

Glyn wondered about the parents of the three younger kids.

If they had parents.

He sat down on the bench, but Lonny went right to one of the younger kids. He waggled his board at the boy.

"You a beginner?" Always the challenge.

Glyn stood up. "Hey, Lon. Come here, I need you."

"Just a sec."

Glyn moved away and pretended to look at the area behind the near pillar of the bridge. He knew Lon couldn't stand to be out of the action. If he thought Glyn had found something, he'd leave off jawing at the kid.

Lon came right over. Just then, a train came down the track that ran past the bridge and beyond the main streets. Its long trail of cars passed the grocers, lumber and hardware district of southeast Portland. It headed for the area near the car park behind the science museum.

Over the train noise, Lonny said, "What you got?"

"We want to make friends, get information. The coolest dude doesn't talk. He listens."

Lon gestured back toward the kid. "But he's just slipping and sliding, doing nothing with that board."

"Sit and watch him learn."

"He doesn't deserve the space."

"We're here to find Trace. Keep that in mind."

"What's back there?" Lonny poked his head back of the pillar, between the edge of the skate park and the next hardware store.

"A tent," Glyn said.

"Maybe that guy knows something."

"Maybe. If he comes out, we ask. If not, he's asleep."

"Boy, are you a do-nothin' guy."

"Yup. Do no harm. First rule of investigation."

"Thought that was doctors."

"Works for them, too," Glyn said.

They turned around and found two of the older skateboarders coming toward them.

"Hey," one of them said.

"Hi," Glyn said, putting a hand on Lon's arm as he felt him tense for confrontation.

"You got a funky old board." one fellow said.

Glyn held his scuffed board up. "Transportation," he said. "Actually, we're writing an article for the school newspaper on skate parks, kind of a way to encourage the city to build more of them." Glyn figured he really could write. Published?

Maybe.

"Yeah?" the biggest guy tucked his board under an arm and looked around. "This was one of the first," he said.

"Perfect place," Glyn said. "All this light and a roof against the rain." He gestured up at the bridge and all the cars whizzing overhead. "But adults always ask, 'How safe is it?' Anybody get hurt? Bothered by transients?"

"Naw," the big guy said.

"Some kids just ask for trouble," the other one said. "You know, flirting with guys, letting cons take them out to the Yo- Plait and like that."

"So, advice on what not to do at the park would be good," Glyn said.

"Sure," the big guy said, and he looked at Lon. "Don't come on to the young ones."

Glyn saw Lon's jaw muscles bunch, so he nudged him. "Any young ones gone missing?" Glyn asked.

"Some don't come back from the Yo-Plait, if that's what you mean." The guy dropped his board as if to get back to practicing.

"Any idea where they end up?"

"I didn't follow them, but they went in the wrong direction for ice cream – off toward the tile factory and the lumber yards."

"So, just like at the game stores, some guys come to play, some come to pick up," Glyn said.

"Some come to take you off to California."

"California?" Lon asked. "That'd be great."

The big guy stared at him. "Not sunny California," he said. "You mean up in the mountains?" Lon said. "Skiing and like that?"

The two fellows looked at each other. The smaller guy said, "Yeah. Like that."

But Glyn said, "Lon, I think he means more like indoor recreation."

The big guy looked at Lon with narrowed eyes. He said, "You don't want to tell your naïve friends about indoor recreation. That might burst their bubble."

Lon bristled, but Glyn spoke quickly. "So, what's the trail to California. It starts here with the pick-up and goes off to the not-so Yo-Plait, and then what?"

"Then into a truck and off on the big adventure."

"You wouldn't be telling this if the big adventure were your business. Do you know some who've been taken on that route?"

"We're just guessing. But the lost ones are the reason we stay till the last kid goes home."

"These kids have a home? Someone picks them up?" Glyn asked.

"Naw. We finally tell them the park is closed and to get to the bus. We're not here to worry about anything but the rep of the park."

"This park never closes." Lon dropped his board as if to challenge someone to a skate duel.

"This park closes in half an hour," the guy said, squaring off with Lon.

"Lon, we got a job. I think we've got to go write it up."

Lon didn't really want to challenge the big guy, so he stepped on his board, flipped around and skated off.

"Thanks for your help with our article," Glyn said.

"Bet the school principal won't let you print most of what we talked about."

"True. By the way, you know a guy named Trace? Skinny, black, dreads…"

"And a habit?"

"Last few months, yeah. I'm worried about him. Seen him in the last couple of days?"

"We told him to steer clear of this place. He's got bad-news friends."

"You know where they hang?"

"Used to sell down here, but we call 911 when they show. Some policeman named Bailey, the first cop they sent, he didn't care and didn't get it. He thought we were the trouble. But we kept calling, and now, the horse cop comes every day, so they disappeared to a little further north. Not sure where.

You think he's crosswise with them?"

"I do."

"Stay out of that. He earned it."

"He's sick."

"By choice."

Glyn ignored that myth. He asked, "Further north? You mean up Grand Ave?"

"Seen a couple of them on Weidler Street the other day, but they move."

The smaller guy said, "I seen em near Second and Flanders."

"Flanders," the big guy said, "Poppy fields. That fits."

Glyn didn't know exactly what the guy meant. Were there really poppies somewhere along Flanders Street?

He didn't want to ask, so he said, "What do they look like?"

"Their leader has big guts, too small pants, curls like a I-talian, and dinky fingers."

"Thanks. You see Trace, please tell him Glyn asked for him. Call home."

"Home?"

"His mom's worried, and me, too."

"Glyn, better catch your friend, Lon. He's a walking trouble machine."

"Don't take him seriously."

"You should."

*   *

Within two blocks, Glyn knew the guy was right about Lon.

He turned the corner at Second and what might have been Davis to find public land had been turned into a small village of tiny houses with an herb garden, and an awning for a kitchen.

Near the awning stood two rows of seven wooden structures, each with an address and a front porch. Two port-a-potties sat near the homes, but a little behind them.

Six angry people surrounded Lon. Two of them were women, the other four were men, some as old as Glyn's Grandma Willie.

One of the old men shook a finger in Lon's face. "Don't keep knockin' on my door when I tell you to go away."

Lon's face screwed as tight as his fake cornrows. "Was that a home? Thought it was a outhouse," Lon shouted.

Glyn walked to the edge of the group. Lon looked up at him and said, "Isn't that right? Looks like a outhouse to me."

"You're way behind the times, kid," Glyn said to Lon. "That is the newest kind of home, and the best. The crowd now surrounded Glyn as well. "So," Glyn said to Lon, "why don't you apologize and leave here with me."

"I don't apologize to some geezer comes bargin' out like I've no right to knock."

"It's probably how you knocked, plus, it's after dark, let the man sleep."

"His light was on."

"So, let him read."

"You're a dick, Glyn Jones."

One of the women stepped up to Glyn and said, "Take your friend out of here and don't let him come back."

"Yes, ma'am." Glyn took Lonny by the arm. "You're coming with this Dick, right now."

Lonny swung hard and connected with Glyn's jaw. As he fell backwards, three of the men picked Lon up and sent him sprawling at the foot of the outhouse. One fellow swung the door open, and three others picked him up, holding him over the port-a-hole.

The woman who had talked to Glyn ran over there and pulled at one man. "Put him down, Jake. You wanna go to jail for this punk?"

"Nope," Jake said and dropped Lonny's left arm. The other two held on and said, "On Three."

From the grass, Glyn yelled. "He's not worth the trouble. Let him come home with me and we won't bother you again."

"Not worth the trouble, but this is a message to all like him."

They dipped him down into the port-a-hole. "Far enough," said the other woman.

They pulled him out and dropped him on the ground. Lon's hair was covered with shit, and some of his face. As the men stepped back,

Glyn pulled Lon's t-shirt over his head. He mopped his eyes and then his hair.

"Lie still so it won't drip," he said, noting for the first time, how very skinny Lon really was.

He couldn't get all the shit out of the hair, and he knew they should go to urgent care for the eyes, but he got enough that it wouldn't rain down on his shoulders when he rose.

"Stand up and walk," Glyn said. Lonny lunged at him. "Not worth it?"

Glyn stood up. "Getting more worthless by the minute. Come get me when you learn not to start fights just because you're feeling small."

He walked away. The men and women stood nearby, but they just watched Lon leave. Glyn saw that one man had a shovel in his hand.

Lon stood up, swung his hair around like a dog and splattered the nearest small house with shit.

The old man lifted his shovel like a pole axe. Lon backed up and started running. The man chased him a whole block before giving up.

Glyn let him go. He foresaw a lot of trouble if he followed to make sure Lon got home safely. Let him live with what he bought himself.

CHAPTER TEN

As Glyn started up Burnside toward home, he saw that all of this action had been watched by an inebriated fellow and also by the younger three kids from the skate park. They all waited for the bus at Burnside Street and Martin Luther King Avenue.

"Your friend's not comin' here, is he?" one of the kids asked.

For the first time, Glyn realized these skaters were only about ten or eleven years old.

"I hope he's not coming this way," Glyn said. "Here comes your bus. Best get on and duck him. I'll keep walking and hope he follows me."

"That fat dude is following you," one kid said.

Glyn glanced back across Martin Luther King. On the northwest corner of Burnside and MLK, Glyn saw a man with a huge belly hanging over his pants. The man turned his curly head from watching Lon to watching Glyn.

But Glyn and Lon were split up. The fat fellow with the too small pants seemed to be debating which to keep an eye on.

Glyn figured Lon didn't notice this fat man, and didn't know even to watch for him – that information had come to Glyn after Lon left the skate park. And Glyn knew there were probably partners to the man, maybe nearby, maybe on each corner.

Back at the Tiny House settlement, the people were busy cleaning shit from their friend's house, and didn't care what happened to Lon.

If this guy were aware of him and Lon as friends of Trace, Glyn needed to get to Lon and make sure he got home safely.

Glyn picked up his board and crossed Burnside to the southeast corner, ready to go back and escort Lon home from afar. However, nobody seemed to be following him or Lon. And no one moved in on him.

Yet.

Just then, the bus passed Glyn. It stopped at the northeast corner. The three kids got on, but the wino suddenly wasn't a wino. He jumped onto the bus as agile as any sober man.

At that moment, Glyn realized it was the kids that Small Pants had been watching, and the wino was his confederate.

Glyn ran around a screeching Subaru while re-crossing Burnside to catch up with the bus. He raced the bus for two blocks, dodging bicycles and pedestrians. Finally, he caught up with it at the next stop.

He lifted his skateboard and jumped on the bus, pulled out his monthly pass, and discovered Fatman's confederate sitting behind the three young skaters, engaging them with jokes.

Glyn sat across the aisle from the confederate, hauled his board into his lap, and just listened. The rumble of the once- drunk man's knock-knock jokes led to Three-men-entered-a- tavern jokes which the kids seemed to laugh at as if they weren't quite sure what was funny about a rabbi, a minister and a priest.

Glyn studied the guy, so he could remember him again. There wasn't much unusual about him – about Glyn's own height, brown, straight, dirty hair, ragged levis, Nirvana t-shirt, converse gym shoes.

But the fellow kept his face in an almost perpetual grin.

After a few moments, Glyn realized the grin disguised the fact that the man couldn't open his left eye all the way – as if it had been knife-slashed.

The guy turned from three men jokes to condom jokes, and then rolled down the mud road to breast and titty jokes.

The kids squirmed.

Finally, Glyn said, "Fellow, give it up. Your jokes aren't funny, they're just dirt rolled in shit."

"What?" the guy said. "You got no funny bone?" he turned to the kids, jerked his thumb at Glyn and said, "Here's a real pansy."

One of the three giggled.

Glyn said, "You kids know this guy? Or is he just hitting on you?"

Three sets of young eyes widened with understanding. They ducked their heads, two pretending to look out the window and the third opening a comic book.

"What are you saying?" the guy asked. "We were just enjoying some humor until you barged into the conversation."

"After you hit on them, then what? You leave the bus with at least one of them in tow, and you're off to the whorehouse with a new cute kid for older men to play with?"

Glyn said this so the kids could hear and understand, but a woman passenger nearby glared at Glyn and said, "Why do you talk so dirty?"

Glyn turned her comment on the other guy. "Why the dirty jokes?"

"They're funny," the guy protested. "These guys weren't laughing."

"Yeah, they were. Weren't you, fellas?"

The comic book boy said, "Not really. You're just talking. Whyn't you quit?"

The other boys finally got up their courage. "Yeah."

"We want this space to ourselves."

The guy turned on Glyn. "We can take this outside."

"You can take it outside. I'm on the bus till home."

The guy grabbed Glyn's arm. Glyn reached up and pulled the brake line on the bus, yelling. "Pull over and stop this guy from fighting."

The guy drew back his arm. Glyn stuffed a fist in the fellow's stomach.

The bus lurched to the side of Martin Luther King Avenue.

The bus driver was a woman, but she came back holding up her cell phone and dialing a number. He could tell she'd take no guff.

"Both of you get off," she hissed

"No," said one of the young boys, pointing at Glyn. "That guy helped us."

The lady passenger said, "He was talking dirty. Said 'whorehouse and stuff."

"No!" the boys chorused.

"I don't care who said what. Get off."

Glyn turned to the boys. "Tell your friends about guys like him. Don't let them get taken in and then stolen."

Then he and his board swung off the bus and ran up the street before the other fellow could get out the door. When he looked back, the other man stood on Martin Luther King Avenue and stared at him.

As the bus passed him, the boys rose up in the aisle and waved.

*   *

The bus had been going north, so now Glyn was near Weidler Street and not too far from the Lloyd Center Shopping Mall. Holly Hill Retirement was just to the east, so he ran through the park south of the mall. He arrived at Holly Hill Retirement Home in time to find the person at the front desk deep in conversation with Grandma Willie.

Glyn sat on a sofa nearby to wait.

"Oh, I'm certain Geneva Oppenheim will calm down," Grandma said. "Something has begun to remind her of the old days."

"She sure doesn't remember much about these days," the receptionist said. "Yesterday she forgot to eat at all. And that policeman, Bailey, he's been back here three times, kind of egging her on to accuse you."

Grandma Willie sighed. "I'm not too worried about Bailey, but if he's encouraging her fears, he should be told to stop."

"Well. if he comes, I can't exactly tell him she's not here."

"No," Grandma Willie said. "There are other things we can do. Meanwhile, I'll try to get her to join me. It's hard to come to the dining room when everyone is talking about you, and no one wants to sit with you."

"Rolly told me she's now accused him of killing her uncle in some town in Germany, and Leah Müller thinks we should send her off to the nut house. I didn't say 'nut house'. Leah did."

Grandma Willie said. "I'm sure everyone who talks about Geneva thinks they are not gossips, but they are making things worse for her."

"I'm only telling you what people tell me."

"Uh-huh. As a kid, did you ever play telephone?"

"I'm quoting exactly."

"But Beverly, that's what everyone in the chain of information believes they're doing. We're human, so we don't remember every word, and the words we don't remember, we fill in with something close. Close may have many meanings, so two or three links down the chain, the meaning may not be the original meaning at all."

Beverly gazed off into the distance, and said, "Well, I'm not sure why you think you have to stick up for the nastiest person in the building."

"Would you want me to stick up for you when you're having a difficult time?"

"It's not the same."

"I see." Grandma turned toward Glyn and said, "Mr. Jones, could you come take care of that bookcase we started to move yesterday?"

Glyn knew this was her signal to come upstairs. "Sure thing, Mrs. Stamps. I think we can finish that job soon."

He followed her to the elevator. A few yards down the hall, he whispered, "People are really getting on Mrs. Oppenheim's case, eh?"

"Yes, they are."

"Who is this policeman, Bailey. I've heard his name before."

"Oh, he's a guy who was in my writing class three times."

Glyn watched her face as he asked. "Got a way to keep him out of here?"

She puckered her mouth, resigned, as if she'd dealt with such problems many times. "Possibly. You look like you ran the marathon."

"Maybe the five-mile. Lonny and I checked the skate park under the Burnside Bridge, and Lonny loves to mouth off."

"Got chased out?"

"Not from the park, but from the Tiny House neighborhood just north of the park."

"What did you learn?"

"Not to go anywhere with Lonny again."

"And about Trace?"

"There's a guy down there that Trace used to hang with. This guy used to sell drugs at the park. He was kicked out by the police and the bigger park guys, but he hovers around the place still, and he was there this evening."

"Might he have been selling to Trace?"

"Maybe, he fits the park guys' description, but he doesn't fit Jon's description of the two guys that are looking for me – and for Mom's car."

"What's this seller look like?"

"Too big for his britches." Grandma raised an eyebrow.

Glyn said, "Sorry. Couldn't pass it up. He's so fat his belly hangs over his pants. And he's got curly black hair on this over-sized head.

Big arms, short fingers. That's how the older guys at the skate park described him. And there he was."

"You didn't get a name, I suppose."

"Nobody knew it. Come to think of it, that's how Felipe described the guy that came looking for Trace's Taco Bell sack."

Glyn had never mentioned the bullet holes at Felipe's station. Grandma would definitely bring in the police on that one.

"But," Glyn said, "I also met one of Big Belly's helpers.

That second guy tried to pick up three young kids who'd been at the skate park."

"They got away from him?"

"Not exactly. They got wise to what he was doing, and the bus driver got him off the bus."

"The bus driver, would he also recognize this guy?"

"She might."

"Okay. Now describe that one."

"Blue driver's uniform."

Grandma Willie turned her teacher frown at him, but Glyn kept going. "Arm on her like the handle of an axe. Face like putty left out in the sun."

"You know who I meant."

"Oh, Pick-Up Guy – pretty common looking. Medium height. Brown hair that's straight and not exactly clean. Wears old levis, converse shoes and t-shirts. The only thing she might remember is that he has one squinty eye – can't open it all the way. Knifed, maybe."

"So, the bus driver on the MLK bus going …?"

"Going north at 7:30 p.m.. You got a friend in the force who might check around for the two guys?"

"Seems far-fetched for finding Trace," Grandma said, "but for the sake of other children, might as well give these two people the police hassle."

"There are lots of folks selling drugs. As I ran through the theater parking lot across your own street, I saw a sale going down."

Grandma sighed. "Still? That's been prime selling real- estate since before your Grandpa died. We used to walk past sales, go to the nearest phone (we didn't have these cell phone gadgets in those days) and report the activity."

"Yeah? So, did the police swoop in and everyone scattered?"

"Yes. No arrests, just run a police car past them slowly. It only moved the sale temporarily."

"I hope you watched from somewhere not too obvious."

Grandma Willie just smiled at him, and said, "Go check on the kitchen. I suspect there's a dish washer still working."

As Glyn took the stairs down eight flights, he wondered how his grandma knew he was interested in the dish washer.

CHAPTER ELEVEN

Glyn arrived in the kitchen at 8:15p.m., almost time for Violeta to go home. She had stacked clean pans about as high as they could be stacked. When Glyn arrived, she handed him a towel and said, "Tonight we learn cooking terms."

"Great. Before we start, could I ask you a couple more questions about your sister?"

She put down the dishrag. "Yes."

"You told me about the bus, but is it possible she got off the bus early for some reason?"

"She wasn't on it when it arrived in Newberg, so she had to have gotten off. Maybe she thought she'd arrived when it stopped in a different town, but Papá has gone to the bus stations of the towns along the way, and they have no record of her in those towns."

"Who does he ask? I mean he doesn't talk to policemen or sheriffs, so ..."

"He asks other people like us, you know, people from South America, Central America."

"So, nada?"

"Nada. Have you been looking for her?"

"Yes," Glyn said, "but what is puzzling is that she speaks English and would know when she arrived in the right town, so…"

"Where were you looking?"

"I told you about my friend – also missing."

"Trace."

"I'm hoping the drug people didn't get him and he's just hiding, so I went to the Burnside Bridge Skate Park."

"Rosaria doesn't skate."

"Well, my search tonight was a bust for Trace as well, but I did meet a couple of fellows who had seen someone like Trace weeks ago, and the fellows who sell drugs down that way.

Mean and scary. One of them hopped a city bus and tried to hook up with kids too young to know what a sleaze he was. It occurred to me that somebody on Rosaria's bus might have forced her off."

Violeta's eyes filled with tears. "Papá's contacts wouldn't have even seen her, then."

Glyn stepped closer to her. "We gotta hope that's not what happened, but if it did happen, who would know where they might take her?"

"One of the ladies here is also helping me. She asked about Rosaria's friend who offered her a ride to school with her boyfriend. I am to find that address, but I haven't had a chance yet."

"Was that what we were going to do tomorrow morning?"

"Yes."

"Is it far from here?"

"No, but I don't go there alone after dark."

"Leave the rest of the pans. I'll wash and dry them later.

Let's walk there and be back in time for your dad."

Twenty minutes later, they had an address for a house on Multnomah Street, just east of Holly Hill Retirement.

As they walked back to meet Mr. Aguirre, Glyn asked. "Who's this other person who's helping you?"

"Mrs. Willie," Violeta said. "Eighth floor. Uses a walker. Very nice."

Glyn laughed, "Grandma Willie. I should have known."

"Tu abuelita?"

"Si. Mi abuelita and slave driver."

"How so? Slave driver."

"She's the one insisted I get a job here to pay off my debt to the state of Oregon."

"I thank her for slave driving, then."

"Me, too. Here's your papá."

*   *

After he put away the pan pile, Glyn ran up the stairs toward Grandma's floor. On the way up, he met Leah Müller running down.

"Two times a day?" he asked.

She passed him, saying, "Three times. Six a.m., two p.m. and ten p.m.."

"Why?"

Leah turned the corner to take the next flight of steps. "Long life."

He watched her turn down two more flights and thought, *Long life to you. Don't break anything.*

Entering Grandma's apartment, he expected to tip-toe to his 'library' room, but Grandma sat on her sofa, phone at her ear. She signaled him to sit.

She also pointed at a note. It said, *Got a new lock for my door?"*

He wrote, *Not yet. Hoped to, but got hung up hunting for Trace.*

She scribbled while listening. *Any luck? Not much. Tell you when off phone.*

As he emptied books off the second-best chair, she talked into the phone. "A woman driver, described as having a strong arm and a melting putty face."

Glyn raised his eyebrows at her. She shook her head, and talked to the phone person.

"Yes, very nice metaphor, and probably accurate, given the source. Unfortunately, the same source could only describe the leader of the ring and not such a great description of the bus rider who tried to pick up the kids."

She listened, then said, "White with brown hair, old jeans, t-shirts, converse shoes."

She cocked her head at Glyn. He wrote on her note pad "Squinty right eye, maybe knifed.

She nodded and added that description to the other person.

She spoke into the phone. "Okay, that helps."

After a silence, she said. "I appreciate you working on this.

That kind needs to be plagued and harassed, but young kids need to know more about their type, as well."

Silence.

"Well, as you know, facts are not always the whole truth.

Some of truth is emotion. Fear at a park breeds less community and more reason for fear."

Silence.

"Thank you. I hope we can find both children." When she had hung up, Glyn asked, "Who?"

"A past writing student now a police captain."

"Think he'll search the data base for Small Pants and his Pick-up Guy?"

She nodded. "Yep. A clear-sighted member of the force who writes colorful letters to the editor under a pen name."

"May I ask …"

"No."

"Okay," he said, and handed her a Post-it Note. "I have an address for you from Violeta. She describes you as very nice."

"Pushy is more what I am. This is Liza's address?"

"Yes."

She studied it. "It turns out that no Liza Cramer ever arrived at George Fox campus either."

Glyn felt his neck cool. "Geez. That's not good. How'd you find out?"

"I know how high school placement counselors talk, so I called the college to see how Liza was succeeding."

He stood up and paced. "Do you recommend lying as a tool?"

"Acting. I act like someone; they make the assumptions.

Tomorrow, I will try to talk to her parents. The police already have her as a missing person, and are looking for the boyfriend."

"Got a description of him? And a name?

"White. Blond curly hair. Six feet one or so. Runner, or at least she met him at a track meet."

Glyn checked his reflection in the nearby window. "White.

Blond curly hair. Six-one, but Not named Glyn Jones?"

"No, but you'd best not be seen near that house, because all you curly blonds look alike. His name is Chuck, and that's all they know."

"Chuck. I'll ask around the track team."

"Older. Probably an alum, if he finished school."

"Maybe Arwain would remember such a guy."

"Call your sister and check."

Glyn nodded. "She's around town a lot, takes busses and the MAX train to college."

"So, give her the descriptions. And next time you see the fat guy and his buddy, take photos."

"That'll go over with the perps. Nice request. Please stand still against that wall."

"You know how to photo with stealth."

"Grandma, I'm getting the idea that you use stealth a lot."

"Blowing my grandma image, am I?"

"Big time."

She chuckled. "When I do it, it's called 'strategic action', and it is done to benefit others."

He looked at her, a big question in his raised eyebrows.

"So, that's your fifty-minute lecture on ethics in sleuthing."

"Got it." He hauled out his phone and dialed Arwain's number. She answered. "Bubba?"

"Sista, I got something I need you to watch out for."

"This about the reason Mom's now buying a truck?"

"Yep."

"Whatcha got?"

Grandma waved goodnight and went into her room.

Ten minutes later, Arwain had been brought up to date. "I remember Liza Cramer," she said. "Pretty. Did the eight- hundred meters. Lots of stamina. But I don't think I knew a Rosaria Aguirre."

Glyn said, "Violeta, her sister, speaks great English, and Rosaria was a DACA student, headed for George Fox College, so probably a good student."

Arwain didn't remember a tall blond Chuck on the track team or from any of the meets she'd been to. "I'm into Skype mode tomorrow with Phip" she said. Their big brother, J.P., John Philip, AKA Phip, had become a Marine and had been in Iraq for ten months, so they tried to keep up with his life. He preferred joking and talking about old memories, but there were times when they got hints that stuff around him turned scary.

Since Phip had been an astounding runner, a track and soccer star, it was possible he'd know more members from other teams. Arwain's rep was from the javelin and the long slow races that required persistence. Phip was All-State speed.

After they hung up, Glyn flopped into bed, where he dreamed about Trace and Violeta being chased by cougars. He kept trying to distract, but the cougars focused on their prey.

CHAPTER TWELVE

The next morning, Glyn awoke to the sound of Grandma Willie in the hall talking to Geneva. It didn't sound friendly.

He hopped into his levis and pulled his t-shirt over his head. Glyn barely had his shoes on and seemed to be moving books into a new bookcase in Grandma's living room when Geneva swung open the door.

"I knew you had that kid in here."

"Hello, Mrs. Oppenheim," he said. "How do you like Mrs. Stamps's new bookcase?"

She barged in, leaving Grandma in the hall, watching.

She shook her long fingers in his face. "Rolly Goforth hired you, didn't he? Wants to spy on me."

Glyn stayed on the floor near the stack of books so she wouldn't feel more threatened. He said, "I thought you were Mrs. Stamps's good friend."

"So, she claims. But I know she was the cook. Willamena, the cook at Mittle-Bau Dora. And that Goforth man ..."

Glyn said, "How old do you think Willamena the cook was when you were four or five years old?"

She stared at him. "She's of the super race."

That surprised him. Had she really bought into that portrayal of the Germans?

"I don't think even super races stop aging and then dying.

So, was she maybe thirty back then in 1945?"

Mrs. Oppenheim leaned down and said, "You're trying to fool me. They passed on their genes and their ideas. I know them. They are at it again."

"What are they doing?" Glyn asked.

"Keeping children for the train to Peenemünde. "Can I get to the train and release them?"

"Never. They are locked in the building and hurried out to the train. No one can get close to them."

"What could Mr. Goforth have to do with the train?" Glyn asked.

"He pretends not to be a Nazi, but I have him identified. He might as well turn himself into the Wiesenthal Center and confess."

"Wiesenthal Center? What's that?"

"They are rounding up the last of the Nazi killers and sending them to trial." She continued, but in a muttering tone. "They should send them all to Israel, but they don't."

"Nazis? Aren't those guys all dead by now?"

"Not this so-called Goforth fellow and Müller, and this new Stapleton guy. He was a scientist at Peenemünde. Then he came here, worked for NASA and pretended he never believed in Hitler."

"Stapleton?" Grandma said from the hall, "You mean the new choir director here at the center?"

"He's from California," Glyn said.

Mrs. Oppenheim snarled at him. "He's German. I know it."

Grandma seemed to be deep in thought. "But Stapleton has no accent."

"He's that scientist. I saw him for sure. People say I was only five, but you don't forget evil people."

"I'm sorry, Geneva," Grandma said. "Can I help you search for the truth about these people?"

"You? You're one of them."

Glyn said, "Grandma was born in Levi, Texas. How could she have been a cook in Germany in 1944?"

Geneva waved his voice away and faced his grandma. "You told me yourself that Texas doesn't have a copy of your birth certificate."

"Sure, and we laughed together about how both our births were unrecorded."

"Likely story – burned courthouse."

Grandma seemed to sense it was time to change the subject. "Geneva, do you remember when you and I exchanged keys?"

Geneva glared at Grandma. "I never would have trusted you."

"But I trusted you. Do you still have that extra key of mine?"

"I never took such a key. You are just trying to slur my character."

"No. Your character is impeccable. Shall we go to breakfast together?"

Geneva turned to look down the hall. Glyn could hear the breakfast crowd gathering at the elevator.

"I will eat in my room. You, Wilhalmena, you have a choice to make."

The elevator arrived, but none who waited for it got on. Grandma said, "And that choice is . . .?"

"Will you continue to deny the truth of your past? Or will you help get those poor children off the train?"

"Can you tell me where the train is, so I can help them?"

"Right next to the Reichsautobahn, between the autobahn and the river."

"What town was that? And what river?"

Geneva began to get very loud. "This town. And the Willamette River of course. I have told you over and over."

"I understand," Grandma said. "I will look into that."

By now, Geneva shouted. "You lie. You have been bought. You skim the food supply. No one but your crew gets enough to eat. And for all you care, those children will stay in that building and be moved out by the train without you lifting a finger."

Glyn stood up to protect Grandma in case Geneva got angrier. The elevator arrived yet again, but still the crowd in front of it grew and no one entered it.

A voice in the hall made both women turn around. "May I help you ladies?"

Glyn turned. It was Christopher Rylant, the nephew of Mr. Corrigan.

Grandma spoke quietly, "No, thank you, Mr. Rylant. We will be all right in a minute."

Geneva yelled. "Who are you? Another Nazi?"

"I'm Irish, Ma'am."

"That doesn't mean piss," Geneva said. "Stay out!"

Grandma said, "We're fine, Mr. Rylant, and it would be best if you take your uncle on down to breakfast."

Then Grandma spoke abruptly to Glyn. "Glyn Jones, I expect you need to get to school, so I will see you at dinner time."

Worried that Geneva would attack Grandma Willie, Glyn said, "I'll lock up and finish your book project later then. Can you come downstairs with me?"

"Good idea. Geneva, will you come to breakfast?

"Certainly not." Geneva ducked back into her apartment and slammed the door.

Grandma looked at Glyn with her "Say nothing" gaze and pushed her walker down the hall toward the waiting crowd.

As they arrived at the elevator, Grandma said, "My goodness. All of you missed the elevator every time it arrived?"

Then she turned to Glyn. "After school, and before you start to work in the kitchen, perhaps you could complete my bookcase project."

"Yes, Mrs. Stamps."

CHAPTER THIRTEEN

An hour before school, Glyn glanced out the window from inside his darkened first-floor history classroom and whispered to Mrs. Price, "Don't look suddenly, but there is one of the guys."

"Put your sunglasses on," she said.

Confused, he did what she told him. He knew she had a reason.

"Okay, now look at him," she said. Her gaze went to his glasses. "Ah! The guy with the curly hair and the tormented belt-line?"

"The very one. Have you done this before?"

"Lived in a neighborhood where you had to keep an eye on your back. I'm turning and taking a photo."

Glyn held very still so that her turn was the only movement.

He was glad her room lights were out, and the door closed. Maybe the guy wouldn't notice her in this room.

Her phone camera clicked several times and then she turned back to him.

"Ten times magnification. Let's back toward the non- window side of the room. I've got homework for all the band members for tonight, including from Mr. Ventura."

"Really? Gee that's something. He doesn't give that out lightly."

"He understands 'threat to school population'," she said.

Glyn thought Mr. Ventura was more likely to understand Mrs. Price's brilliant smile and sense of humor. She often used those weapons in class to get the attention of her students.

He turned his attention toward the guy out on the sidewalk in front of the school.

"So, the fat guy is here," Glyn said. "That means he knows Trace and the other Ancient Nation members go to Eisenhower High School."

"And I've got a feeling his helpers watch other doors," she said. "Skinny, you said, yes?"

"His helpers? Yep. Skinny like don't eat because they're high."

"The helpers are probably out there somewhere, too. How can we get you out of here?"

"I know how to get into the tunnels from here to the incinerator tower out by the pool."

"Can you show me?" she asked. "I may need that myself."

"What? You need a quick escape from an irate parent?" She laughed. "No. More from a boring meeting.

Mrs. Price fished in her huge bag, thumbing through multiple small, zippered bags. Puzzled, he watched her baggy process. At last, she produced a flashlight, held it up, and raised an eyebrow at him.

"Yep," he said. "That'll definitely help."

"Be prepared," she said.

He laughed.

Half an hour later, Mrs. Price handed him an envelope with all the homework papers. She turned off her flashlight and opened the door near the bottom of the old incinerator.

"Good thing these burners aren't used anymore," Glyn said.

Mrs. Price said, "Haven't been for years. I don't see anyone out there that I don't know already."

"Thanks for the papers."

"I'm not going to ask how you discovered this route out of here, but I'm glad to know about it."

"See you in a week."

"Tomorrow is Jon's turn to collect homework, right?" she asked.

"Yes. I'll tell him to get there through the tunnel."

"No. I'll meet him at the incinerator door. Seven-thirty, sharp."

"Great." Glyn waved a good-bye and headed toward the hardware store for a new door lock for Grandma's door. All the way, he looked over his shoulder for any followers of Curly- haired Big Gut.

*   *

In the afternoon, Willie Stamps sat with the other sopranos in the Holly Hill Choir and watched Mr. Stapleton give the final beat of the rehearsal. She saw exactly why Geneva believed him a German scientist. His bush of white hair stood out from his head as if electrified. His jaw line might be described as heroic, or a timid person might say his jaw seemed belligerent.

However, Jack Stapleton knew his music, and he knew how much voice an old person could produce, with the right encouragement and explanation for supported breathing, and proper use of mouth and head space.

And, as with all of Geneva's supposed Nazis, Mr. Stapleton was too young. Geneva herself had been a six-year-old child at the end of World War II. No one presently near her age could have been responsible for what happened to her.

However, as her mind went back over frightening times, Geneva lost her perspective.

Willie couldn't change Geneva's mind. Only Geneva could do that.

Now, however, Willie worried about what she'd discovered for Violeta. With both Rosaria and Liza missing, it had begun to look as if the trail between Portland and George Fox College endangered students. Her friend, Captain Reese worked to find out more about

Liza's trip. Also, he worked with the college to know if any other students were missing.

As Willie picked up her song book and prepared to say goodnight to others in the choir, she found Rolly Goforth and Leah Müller descending on her.

Leah spoke first. "We're sure you'll join us in this. We insist that the management put Geneva Oppenheim in the Alzheimer's ward. She can't be allowed to screech about the war anymore. Enough."

Before Willie could say anything calming, Rolly chimed in. "She's a danger to all of us."

"How so?" Willie asked. "What has she done other than mistake you for a German she once knew?"

Leah said, "Others will think she may be correct."

"Others will know that's impossible, Leah. You weren't even born."

"She's clearly losing it."

"As we all are. We wouldn't have moved here if we weren't slowing down mentally and physically. We learn to accept our frailties and those of our fellows."

Willie stared at these two quietly, letting them think about the truth of the situation. Neither Rolly nor Leah appeared to be taking it in.

Willie said, "You are both working hard to avoid that slowing, or even to think about it. But it is happening."

Leah hissed, "She has accused you of being the cook in the camp."

"She has. Evidently, the cook had a similar name. Geneva is not dangerous. Leave her alone."

Rolly leaned in and whispered, "We'll see what management thinks about that."

Leah swiveled to go. Rolly puttered after her. Willie again picked up her music, but saw that Jack Stapleton stood nearby talking to Don Corrigan, who hovered next to where the choir had been practicing, head in hands. Jack waved her over.

"Mrs. Stamps, Mr. Corrigan is confused about where he lives."

Willie sat down next to Mr. Corrigan. "Don," she said. "I've seen you listening to my readings on the second floor. But I've also seen you walking with your nephew on my floor. Does floor two or eight sound right to you?"

He sat up and smiled at her. "Eight. I think it is eight."

"Do you have a key in your pocket?"

He began fishing in many pockets. Papers fell to the floor. Willie picked them up and held them as he continued to fish. After a few moments, he came out with an official Holly Hill key chain, a logo of roses entwined with holly.

Everything in Portland, Oregon somehow came up Roses. The number on the key was 808.

"There you have it," Willie said.

Don stared at it and then smiled at her. "I have it."

"Would you like to ride up in the elevator with me?" His smile grew even more brilliant. "I would."

Jack Stapleton nodded and began collecting his music from the piano top. "Thank you, Mrs. Stamps."

"I am Willie. We're glad to have you here, Mr. Stapleton. Singing, however wobbly, is very good for us all."

He glanced up from his music. "I'm Jack. I enjoy being able to work with you. I enjoy singers at every age. They love music as much as I do."

Willie turned to Don. "I see you like to listen to the rehearsals."

He looked puzzled. "Rehearsals?"

"Practice. For the choir."

"Oh. Yes, I like that."

As they approached the elevator, Willie noticed that Leah and Rolly were down the hall talking to the administrative secretary of Holly Hill.

She glanced back at Don and saw that he had already punched the 'up' button near the elevator door. She remembered how children always wanted to be the one punching the buttons on an elevator. At least he hadn't forgotten that early fun.

When the elevator arrived, they went in. She stood at the elevator's back and waited. He pushed the button for 8. That also pleased her. He may have temporarily forgotten where he lived, but he was on it now.

When the door closed, Don said, "What was Geneva saying to you the other day about trains?"

Willie thought back and then remembered. "Oh, she was remembering when she was a child. The Nazis kept her and other children in a warehouse before they put them on the train to Mittlebau-Dora."

Don fidgeted with his shirt pocket full of pens. "But she seemed so afraid . . ."

"I don't think you need to worry, Don. It is her past memory."

His hands became stiff and still. "Not here?"

"Well, she fears it is happening again, but it is just memory."

Don began walking back and forth in the space. Toward the door and then backing up as if very worried. "What trains?

Which warehouse?"

"In Germany. Long ago. It's all right."

He glanced at her and calmed a little. "All right?" She nodded.

The elevator arrived at the eighth floor. When the door opened, Don started to turn right and walk toward her apartment.

"Don, you are in room eight. That's the other way and close to the end of the hall."

"Oh. That's right."

"Got your key?"

He waved it in the air. "Great. See you at dinner?"

"Umm. No. My nephew is taking me out to dinner."

"Well, that will be very nice." Willie wasn't so sure about that. The nephew didn't really seem all that patient with Don's forgetfulness.

Willie entered her own apartment and lay all her music and her new mail down on the overflowing coffee table.

A knock on the door, stopped her from sitting at last.

She assumed it would be Glyn, but when she opened the door, there stood Geneva, holding out an envelope.

"Did you put this under my door?"

Willie looked at the envelope, and said, "Geneva, I don't use that kind of envelope. I use number tens. They are business envelopes and not for invitations."

"Threats!" Geneva said. "This is a threat that I should watch my step and stop talking."

"My goodness. I don't suppose it was signed."

"Signed! Do you think I'm an idiot?"

"No, of course I don't. Mine was a stupid question. But it has to be someone who lives here."

Geneva snorted. "Haven't you ever walked past the front desk when the receptionist was gone?"

"Yes. I guess I have."

"So, someone who doesn't live here, or…" Geneva stared into the apartment behind Willie. "Or someone who works here."

"You should call the police and show this to them," Willie said.

"Hmmph. I know you are friends with police."

"Some have taken classes from me. And some wish they hadn't had to do that."

"I have other resources," Geneva said, waving the envelope. "You tell that young man, Glyn, that he can't get away with this."

She turned and strode into her room, slamming the door.

CHAPTER FOURTEEN

Glyn took the roundabout way from the meeting with his teacher, Mrs. Price, to the downtown library where he researched newspaper stories on gang enforcement and drug selling in Portland and its nearby cities.

He'd begun to pick up on a pattern. Everyone talked about drugs being a youth gang thing, but he was pretty sure the gangs were working for older people. And the people who got arrested were the victims like Trace.

He called Leneld and Jon to check in on the search for Trace.

"While we're looking," he said. "We've another missing person…" and so he told them his worry about Rosaria Aguirre.

"We'll keep an eye out," Leneld said, "but our priority is Trace. If she turns up, too, it'll be a miracle, since they disappeared in such different ways."

"I know," Glyn said. "But more eyes bring more information."

"By the way," Leneld said. "What do you know about Lonny's black eye?"

"A black eye, too?"

"What do you mean, 'too'?" Leneld asked.

So, Glyn explained about the skate park and tiny house incident.

Jon said, "Let's not tell Lon about Rosaria. He talks without thinking."

They agreed.

By the time he got on the bus back to the east side of town, he was bound to be late for kitchen detail and Grandma Willie would tan his hide.

She'd promoted his 'good name' and gotten him the marvy job of peeling potatoes and delivering meals to all the old folks. He knew it was a good deal, and he didn't want to disappoint her.

He banged on the kitchen door. Pretty soon, the head chef, Judson, yanked it open.

"You're late. Violeta is setting up for you."

"Sorry, I'll get in there and help her."

Judson put up a hand. "Wash and comb first. Otherwise, everyone will know you just ran in here."

Glyn nodded. He hadn't thought Judson was alert to appearances and how people read them. Judson himself had on an apron covered in blood and swung a meat cleaver as if it were a baton.

"Thank you, sir." Glyn marched to the sink in the nearest bathroom, washed his face and let water settle his hair, mostly. He practically ran out to help Violeta. Didn't want her worrying about him.

She glanced up from putting around silverware. "Your grandma is talking to Liza's parents this afternoon."

He grabbed a stack of placemats, silverware and napkins, and followed her around the table. They had thirty tables of six place settings each and she had already finished about eighteen of them by herself.

"I'm sorry to be late," he said.

"Did you get the band's homework?"

"Yes, and some information about recent drug trafficking."

"Oh!"

He wished he'd put that more smoothly. "I mean, about Trace and the drugs he uses. Not Rosaria."

She leaned hard on a chair nearby. "But what if…"

He wanted to touch her shoulder, help her stop fearing, but touching wasn't good here, and he worried about the same thing that she feared. *What if?*

"Violeta, anybody who tries that on her, we'll get her back and get the drugs out of her."

He hoped he wasn't just whistling Kumbaya. He hoped that working together on Trace and Rosaria, they might really find and rescue them both.

Two disappearances might not be related. Even three with Liza Cramer. But there might be a benefit in having all of them looking together. He sure hoped that would be true.

People from Holly Hill began lining up outside the dining room door.

"Wow," he said. "You'd think we had tickets to Blazers' basketball or Thorns' soccer in here, the way they line up."

Violeta glanced up. "Dinner is the best action of the day. You get to see who sits with whom. You get to see the visitors and comment on how cute the grandchildren are…"

"You get to grouse about the help and the food," Glyn added.

"Some do that. Most don't look for things to complain about," Violetta said.

"Ah, here comes Grandma Willie," she said.

Glyn glanced out the glass doors to see Grandma talking with Mr. Goforth and Leah Müller. He also noticed how quickly his grandma had become Violeta's Grandma Willie. He liked that.

May she be Grandma Willie for Rosaria someday, he thought. And knew he would search anywhere for Rosaria, because she was important to Violeta.

CHAPTER FIFTEEN

Out in the waiting area, Leah Müller and Rolly Goforth descended on Willie. And sure enough, they wanted to talk about Geneva.

"The admin has called in the doctor. He's going to test her now," Goforth said. "All you have to do is tell that she accuses you of being the cook."

"All I have to do?" Willie said. "And what happens to Geneva?"

Leah at least was a little bit more concerned with how things looked. She had the good taste to say, "Poor Geneva needs this visit to the hospital mental health unit. It will help her regain perspective."

Willie asked, "What perspective should she have?"

"You know it's not good for her to be afraid of everybody," Leah said. "Very tiring."

"Very tiring for you, at any rate," Willie said.

Goforth said, "Come on, Wilhalmena, don't tell me it's not bad for you as well."

"Rolly, do you have other reasons for worrying about your reputation? If not, then what harm can Geneva's accusations have?"

Rolly backed up.

And to Willie's amazement, so did Leah. *What reputation did Leah worry about?*

But Willie was more worried about Geneva. "What doctor?" she asked.

Rolly said, "I've got to get to work."

Rolly work?

Leah said, "Wilhalmena, you'd best be careful. Geneva is getting dangerous. You've been yelled at. You should know."

Willie softened her voice. "Leah, if you had fearful memories, you would also be mixing up old memories with new faces. I look like the cook and have a similar name. The mix up shouldn't be a surprise."

Leah shook her head. "I'm not going to put up with her craziness."

"Did you or Rolly put an envelope under her door?"

Leah looked surprised. "I don't even go to her floor except to run past it."

"Okay. How about Rolly?"

"I don't control him. What envelope?"

"A threat," Willie said.

"Are you aware of how many might want to threaten her?"

"You and Rolly are the most vocal."

"But too smart to do that," Leah said.

Willie saw that she would have no sway with Leah, so she left to find Geneva.

And discovered that Geneva was just leaving the area, getting ready to climb eight flights of stairs.

Willie wondered if she had been aware that Rolly and Leah were talking about having her sent to a hospital. She couldn't have been too far away.

*   *

After dinner, up on the eighth floor, Willie found her friend sitting in a chair outside her room, her biggest purse on her lap.

"You're not invited in," Geneva said, trying to make herself look bigger than normal by raising her shoulders and pushing her head forward.

Willie turned her walker around and used the seat part of it to sit with Geneva. "This is a nice place," Willie said.

"You called the doctor," Geneva said.

"No, that was not me. I'm sorry that happened."

"Who did it, then?"

Willie settled into her chair and said, "I believe there are several people who are worried about you. Did a doctor come talk to you?"

"No. She called and asked me to come down. I'm not going."

"Okay. Can you come to breakfast tomorrow?"

"You already eat too much," Geneva said.

"Yes, that's true. Eat too much and don't exercise enough. Let's go for a walk."

"Nobody's getting in my apartment."

"Right," Willie said. "You're here to guard it."

"Nobody believes me, so they can't have the papers."

Willie stopped moving. A feeling of cold settled into her spine. Geneva had not mentioned papers before. What papers?

After a moment Willie said, "No one can get the things you guard. That's good."

"I don't want to go to the hospital," Geneva said.

"No," Willie said, "None of us wants to go there, but if we break a leg or hurt our head, we're glad they can take care of us."

"Doctor Sartan is Jewish, too."

"Is she? That's helpful."

"She says I have memories I need to share."

"She may be right. Sharing memories helps us think clearly about them."

Geneva's hands scrabbled with the rose print of her dress. "Doctor Sartan believes me about the warehouses and the railroad. Her mother was there."

"Oh!"

"But her mother wasn't here when I discovered what they are doing. She wasn't there when I knew they thought I had figured them out."

"But you were there," Willie said.

"You have to keep them out," Geneva said, glancing down the hall. "Don't let them find my papers, Willie."

Willie listened with her heart and her mind. This was the first time this week that Geneva called her Willie instead of Wilhalmena. Did Geneva mean to say this to her old friend? Did she no longer think she was that cook?

"I said 'yes'," Geneva said. "Yes?"

"I said 'yes'. She's coming in a few minutes. I have my suitcase." Geneva reached under her chair.

For the first time, Willie realized her friend had a briefcase under the chair.

"She's coming in the evening? Do you have all that you need?"

Geneva lifted her heavy purse. "I'm just going to share my memories. I won't be gone that long."

Now, Willie became alarmed. The nurse here told Geneva her calming pills were vitamins. What lies had Doctor Sartan told?

"When did you meet Doctor Sartan?"

"Last week. She's very nice. Jewish, too."

Willie nodded. "What hospital are you visiting?"

"I'm visiting the patients at St. Agnes, over on Halsey."

Willie knew the reputation of St. Agnes. One of her students with Bulimia had stayed there for a time. Now that student was a nurse. St. Agnes sounded like a hopeful place to go to, but not if it started as a lie of just visiting to share.

Just then, the door opened on the elevator at the other end of the hall. Several others who lived on this floor came up from the dinner that Willie had just missed.

"Oh, I hate these people," Geneva said.

Willie looked at the crowd. Mostly, these were people Geneva had liked, played dominoes with, or Scrabble.

"Did you want to take a walk?"

"Are you nuts?" Geneva asked.

"You don't want to talk to them, so we can walk up and down this end of the hall. You can keep an eye on the door while we exercise."

As they sat there, the others waved good night to each other, or made plans to meet for a card game or the evening movie.

Finally, they each moved into the apartments.

The elevator opened once more. A young lady in a business suit came out of it.

Geneva stood. She leaned over Willie and said, "They will try to find me, so I'm going away. Tell anyone you know that I'm at Emmanuel Hospital. Emmanuel. Got that?"

"Emmanuel it is," Willie whispered.

"And no one in my apartment. They want that proof. They get that proof and I'm as good as dead."

"All right. For you, my friend."

Geneva lifted her brief case and marched toward the elevator, where the young lady in a suit had come out and waved.

CHAPTER SIXTEEN

illie strode after Geneva and met Doctor Sartan at the elevator. "I'd like to be able to visit my friend while she is in your care," Willie said.

Geneva glanced at Willie and then at the doctor. Willie feared the balance of Geneva's paranoia was about to turn, but she had to try for her friend's sake. As far as she knew, she was Geneva's only friend.

Doctor Sartan said, "Mrs. Oppenheim, is this what you want?"

Geneva looked down at Willie. "I know you are not the cook. I know you are my friend. I heard you defending me to Leah and Rolly." Then she turned to the doctor, and said, "Yes, I want her to visit."

Willie cheered inside, but knew she had to remain calm on the outside. So, she said, "I will take care of things, bring you things that you need, and I'll be glad to have you home again when all is safe."

The doctor smiled and fished a card from her pocket. "This number should not be shared with anybody else."

"Yes," Willie said. "I understand." She punched the button on the freight elevator instead of the resident's elevator across the hall. "May I suggest an exit through the kitchen. Leah and Rolly are hovering around the mailboxes and looking for a doctor to visit you."

"Good idea," Geneva said. "Virginia," she said to the doctor, "the kitchen staff are safe. One is Willie's grandson."

This surprised Willie. She didn't think Geneva had understood this. Perhaps her fears were fading, and this young woman helped her.

"We will look for your visit," Doctor Sartan said, and then the doctor and Geneva got into the freight elevator.

When Willie turned back to her room, she saw two ladies watching from their doorways. As she walked down the hall, she said, "Isn't that nice. Geneva's young friend has come to visit her. They will be on a vacation together for a little while."

The two neighbors made appropriate exclamations of celebration for their neighbor, and went back into their apartments.

Soon after that, she heard the residents' elevator door open.

Mr. Corrigan and Rolly Goforth exited the elevator.

Willie just kept walking toward her room. Then she realized that Geneva had left her chair in the hall. Goforth would comment on that as further evidence that Geneva was losing it.

She sat down in it until Rolly came by. Rolly said, "Why are you in the hall?"

"I like to watch people," Willie said. "They do and say the most interesting things."

Rolly looked at Mr. Corrigan and said, "Don, I think we need to get you in your room."

Mr. Corrigan looked blankly at Willie and at Rolly. "Okay," he said.

As soon as they were inside Don Corrigan's room, Willie moved Geneva's chair into her own room, meaning to take it back to Geneva's later.

She sat down on her sofa and began straightening magazines, thinking about what Geneva had said this afternoon about papers.

She had been very different this afternoon. Not confused about who Willie might be, not uncertain about Doctor Virginia Sartan, and very certain that she wanted no one to find certain papers in her room.

CHAPTER SEVENTEEN

As Geneva and her friend walked through the kitchen, they found Violeta, Judson and Glyn working to clean up after dinner.

Geneva sidled over to Glyn. "I know how you got this job."

Glyn looked up and decided she might be trying to see how he would take bullying.

"Nepotism. Pure and simple," he said. "My grandma wanted me to pay a speeding ticket."

Geneva's friend smiled, but said, "Geneva, we should go."

Geneva sidled over to Glyn, and said, "Virginia, do you know how many Nazis there are in this world?"

"I suspect there are always people who want to control others, and exclude certain groups," the friend said.

Glyn said, "And there are always people who accuse others with little evidence."

Geneva straightened her back and said, "There is evidence. Lots of evidence."

Her friend frowned and said, "Geneva, we should get going."

Geneva said, "Let's go tell our story."

"That's a great idea," the friend said as she opened the door out the back of the kitchen. "My car is right out here."

*   *

Later that evening, Glyn appeared at Grandma Willie's door with his mother and dad, Susan and Merlyn Jones. Behind them stood Leneld, of the Ancient Nation, Violeta and Judson.

Judson's apron of blood was nowhere to be seen. He cleaned up pretty well for a guy who whacked and steamed things all day.

Grandma invited them in. "What's going on?" she asked. While clearing magazines off chairs, Glyn answered.

"Geneva and her friend went through the kitchen this afternoon. Who was that lady?"

Grandma said, "She is a friend of Geneva's. They are going on vacation. And, she and I are friends again."

Glyn said, "At our Ancient Nation meeting, Markus said, 'Just because you're paranoid doesn't mean no one's after you.' That made me think we really need to follow Geneva's thinking more carefully. Geneva's always talking about children in jeopardy. And what we have is children in jeopardy, so following her thoughts might be useful."

Judson said, "I think that's right. A slim chance, but we should take that chance."

"Grandma," Glyn said, "can you write down what all she has said about those old fears?"

"Got that verbatim in my diary."

Glyn said, "Still keeping a diary? Red covers every year?"

"Yes," Grandma Willie said. "I've had to move to peach and rose some years."

Violeta coughed and tried to bring them back to the main matter. "So that person is okay? Geneva is not being kidnapped?"

Willie thought about this. She wondered if Geneva knew what it meant to go to the hospital to share her story. If she didn't know, wasn't the lie a kidnapping?

"I will be visiting her soon, where they are vacating."

Glyn looked puzzled. "Vacation, but close enough to visit?"

Judson said, "Glyn, how about if you and Willie track through Geneva's ramblings and see what you can come up with. Meanwhile, shouldn't we be bringing the police in on this business of Trace and Violeta's sister going missing."

Grandma Willie said, "I've got Captain Reese checking out the drug-sales people that Glyn met."

Glyn's mother, Susan, started out of her chair. "Met where? Glyn?"

Glyn felt like he'd been gone from home for weeks. He'd never told Mom and Dad about his escapades.

Leneld said, "Glyn and us guys, we divided the bridges and Glyn took the skate park under the Burnside Bridge."

And then, of course, Mom and Dad went into their parental hovering down mode.

"You've all been trying to solve these things without help from the police?"

"You can't be taking these chances …"

Grandma Willie now took charge. "Susan and Merle, listen up. The kids know the police won't search for a kid for twenty- four hours, maybe forty-eight if it's a weekend. And I can tell you, the police bumble through these things in uniform and with attitude. So, dividing up the bridges was a start on getting some evidence without tainting it with blue wool and gold chest medal."

She turned to Leneld and Glyn. "However, we have a good idea that Trace was taken by the guy with the overworked belt. And Captain Reese now has a name for him and a call out to pull him and his boys in, especially since his ally was caught trying to seduce minors on Tri-Met."

Violeta let out a moan. Grandma Willie turned to her. "Your parents have given me the name of the boyfriend and a photo of him and of Liza. These photos came to them from Liza's parents. They have been very helpful. Captain Reese has people tracking him down as well.

"So, you see," Willie continued, "Glyn and the band have given the police something solid to go on."

"Now wait a minute," Susan said. "This is our son you're roping into this."

"Mom," Glyn said. "You should come live with us. The guys who took Trace know where you live."

A free-for-all ensued with everyone talking at once. Glyn noticed that Violeta sat there blinking and thinking. Suddenly, she stood up and said, "No hablen tanto."

Everyone else stopped talking and stared. "Susanna y Merlyn pueden vivir en nuestra casa. Glyn y Senora Willie en …"

She suddenly realized she needed to speak English and seemed at a loss, so Glyn said, "Violeta has invited you, Mom and Dad, to stay in their house for safety."

"Si," Violeta said.

Leneld said, "How about if Glyn's sister stays with her girlfriend."

Dad nodded. "Claudia Ash. Maybe she could stay there."

Silence followed. Then Mom said to Violeta, "Perhaps we should talk to your mother."

"Si." Violeta pulled out her cell phone.

Leneld said, "Mrs. Stamps, can we also talk to this Captain Reese?"

"I'll be glad to introduce you."

Violeta handed Mom the phone and a whole conversation ensued in English and Spanish with Violeta's Papá Aguirre.

Dad looked awash in all the activity, going on without him. "How'm I going to practice if we're gone all the time?"

Violeta said, "My dad has a guitar. He can play while you sing, or whatever..." She trailed off.

"That's a great idea," Merlyn said. "Always wanted to learn some new songs. But I need to help him hunt for your sister and her friend."

"Yes, in the little towns along the bus route, he cannot talk to the police. Only you."

"We'll be a team. I'll get a copy of that boyfriend's photo, too."

CHAPTER EIGHTEEN

Of course, Grandma Willie intended to keep on teaching, so Markus signed up to accompany her to the police academy and Leneld to the corrections facility. Markus thought of himself as Grandma Willie's protection, but Leneld said, "I think you're under-estimating the power of old ladies."

Markus laughed. "I'd do whatever she tells me, but I don't think that covers all the protection she'll be needing."

* *

"A great way to see jail as an outsider," Leneld quipped a few hours later, as he and Grandma Willie entered the corrections facility.

"Because you are never going to see it from the inside," Grandma Willie said, looking over her half glasses at him. They walked into her concrete and windowless classroom.

The guys in the class stopped talking as soon as they saw Grandma Willie. They turned their small desk-chairs toward the front, but there were no rows, only a flotsam-like collection of big feet hung on chair rungs at all angles.

The guard who had let them in, whispered something to Grandma Willie.

She glanced at him and said, "And have you worked with Officer Bailey?"

The man straightened. "Not long. And only when he's here for some prisoner."

"Let me know about his veracity when you have had a chance to test it."

The guard leaned against the back wall. Leneld looked at her, puzzled. She said, "After class on the way home." He accepted that.

Leneld saw that most of the guys in the class were about twice his weight, though Leneld was taller than many. About half of the class looked to him, what his mother would have called "varied flavors of chocolate." A few were chocolate with paprika and three or four were white chocolate.

"New kid," called one guy with a big fro. He waved toward Leneld. "Sit over here. And keep your head down. Gonna learn how to write like a straight-up politician."

The man pulled around a chair where his feet had been resting, wiped the boot marks off the seat and gestured welcome.

Grandma Willie laughed. "Gentlemen, this is my friend, Leneld Abu. He'd like to learn to write like a philosopher, but without the plodding pedantry."

"Plodding pedantry," shouted one of the fellows. "An alliterative alternative."

"Correct, Mr. Art, we can write like the Irish poets and the Zulu troubadors."

Another guy said, "Can we get this kid some paper? Ain't gonna write nothin' standing there."

Grandma Willie reached into her oversized teaching bag and said, "Mr. Abu, go ahead and take the offered seat next to George Wilson. Here is paper and pen."

The alliterative fellow in the back said, "I got it. Zulu zitherists and Irish incidentalists."

"Good work, Mr. Artimus. And let's be certain our alliteration doesn't stretch so far that our reader cannot relate to our thoughts."

"Yeah," said George, the guy next to Leneld. "Them Zulus didn't play the zither. More like some kind of stringed banjo."

"A Kora," Leneld said.

"You got one?" George asked.

"My dad plays one. Kind of hard to find a band to play with, though. Not too many Zulu or Mandika in Portland."

"I play plastic-tub drums," George said. "Get your dad to come live here. We could practice all the time."

Leneld smiled. "I'll tell him."

"Well, at least a visit. Get him to come with Mrs. Stamps.

I'd like to hear the Mandika Kora."

"I got it!" Mr. Alliteration shouted out. "Mandika Kora.

Inner alliteration, right, Mrs. Stamps?"

"I like the rhythm, and the repetition of the K," Grandma Willie said. "Who has some writing to share today?"

Six out of ten hands raised. Leneld settled in.

What he learned over the next half hour was that the fellows inside came in all levels of self-doubt and self- confidence. The assignment had been chosen by them the week before, expressed as 'What I'm going to do with myself while I'm in this joint.'

Some were focused on disproving the charges against them, which Grandma Willie said meant that they were going to learn a lot about how the law works.

Some were going to earn library privileges and study the classics.

Leneld asked, "What are the classics?"

George said, "That stuff we shoulda read in high school, and the stuff we might of got to read if we'd gone to college."

One of the guys asked what the classics would do to improve their lives, and Mr. Alliteration said, "You'd learn a lot about how the suits think and how they justify themselves."

"Aren't there African classics?" one fellow asked.

"There are," Willie said. "And modern writers who will be classics."

George said, "African-American classics, too. Langston Hughes."

"Yes," Willie said, "Zora Neale Hurston.

"W.E.B. Dubois, Countee Cullen," one of the fellows said. Artimus Alliteration shouted, "Maya Angelou! Toni Morrison!"

"Yes!" George pumped his fist.

Grandma Willie smiled and repeated "Yes! Let's read what we can, and who you suggest, and then write about what we read or about incidents of which the reading reminds us."

"Library here is pretty thin," pointed out one man. "Maybe Leneld and I can bring in some good books, and books you could suggest."

"How about PlayBoy?" suggested someone. "That magazine died," someone said.

"Not my old copies. They are still alive in my storage space back home," another said.

Everybody roared at that one.

As the laughter died down, Grandma Willie said, "You know, I've never read anything in that magazine. I only look at the pictures."

Leneld sat straight up and stared at her, as the whole class laughed. It seemed to him that these fellows were used to Grandma Willie saying the unexpected.

"Now, Gentlemen," she said, calming them down with her hands. "I find your plans very interesting. Maybe some African instruments like Leneld's dad's. And let's see if we can get a speaker in here to tell us a little more about how to study the law, and another time, let's bring in someone to help us add to and build a library of helpful and interesting reading."

"What we gonna write about for next week?" Alliteration asked.

"I've got a problem," Grandma Willie said, "and I hope we can discuss it and then write about it."

"What? You have problems?"

"I do. A young friend of mine has disappeared while standing on a street corner here in town. Another young friend disappeared while riding a bus between Portland and another town down the valley. Could we speculate on ways to track these missing people and restore them to safety?"

"Do they want to be found?" George asked.

Grandma Willie nodded. "Good question. I believe the person on the bus for sure wants to be found. The person from the street corner may be hiding from dangerous associates."

"He owes somebody money or product, eh?"

"A distinct possibility."

"Dead man walking," said George.

"Better find him before they do," said another man. "Why would the bus kid want to be found?"

Grandma Willie answered, "The bus was taking that person to college, and they were looking forward to that experience."

"Uh-oh." Alliteration said, "Off to California."

"Do you mean to the sex trade?" Grandma Willie asked. Dead silence followed, as if the guys didn't think their Mrs.

Stamps could even guess about such things. Uncomfortable chairs scraped the linoleum floor. Finally, George spoke up.

"Girl, huh? I'd be chasing every bus and truck between here and the California border. Have you gone to the police?"

One of the guys snorted. "The police? What do they care?

Specially if she's not from money. For money they find heiresses that go missing."

The noise next came from all sides. "Look at the rape kit bit."

"Yeah! Oregon be one thousand kits behind in testing them rape kits."

"Does that show any sign of care for girls?"

The guard in the room stood away from where he'd been leaning.

Grandma Willie held up her hands, asking for quiet. "Gentlemen, I appreciate your outrage."

"Some of us have got daughters, too, you know. And sisters and…"

Grandma Willie nodded. "Yes. I hear you caring about the women in your lives. That's very important to them that you care. Since my friend is an immigrant, her family fears the police, so the help I need is ideas about how to find her. What's the process for taking and hiding and … and selling?"

Leneld hunched forward. He'd never thought anybody's grandmother but his own could be this strong and face this much truth. He needed to take another look at all grandmothers.

The guys all looked sideways at each other. Some stared at the desks or their shoes. Some glanced at the guard.

Finally, Mr. Alliteration Artimus said, "This is all speculation, you know. And stuff we've heard on the street. But I think they gang them together before they take them anywhere."

"That's what I hear, too," another man said. "Ten to twenty depending on the size of the truck they got."

"So," Grandma Willie said, "They might not have gone yet."

"Trouble is," George said, "You … I mean they got to find a place big enough, or enough places they trust."

Grandma Willie nodded. "Where might be good places to look?"

"Cheap hotels."

"Guys apartments that want …"

"Naw," one guy said. "You don't want 'em used up before you sell them to the next guy."

"Brings down the value."

Grandma Willie said, "What about boys."

"There's a market," Mr. Artimus said. "Least ways, I think there is."

"Okay," Grandma Willie said. "How about if we write. You don't need to sign your name. But I sure could use any ideas you've got."

The fidgeting went on for several minutes. The fellows folded and unfolded paper, clicked pens and finally got down to it.

Leneld began writing what they knew about Trace and Rosaria.

Trace Owes money to Small Pants and his gang.

Small Pants (SP) knows Ancient Nation connection, so follows members to high school.

SP knows the home of Jon

Ask Jon more questions about how SP made his home.

SP works around Martin Luther King and Mississippi, Denver Ave and Killingsworth, but has been seen at skate park farther south

Skate Park ranger types banned SP from park for picking up and selling to kids

SP and gang take kids north on Second Ave. to get fake Yo- Plait and don't return

SP's guy tried to pick up kids from north-going bus on Grand Ave.

So, hunt for places along Second, Mississippi, MLK, Grand, Interstate (lots of motels) and nearby streets.

Make flyers with Trace's face

Ask Violeta's parents about flyer for Rosaria Give up looking under bridges

Speed up search of motel and cheap apartments that rent by the month along these places.

For Rosaria, spread around photo of Liza's boyfriend and spread it around other rappers and friends.

Look at map and figure where along that bus route they may have a stash of girls

Check motels in Tigard or Tualitin and other small towns near Newberg.

* *

At the end of the hour class, the guard started forward to whisper to Grandma Willie. She pulled out a large card and read it out loud to him.

"By order of the Director of the Federal Prison, Sheridan, Oregon, all writing that takes place in Mrs. Stamps's classes is the property of the writers and of Mrs. Stamps. No one else may read or take possession of any of the written material produced in this class."

The guys sat in their desks, statue silent, watching.

The guard's face faded from red to white. Grandma Willie straightened from her walker and looked him in the eye.

"I understand that you believe you will learn something by reading these papers. We all understand that you also want to stop this business of selling children.

"We all appreciate that you care, along with all of us, about the women and children who are damaged in this way. But what you will learn from any paper here is only guesses and suggestions, not incriminating evidence. And believe me, you will also learn that this rule about writing ownership is sacred to the Director and to me. I would not be here, if I didn't believe he would back me up in this."

The guard leaned forward, "I don't like this child stealing business. I want it stopped."

"Then leave these men and their paper to me. They are helping to stop it. For their loved ones, they also want it stopped. They are helping by imagining how it might be done. They are not telling us how it is done."

"Okay, Mrs. Stamps. But some of these…"

She whispered something to him. He nodded and backed off.

Everyone in the room relaxed. Leneld took a deep breath, and put his name at the top of his paper, handing it in with everyone else.

"Thanks for the desk and chair, George," he said.

"Anytime, Kid. But don't be back for cause."

"I'm working on it."

George gave him the 'got your back' nod and they parted.

*   *

Leaving the correctional facility near Sheridan was a maze of slamming doors, friskings (especially of Leneld) and careful watchings. Back in the old red and white Buick, Grandma Willie put what she called her portmanteau, in the red-vinyl back seat. The 'portmanteau' thing looked like a big bag to Leneld, but whatever.

He folded himself into the cushy driver's seat, glad she trusted him to be careful in traffic, because this car was smooth.

He glanced at the dashboard where Mrs. Stamps's husband once had glued a saying. "*Believe in the Lord, and drive the speed limit. God cares for others.*"

Leneld knew he would have liked her husband, Clifford.

He'd seen Grandma Willie's painting of the guy, laughing and happy. And, Leneld liked her. He was glad for his detail to chaperone her – like she needed chaperoning.

"What did you whisper to that guard?" he asked. "Let those without sin cast the first stone."

"Jesus, the year thirty-two or three. Somewhere in Mark or Matthew, I expect."

"You been footnoting papers in high school?"

"Sure. Crandall lets no attribution go un-noted."

"Good for him."

"You got something on that guard? Did he know what sins you referred to?"

"What he doesn't know is what I don't know. He has to assume I know something. After all, the guys are there writing twice a week."

"You ask for dirt."

"Never. Always ask advice, or pose a situation that has come up in our reading. What would their characters do?"

"Never ask what would they do themselves?"

"Better to let everyone write their best self and then live up to that imagined person."

Leneld nodded, thinking about who his best self might be.

After a moment, he said, "I narrowed the places that we need to look, if Trace is still in Portland."

"And alive."

Leneld swallowed hard. "We have to go forward on the assumption he is alive."

"I agree," Grandma Willie said.

As silence descended, they could both hear the flapping of the old Naugahyde fabric of the car's top. The top was in the process of disintegrating on Mrs. Stamps's ancient Buick. Since she didn't drive, and evidently never had, he kind of wondered why she kept the thing. And then he looked again at the saying on the dashboard. She must have really loved that guy.

Then Leneld asked, "Back at the beginning of the class, you talked to the guard about somebody named Bailey. What was that about?"

"Officer Bailey failed my class and then discovered that passing it was necessary to getting a badge. He passes on the story of Geneva's accusations because causing trouble is easier than admitting he made a mistake."

"Did he ever pass the class?"

"Third time's the charm."

"Was he charming?"

Willie laughed.

*　*

They drove into town from the south. On Grand Avenue, Leneld said, "I'm pulling over. I've seen something."

He parked on the shoulder of Grand Avenue. "What?" Grandma Willie asked.

"Don't turn around," he said. "I'm watching in the mirror.

Your Granddaughter."

"I see her too."

"Name's Arwain, right?"

"Yes." Grandma Willie said, "What the deuce is she doing?"

Leneld tensed as he stared into the rearview mirror. "I think she's following someone, and pretending to just be shopping."

"It's after school. Maybe she is shopping."

Leneld shook his head. "He's in front of us. He stops. She stops a block behind him. Skinny. Anorexia or drugs."

"Never!" Grandma Willie said. "Him, not her."

"Okay. I see the guy you mean. If he notices her, she's up a creek on this street."

"Unless we stick close. Got anywhere to be?"

"Shall we move up a block?"

"Wait. It looks like he has a buddy who's behind her. Let me get out"

"Len!" Grandma Willie said as he rolled out the driver's door.

"Gonna distract and maybe learn something," he said. "Get your phone out."

"Watch for knives."

"Yes."

Leneld crossed the street behind the first skinny guy, stood on the corner next to Andy and Bax Outdoor Store. He waited for Arwain to come by, shook his head at her and said, "Keep going. Don't turn around. I'm watching the one who's following you."

"Thank you. I'm following a guy who keeps appearing near the high school. Mrs. Price, Glyn's history teacher, pointed him out to me."

"Watch, but don't approach."

"Right." She kept walking as if she had no idea who Leneld might be.

When the guy behind her came by, Leneld greeted him. "Got a roll?" Leneld said.

"Outa my way."

"Sure, but can't you help out a fellow? I need something to take the edge off."

The fellow stopped, glancing up the street toward Arwain. "I got some product," he said. "How much you want?"

"Got five dollars in change," Leneld said. "That won't get you much."

Leneld nodded, "Whatever it gets that's what I got." He started pulling a bag of change out of his pocket. At the same time, he motioned Grandma Willie to stay where she was.

Leneld saw her get out, hauling her walker from the back seat.

As Leneld started counting out coins he saw Grandma Willie pushing her walker toward him. The way she was hunched over, she seemed to be just another tired old lady who might live in the upper reaches of any of these tired buildings.

Leneld started counting coins faster. His plan had been to stall this guy, but he didn't want Grandma Willie coming anywhere near the man.

"Come on, come on," the guy said. "I got places to be."

Just at that moment, Grandma Willie walked past on the guy's right, reached over and snapped handcuffs on his skinny wrists. "Sit down on the ground," she said. "You're under arrest for selling drugs."

The guy stared at her.

"Down now," she said, lifting her walker legs toward his chest.

He collapsed onto the sidewalk.

Grandma Willie handed Leneld a bigger pair of cuffs. "On his ankles and then you go up the street."

"What right you got?" the guy sputtered.

She held out her billfold at the guy's face. Leneld shackled him.

"Give me the baggy and get going," she said.

So, he handed it to her and went. In a block, he caught up to Arwain, who stood outside a drug store.

"He in there?" Leneld asked.

"Upstairs. Used a key. His apartment or his office," she said. "Your grandma is back a block. Arrested the other guy for selling drugs."

"Grandma?"

"Yup."

Arwain held up her phone, saying, "Let's go help her. I've got the address and photos of him and everyone he's talked to on Grand Avenue since we got off the bus from Eisenhower High School."

Leneld turned back and saw that a police car had pulled up next to Grandma Willie.

"Come with me, "Arwain said, and took off running.

Arwain was swift, but Leneld caught up to her in half a block and said, "Geez! Don't run at the police."

"Sorry. Wasn't thinking."

She slowed to a walk. As they approached the scene, Arwain called, "Ma'am, we're here. Do you need help?"

A red-headed policeman turned toward them, gestured for them to stop and said, "Jones, right?"

Arwain looked puzzled. "Yes, but…"

Grandma Willie said, "Captain Reese will finish what we're doing here. Then I'll explain." She turned toward Leneld and said, "This is the young man I asked to try to make the buy."

Captain Reese said, "I'll need a statement from you, sir. But first," he straightened to his whole five-foot-five height and called toward the police vehicle. "Officer Seneca, can we get this man into the vehicle."

A second officer appeared from behind the police car. The officer, Seneca, straightened his cap over his spikey dark hair, wiped his face with a long-fingered hand and strode toward the fellow on the sidewalk.

Leneld got a kick out of the appreciative glance that Officer Seneca sent toward Arwain. The guy clearly was impressed by what he saw, and Leneld, thought, why not. Glyn's older sister had always been a stunner.

Seneca took one more look at Arwain, and then bent over to lift the arrested man from the sidewalk and help him walk into the back seat.

He pushed the man's head down to get him below the car top and then buckled him in.

Door closed, the officer rang the keys at his captain and said, "I'll be in the vehicle. Nice to meet you finally, Miss Jones."

Arwain stared at him and then back at the captain. Her grandma shook her head. "Later."

As soon as Officer Seneca sat in the driver's seat and had the door closed, Grandma Willie said, "That was Officer Sidney Oberon Seneca. This is Captain Rob Reese. My granddaughter, Arwain Titania Jones, and my friend Leneld Abu."

"Good to meet you all." Captain Reese said, and then towered over Grandma Willie. "Explain. The man said you assaulted him."

"I told him to sit. He wouldn't, so I lifted my walker and pointed it at him. He fell from shock. Didn't have a clue what an old lady might do."

Reese said, "I'll bet. Now tell me what Miss Jones is doing here."

Leneld let Grandma Willie do the explaining. He heard the said and the unsaid and decided to act accordingly.

According to Grandma Willie, Leneld had been sent by her to stall the guy who was following Arwain. The suggestion to buy drugs had been made by her as a strategic move to keep Arwain safe. When the man actually produced the drugs from his pocket, Grandma Willie thought she ought to do her duty as an honorary deputy of the County Sheriff's office.

"In the jurisdiction of the Portland Police?" Reese asked. "Well, of course the jurisdictional problem was why I called you before I got out of the car."

Finally, Arwain spoke. "Captain Reese, I'm sure the man in your car, and the man I followed to the apartment door near the pharmacy, both know something about our missing friend. I hope they can be questioned separately about that."

Captain Reese lowered his head and then looked over his glasses at Grandma Willie. "Mrs. Stamps, what is it you have not been telling me?"

CHAPTER NINETEEN

At the police station, Grandma Willie, Leneld and Arwain waited for Glyn to arrive from Holly Hill, so the whole story could be told to Captain Reese and Officer Seneca.

The benches where they sat were not exactly designed to put visitors at rest, so Arwain rolled up her coat for Grandma Willie to rest her head and Leneld covered her with his coat. He and Arwain sat on the other bench.

"Arresting people takes it out of you, I guess," Leneld said, as he watched Grandma Willie sleep.

"This whole situation probably has finally hit her," Arwain whispered. "She and Geneva were good friends until about three months ago. So, there's a fragile friend and two missing kids that she cares about."

Dark hair now slicked down, Officer Seneca brought them coffee and water and pretty much anything else he could think of.

Leneld noticed. He also noticed that Officer Seneca turned up the heat in the waiting room as he glanced at Arwain.

Leneld whispered to Arwain "Really? Sidney Oberon Seneca? What are the chances, Arwain Titania?"

"Hush your mouth," Arwain said. "You mention that to him, and I'll whup you upside your head."

Leneld laughed. "You were pretty much fated to meet, especially since your grandmother knows both of you. She's probably had this guy in her back pocket for years, just waiting to spring him on you."

"What was his mother thinking?"

"In your case, it was your father. Glyn Dower and Arwain Titania Jones. What a pair of names that makes. Your senior year the awards assembly was a hoot. It got to where the audience could hardly contain themselves. Looked like Titania, the Queen of the Fairies had bewitched the math department, the history department and the athletic department all at once."

"Yeah, well I didn't bewitch them enough. I asked them to drop my middle name out of the records back when I was in first grade, but no… each principal along the way got enough of a kick out of it they had to torture me with it every time I got into trouble, and every time I earned something."

"Just about makes you want to stop earning."

"Name's gone from the records now. It took fifty dollars and turning twenty-one to get that taken care of."

"Trouble is, Grandma Willie doesn't know it's gone, so Officer Sidney is gonna know that name and you're stuck for life."

Arwain glared her disgust at Leneld.

Just then, Officer Sidney Oberon Seneca stood in front of Leneld and Arwain saying, "May I get you anything?"

Arwain put a hand on Leneld's arm and said, "Would you get my Leneld, a coke? He's very thirsty."

Leneld looked at her, startled. Then he smiled up at Oberon and said, "A coke would be great. And I bet Arwain wouldn't mind one, would you love?"

Officer Seneca backed up, "Uh, sure. Sure. Be right back." As he wobbled off down the hall, Arwain watched his back. "Poor Oberon,"

Leneld said, "Titania and Puck have struck again. Now, don't you feel sorry for that guy."

"Not yet."

Leneld leaned back, smiling. He'd always liked Glyn's big sister, but he hadn't really appreciated her wit until this moment.

How'd she do that? He laughed to himself. *All she had to say was 'My Leneld,' and the guy is certain we two are an item even with a big difference in our ages. Arwain is as good at simpering as her grandmother is at playing the old street lady. Two actors in one family.*

Glyn pushed through the swinging door, dropped his change and his keys in the plastic box, strolled through the metal detector toward the clerk's desk and started to talk when Arwain jumped to his side. "Keep your voice down. Grandma is sleeping."

He turned to take that in. "She okay?"

"Exhausted by everything."

The clerk at the desk whispered, "Sir, would you sign in?"

As soon as he signed his name, the clerk picked up a phone and said, "Captain Reese, your man is here."

For a moment, the three of them stood and watched Grandma Willie sleep. Leneld felt each of them thinking, "What is too much for her?"

*   *

As she slept, Glyn saw Officer Bailey rolling down the hall toward them. Glyn said to the desk man, "Bailey here has it in for my Grandma for some reason. Can you get him to leave her alone and keep his voice down?"

"Do my best. But Bailey is his own drum major on the march through life and the law."

Glyn raised an eyebrow at the guy. "Did you take her writing class?"

"Yep. Stick-with-your-metaphor-Stamps, we called her.

She's the band leader, for those who get the beat."

Glyn smiled, but stared toward the approaching Bailey. So, the desk man stepped out from behind the desk, stood between Grandma and Bailey and said, "They want you in records."

"Whaa? Why?"

"Missing info, I guess. Don't know which …"

"Damnation!" Bailey turned on his heel and retraced his steps.

Thanks," Glyn mouthed.

The officer said, "For him, it's always missing records."

Glyn chuckled. He believed he understood Bailey's beef with Grandma Willie.

A few catnap minutes later, Captain Reese came through the swinging doors from the back offices. He glanced at the sleeping form on the bench and said, "Should I be getting an ambulance?"

Willie opened her eyes and said, "Fifteen minutes is enough renewal time." Then she turned toward the desk man. "Nice music metaphor – band leader and beat. Officer Simon, you should take up writing for fun."

He laughed. "When I retire, maybe."

"A diary now will give you a lifetime of stories for age sixty to ninety."

"Ninety, eh?" Officer Simon said.

"If you give up the cigarettes and roll stories instead."

"Grandma …," Glyn said.

She sat up and held the overcoat out toward Leneld. "I know. Business."

Leneld took the coat. Arwain offered the arm, and Glyn grabbed up her 'portmanteau'.

*   *

Hours later, the skinny man sweated in a cell. He'd been accused of selling cocaine. He talked, but Officer Seneca said the guy really didn't know beyond his confederate and Heinrich Strauss, also known as Big Gut/Small Pants. They'd have to get more on Strauss.

"Hard to make Strauss sweat," Seneca said.

As soon as they left the police station, Grandma took a cab, going somewhere to visit Geneva and her friend, she had said, as she waved them all off to their homes.

Geneva taking a vacation somewhere in the city puzzled Glyn, but it was clear to him that Grandma wasn't going to tell him anything more about Geneva.

Glyn sat in the Holly Hill Retirement Home Library doing his chemistry homework. Grandma came back, said hello and then elevated up to read to her friends in the Alzheimers' apartments.

Earlier in the week, Glyn had seen that the chemistry teacher, Mr. Ventura had softened his stance since he understood why his three students were not coming into the building. He helped Mrs. Price gather the homework for them. But he still insisted on high standards of work, so Glyn read the chemistry book with his pencil in hand.

Glyn figured out long ago that he learned best by drawing what the stuffy books were talking about, so he had cartoons in his notebook of atoms banging into each other and then sticking. In his cartoons, of course, they stuck because of a candy coating, but that stood in for the valences of the various atoms. One layer of candy coating for hydrogen, three for nitrogen and four for carbon.

Or so he hoped …

He glanced around the library of the retirement home. He'd already figured out that much of the library content had been donated by his grandfather and grandmother when they closed their house to move in here.

The whole sheet music section had been that of Grandpa Clifford, tenor and piano player. All the theater plays, and the British and American literature had been Grandma Willie's.

But he was pretty certain that Grandma Willie didn't donate the computer that sat on one of the desks. She didn't like things that ran on invisible sources of information. The idea that you could pull information down from a satellite made her suspicious.

"Who knows who put that information up there?" she'd said, "An encyclopedia has been vetted. Who vets the wackos who write on the internet?"

And, of course, she was right. You couldn't always spot a wacko. Some were very clever.

That made Glyn think about Geneva. What if Geneva's Nazi conspiracy ideas came from some place on the internet?

Glyn moved over to the computer table and opened the thing up. He soon realized that he could see the most recent searches that anyone had done, but he couldn't know who had done them.

There were many searches to the Wiesenthal Center, which he thought might have been Geneva's looking. There were searches for the annual financial report of various Portland companies, by who knew which resident, and a recent search into Argentine composers. Maybe that was Mr. Stapleton. Glyn didn't know all the residents, so couldn't guess who else might be interested in music.

Then, he realized that each person who used this computer had his or her own email and could sign in with a password.

He debated for a while, and then decided that if Geneva herself was being threatened and thus become paranoid, he might find the source and the threat. Also, Geneva had accused his grandmother of many things and he should see where she got those ideas.

He opened the email program and signed in as Geneva Oppenheim. The program asked for a password. He thought a moment and then tried Mittle.

Wrong.

He tried Peenemünde.

Wrong again. He probably had one try left on this sign in.

The email program wisely discouraged guessing.

He tried Mittlebau.

And the machine began whirring through its opening motions.

He felt like an intrusive ghoul, and almost closed the machine, but up popped her email inbox and the first email subject line made him stop.

Immigration status of Wilhalmena Stamps.

Glyn opened the email. It was from another person with a German last name, Hensel Heinke.

Wilamena, Wilhelmina or Wilhalmena Stamps turns up no person of her age in the immigration records. A Stamps family once lived in Stamps, Arkansas, but left for Levi, Texas after the war between the states (1860-65). We think your requested search subject may be Wilhalmena, granddaughter of Malka Silverberg and Orin Chapline, daughter of Sidney Arthur Stamps and Edna Chapline Stamps, and sister of the artist, Scott Arthur (who died in the Philippines prisoner of war camp during World War Two.) She married Clifford Wheeler Williams of Colorado Springs, Colorado, but unlike most of her generation, insisted on keeping her own last name.

Glyn realized this Hensel Heinke had done his homework. He had exactly the right Wilhalmena Stamps. Her insistence on remaining a Stamps was spot on. Grandma Willie and Grandpa Clifford had agreed on this. "Her own free spirit with her own name," Grandpa used to say, and then he teased her, "Can't sully the upstanding Williams name when you poke into things, right?"

"And, nobody can give you credit for what I discover either, eh?" she'd said.

And then, they always laughed.

Glyn hoped that Geneva Oppenheim had seen this email. It should help her believe that Grandma was not the enemy.

That one email kept Glyn poking. Pretty soon, as he opened each email, he printed it out, getting up to check the printer each time, because the thing was balky.

He arrived at another Heinke email with the subject *Immigration status of Leah Müller*. At that moment, the library door swung open and in marched Miss Müller.

Glyn signed out of Geneva's email and stood up. He reached the papers on the printer as Miss Müller said, "You are supposed to be in the kitchen."

Glyn didn't turn around, he merely stacked his papers, 'officiously', as Grandma would have described it.

"Knabe, did you hear me?"

He said nothing. Put his papers in his school bag, returned to his desk and sat down to resume his chemistry homework.

"Are you deaf?"

He glanced up. "Oh. Hello, Miss Müller. I'm glad to see you."

"You work in the kitchen."

"I do homework in the library."

"The help…"

"I can help you with something, if you like."

He stood from his chemistry, went to the swinging doors and opened them wide, propped them open and then said. "These are getting squeaky, aren't they?"

A few people sat in the lounge outside the library, which is what he hoped for. They perked up from whatever magazine or nap they indulged. One of them was Henry Crick, the taxi driver.

"Can you bring an oil can?" Glyn asked, Henry. "I think we could use it on the hinges."

"Sure," Henry said. "Glad to be of help."

"Knabe…" Leah said.

"You have the wrong person. I am Glyn. Glyn Jones. We've met before, as you run up and down the stairs."

He returned to his chemistry homework, leaving the doors wide open. "I really need to finish my homework," he said. "I think the books here use the Dewey Decimal system, but I can help you find any if you like."

She glared at him.

"It's basically 100s for philosophy, 400s for languages and 900s for history."

She raised her shoulders as if preparing a loud speech. He added, "Science is in the middle there somewhere.

Probably 500s." She stormed out.

Glyn pretended not to notice, finished his chemistry, put it in an addressed envelope, grabbed his stuff and began on his history homework.

He glanced up in time to see Henry Crick oiling the library doors.

"Thanks," Glyn said. "Where'd you get oil so fast?"

"Always keep it in my taxi-cab just in case."

Glyn frowned. "I thought your daughter was selling your cab."

"My daughter's got nothing to do with my cab. She'd like to control her old man, but she has enough trouble controlling herself, so I'm keeping the cab and she just keeps on talking about getting rid of it."

"I'm glad to hear you still have it."

"Yes, and your grandmother is helping me keep it. Takes taxi rides and writes me checks to prove it is still useful."

Glyn chuckled. "Yeah, Grandma Willie finds a way to solve most problems."

"Including grandsons who speed?" Henry said. Glyn glanced up at him. He saw that Henry was smiling at him, so figured he was just teasing.

"You ever speed?" Glyn asked.

"In my youth. But you get a speeding ticket as an old man, and people offer to yank your license, so no more of that fun."

Glyn laughed.

*   *

Two floors above the library, Grandma Willie talked to her reader friends. "I see that some of you wrote ideas about Little Britches on the question sheet."

"What question?" a woman asked her neighbor.

The neighbor said, "You know. What's the Britches kid got that we all need."

"I answered," said the lady who had brought up the question. "He had grit."

Grandma Willie nodded. "He did indeed. And so did his dad and mom."

"You need grit to live in this place," the same lady said, waving around the room at her neighbors.

"We do," her neighbor said. "We need persistence and pluck to live a good life."

Mr. Corrigan had joined the edges of the group. He sat there watching others, but not saying anything.

"Britches family didn't have money," another said. "But he had family," chimed in another.

"But too many sisters," said one lady, who Willie knew had been youngest in a family of twelve.

Willie asked, "What did his sisters do during the day?"

"They helped Mom."

"They took up space and ate too much."

"We all eat too much," one said.

Willie looked around at the well-fed and the under-eating members of the group. Some ate to pass time. Some didn't eat because it didn't taste good to them anymore. Some didn't eat enough, under the impression that they could put off death if they were thin.

She… she herself had always had a negative relationship to food. Late in life she had learned that her frying and baking habits were good only for those who worked hard in the fields as her grandparents once had done.

"Britches' dad is dying," a man said. "That's pretty obvious."

"Yeah," another said, "but the guy loves Britches, and that cowboy named Hi loves him like an uncle."

Willie asked, "Is love going to be enough?"

"Naw. Family and friends aren't enough. You gotta eat."

"Aren't you going to read. How we gonna know if you don't read?"

So, Willie said, "*Little Britches*, by Ralph Moody, chapter ten," And she began reading.

*   *

Getting ready to go to Holly Hill for work, Violeta knew that family and friends were not going to be enough.

Glyn's mother, Susan, had been helping her mother, Camelia, as they drove everywhere between George Fox College and Portland. They'd checked out all the motels along the way, hoping for a hint that Rosaria might be held in one of them. They found a good deal of sleaze in some, and reported those to Captain Reese.

In others, they found what appeared to be very careful and honest people with nothing to hide. At one of those motels, Glyn's mom asked if there was an association of motel owners along that highway.

The motel owner had said, "Yes, there are many in the group. It helps us advertise and hire good workers."

"Well," Susan said, "What do you know of other motel owners along the highway?"

"Oh, we meet monthly at a restaurant in Newberg. Why?"

Susan glanced at Camelia and said, "Here is what we are looking for …"

Half an hour later, she had a list of motels that never joined the association and had questionable practices in renting.

When Violeta heard this news, she shuddered and cried with her mamá. What was happening to their Rosaria?

Her papá and Glyn's father had gone the other way, checking out the bus route and possible places between the bus station in Newberg and the college, and all along the bus route.

Violeta despaired of figuring out what had happened, and cried herself to sleep each night. Her papa steamed with anger, but Violeta knew that was his cover for fear.

Merlyn, Glyn's father showed the fear in fiddling with his car keys every morning until they were on their way to the next place they suspected of harboring people who used children.

And every day, Merlyn asked Grandma Willie, "How many police are on this? We can't let these children vanish."

Grandma Willie answered, "Captain Reese and Sergeant Seneca are bringing in as many as can be spared."

*　*

As far as Glyn could tell, family and friends were not going to be enough. He couldn't concentrate on United States' history when Trace and Rosaria desperately needed his mind to help them.

He realized they really would have to call in even more than the two policemen who knew Grandma Willie. Otherwise, they wouldn't have any chance of finding Trace or Rosaria.

Violeta's mother had taken a leave from her job as a nurse-practitioner to hunt for her daughter. Her colleagues were all on the lookout for any hint that Rosaria had come through the hospitals of the area.

Violeta had become dejected. Glyn's dad, Merlyn, had interviewed the bus driver of the LeapFrog bus that Rosaria had taken in Portland. The man remembered that two girls got on the bus with tickets to Newberg, but they had gotten off early in Tualitin, saying they had a ride directly to the college.

When Merlyn and Glyn told her family this, Violeta said, "Tualitin? From there they could have gone any direction and never be noticed."

Her father had put his head into his hands and said, "My Rosaria lied to me. She did know someone on the bus."

"Papá," Violeta said, "perhaps Liza wasn't on the bus when Rosaria got on. Maybe she didn't know that Liza would come, too."

"Si, Augusto," Mrs. Aguirre said, "is not certain she lied. Rosaria no es una mentirosa."

So, after that discussion, Glyn came into the library late at night. He wanted to see more about the stops of the LeapFrog bus system. Did it always stop in Tualitin? Where might Liza have gotten on the bus? And why? Her parents believed she had ridden to school with the boyfriend.

Liza's parents had no qualms about getting the police involved in searching, but until Captain Reese and Officer Seneca picked up the drug seller, the other police had no idea that Trace and Rosaria as well as Liza might be missing.

Glyn saw that bad people got away with bad things when whole groups of citizens didn't trust the law to work for them.

As he fingered down the usual routes of the bus, he realized that Liza could have gotten on in Tigard, but the bus didn't usually stop in Tualitin, so maybe they asked the bus driver to make that stop. Did Dad ask that question?

Glyn knew his dad filtered stuff. He may have told what he thought was critical, but not realized the detail of why they stopped in Tualitin could be important. And where did Liza get on the bus?

"I hope Dad has the phone number of that bus driver," Glyn muttered to himself.

Outside the library, Glyn saw a police car whip into the circular drive and park in front of the front door. The police were back, investigating something.

And here he was with evidence of Geneva's thoughts, and maybe ideas about her supposed enemies. He clicked out of the LeapFrog bus routes and into Outlook, typed Geneva's password and returned to her inbox.

Immigration history of Leah Müller. He found the subject line. Who sent this information?

The sender was a search program for people who had been adopted. Hmmm, Thought Glyn, Geneva searched creatively.

According to the program. Leah Müller was born in Argentina to an Anna Maria Müller and a Gervasio Halley, a musician. Anna Müller had died in 2002, but Halley still lived in Argentina.

Glyn got back into the internet and looked up Gervasio Halley. Up came a lot of references to music, including some YouTube videos. Glyn clicked on the first video. The beats and the instrumentation showed that Halley wrote modern tango in the style of Piazzolla, and used primitive instruments like a very old guitar, something called a bandonion, and drums. Glyn saw references to Afro-Tango.

That puzzled him. In an interview, Gervasio Halley referred to the drums as Tangó, saying that tangó was what the drums were called in African Bantu.

And then Glyn saw a small photo of a band playing Gervasio's most famous piece, *Tango Sylphide*. Glyn enlarged the photo of the band Los Cometas de Halley.

And there he stopped, felt his eyes widen and his spine straighten. In front of the band stood Leah Müller, her arms raised, her face suffused with light and her body clearly swaying. She was the band's singer. Glyn's arm jerked and the mouse ran across Leah's face. Auto recognition labeled her *Anna Maria Müller*. And then the auto recognition ran across the man who stood slightly to her right, holding an acoustic guitar. *Gervasio Halley* was dark black, smiling at Anna and clearly proud of what she did as she sang.

Glyn sat there a moment, stunned. Leah Müller was the daughter of these two people. A Rhine Maiden, indeed.

No wonder she ran all the time. No wonder she put on the Germanic façade. No wonder …

Glyn backed off. His hands dropped into his lap. Did Geneva know this?

Glyn realized that finding Gervasio Halley had not been easy. He'd been on page two of the Afro-Tango choices when he discovered this band photo.

So, this computer had not been to this site before. So, Geneva had probably not been to this site either.

Unless someone else had discovered this on another computer and shown it to Geneva. And who might that be?

He looked back at her emails.

And there sat an email from Gervasio Halley.

I believe you have found the wrong Gervasio Halley. I'm sorry not to be able to identify the person in your photo.

Glyn stared at that and then went right to the sent file in Geneva's email. There it was. Did she know how to do an attachment? Where did she file the photo? What he found was a photo of Leah, but were there other photos? Where would she put them? Who else did she suspect?

Just because you're paranoid, doesn't mean no one is after you.

And was this reply the truth?

Did Gervasio Halley tell Leah Müller that Geneva was asking about her?

Did Leah threaten Geneva? Was that the real reason Geneva left with her friend on a 'vacation'?

Glyn felt guilty about getting into Geneva's email. She clearly was not right in her mind, asking about all these people. Was that a good enough excuse?

He didn't even have that flimsy an excuse for invading Leah's privacy. He hovered the mouse over thinking it would be pretty easy to guess her password, then he stopped himself.

Instead, he downloaded several Afro-Tangos of Halley's onto his thumb drive.

At that moment, Rolly Goforth charged into the library.

CHAPTER TWENTY

"What are you doing in here?" Goforth asked.

"My homework," Glyn said, closing Geneva's email and sliding back into his research on tango.

Goforth came and looked at the screen, as Glyn knew he might do. Glyn enlarged the page on how to dance *tango salon*, clicked on the sample steps and said, "Learning about historic ballroom dances."

"What kind of study is that?"

"World music."

"A fluff class you can pass without working?"

"Want to try this dance with me?"

"I don't dance. For sure not with some guy."

Glyn laughed. "It'll make you work up a sweat, that's for sure, but I'm writing about its history, so only researching at the moment."

Goforth harrumphed into the sofa and put his feet up on a coffee table. It was then that Glyn realized neither of them had turned on the library lights. He'd been here since dusk and had not really noticed, but he figured maybe Goforth was just lazy. He got up and walked to the light switch.

"Turn that off," Goforth said.

Glyn remembered the police car. Was Rolly Goforth hiding? "If you want to sleep, why do it here and not in your room?"

"Just turn it off, I tell you. You want the management to fire you for being insolent?"

"I doubt they will. Hard to find help as diligent as me. But you could sleep somewhere else while I finish my homework."

Goforth got up from the couch and hulked toward Glyn, but Glyn stood his six feet and puffed out his arms, the way he had when he startled a bear at the family tree farm.

And just like the bear, Goforth backed down, marched out the swinging door and huffed down the hall to another hiding place in the gift shop where again he turned out the lights.

Glyn turned off the computer, and the library lights. He took his thumb drive down the hall past the gift shop where Rolly hid. He thought Rolly Goforth probably owed money to the state or the feds. His reputation as a careless accountant made that easy to imagine.

Glyn walked into the room next to the kitchen – the room where the musack machines were stored.

He got into the preprogrammed, slurpy old-time and innocuous low-value stuff and upped the well-known classical music. In that music, he copied the Tangos, spreading them amongst the choices around breakfast and dinner time.

He planned to watch Leah Müller's face when her father's tangos came on. If she grew angry, he would know something. Not certain what, but something.

CHAPTER TWENTY-ONE

Leah Müller sat with one of her bleached blond friends at the table nearest the outside windows and directly under the speakers for the dinner music. She exchanged stiff pleasantries with Glyn as he took her order, then turned to her friend and brought up their next *volkwalk* which Glyn gathered was a passel of German-like-Americans hiking somewhere in Portland. As he moved toward the next table, an overture from Wagner came on the musack. Glyn recognized it from his dad's collection – Merlyn Jones, Welshman, a Wagner fan. Hard to explain taste.

Leah didn't seem to notice the Germanic muscle in the music, just kept talking to her friends about their plans to pack a light lunch for the hike.

Glyn moved to the next table and took orders, then retired to the kitchen to put in the orders for two tables.

A half an hour later, he heard the Richard Rogers' Victory at Sea which he knew was just before the Afro-Tango *Dienstag,* by Gervasio Halley. So, Glyn began refilling water glasses closer and closer to Leah.

The last waves washed over the Richard Rogers piece. The rhythm of Afro drums began softly.

Báahn, kĭn Bahn Bahn,
Báahn, kĭn Bahn Bahn

Kĭn Bahn, kĭn Bahn
Bahn Báahn, kĭn Bahn Bahn

The background drums kept up an insistent eight beats. And then the bandoneon began the tune.

Leah's hand stopped in mid-air. Her eyes opened wide as she turned toward the speaker in the ceiling.

Even her friend noticed the sudden change in Leah. "What?" the friend asked.

Leah shook her head and pointed upwards.

"What?" the friend persisted, but Leah stood and moved away from the distraction. The friend stopped and merely watched.

And so did Glyn. Leah Müller danced. She held one hand out as if part of a pair and slightly moved her feet, then caught herself and stood still until the end of the piece, hand still suspended.

By that time, her friend had stood, waiting to help if anything had gone wrong with Leah's mind. At the last beat, Leah smiled and seemed to come from a trance. She returned to her table, leaned over and said, "Did you hear that?"

"That music?"

"Isn't it fun? Isn't it great?"

"Umm … was it Mexican? I didn't recognize it."

"Argentina, Gervas…" and there she caught herself. "A great composer."

Her friend smiled, bland and non-committal. So, Glyn moved in. "I like that music, too," he said. "We should have more of that."

Leah smiled up at him. "Yes, we should."

"I'll ask the supplier," he said.

"Thank you, young man … um…"

"Glyn Jones," he supplied. "May I bring you dessert, now?"

"Oh, yes."

Leah, thin and careful, never said yes to dessert.

*   *

Later, Glyn hiked up to Grandma Willie's. As he hiked, he thought.

Leah Müller hides her father's identity. She was happy to hear his music, though reluctant to say why.

After puzzling fruitlessly over the human heart, Glyn sank into his bed in the room next to Grandma Willie's room and her troubled sleep.

He thought about Arwain, living with her friend Claudia, and Mom and Dad hiding from the gangsters as guests of the Aguirre's, Violeta's parents. And all four of them hunting for Rosaria.

He thought of his band members, those who had visits from the drug gang and were now hiding out with other gang members that might not be known. He thought about Felipe and Anita and all the guys at the Chevron station.

All these people hiding and in danger because of Trace's need for drugs, and the people who made money off that need.

Why couldn't Trace take medicine to kill his need for medicine? Had such medicine even been invented?

And what about Rosaria? Was she just a medicine to feed some guy's need to feel powerful?

Glyn hardly slept all night, wondering about what might be happening to Trace and Rosaria.

*   *

In her bedroom, Willie didn't sleep at all. She attempted to decipher what Geneva told her.

"Please make sure no one goes in my rooms," Geneva had said. "But you go water plants, and you can read my books, too."

Willie had realized that Geneva had lost track of something and couldn't bring it up. She feared whoever threatened, but she couldn't seem to explain why anyone would make the threat. Her doctor assured Willie and Geneva that Geneva was free to leave any time she felt was right, but Geneva had shivered at the idea, then bristled at Willie for asking the question.

"Of course, I could leave. Is that what you want? You want me to be a target of these people?"

"Who are they, my friend?"

"The ones who put us on trains, sent us to build those dangerous weapons."

"I don't want that to happen to you. I want you to stay here as long as you need to."

Doctor Sartan had added, "Geneva, I believe your friend, Willie, is just making sure that you are not at the hospital without your consent."

Geneva had looked at Doctor Sartan and said, "Please, let me stay. I can tell my story, and be safe here."

Then she had turned to Willie. "Read my books. My favorite books. And read anything you find there. It's all part of the plot. Read it."

Willie had begun to ask, "What plot …?"

But Doctor Sartan had shaken her head because Geneva became very agitated. "Let's read and see if we can understand," Doctor Sartan said.

So Willie had gone into Geneva's room, watered the plants and found another computer printed note under the door.

"Keep your mouth shut. We'll send you to Dora again if you talk."

A note from someone who had heard of Mittle-bau Dora, but clearly didn't understand what it was, or what it really had been named. A threat from an idiot? From someone who didn't listen carefully? Who understood only part and not all of what frightened Geneva …?

A someone who thought Geneva might talk about a thing that was a threat now.

Willie had picked up the most recent reading on Geneva's desk – neatly stacked as always, so hard to tell what she felt was most important.

But she had dutifully brought them here and tried to find a hint in any of them.

Nothing spoke of trains from warehouses to workhouses.

CHAPTER TWENTY-TWO

In the morning, Glyn crawled out of bed, opened the door and looked down the hall toward Geneva's.

Geneva was still visiting with her friend.

Grandma Willie came up beside him. "Yesterday, she asked me to take care of her flowers. I've still got a key to her room. You go on down to work in the kitchen, and I'll take care of this."

He looked at her, amazed she would care about the flowers.

But then he read her face. She clearly steeled herself to face whatever the room would reveal about Geneva's fears.

* *

Once locked inside Geneva's apartment, Willie recognized that Geneva's neatness was absolute. However, still on the desk was her ledger for expenses.

The first page showed many donations to the Wiesenthal Center and others to a local reformed synagogue. What caught Willie's eye, though, were the deposits to Geneva's account from the place where she had worked until about eight months ago.

Larson Lumber and Woodland Supplies had been Geneva's home for forty years. The payments stopped eight months ago, and since – only social security deposits. Forty years and no retirement benefits? No health benefits?

Willie saw that donations to the Wiesenthal Center had suddenly risen at the time that Geneva left Larson Lumber. All these donations seemed to have come from her savings. And then there began to be donations to the Holocaust Museum and to a fund for the renovation of the Mittlebau-Dora Memorial.

Willie left the bank statements where Geneva left them.

She stepped over to Geneva's book collection and took out a book by Elie Wiesel, a prize-winning author who had survived both Auschwitz and Buchenwald extermination camps, and had lost mother, sister and finally father to the Holocaust. Willie had seen Geneva reading and re-reading this book.

And in the margins, Geneva had written notes.

Inside the back cover, Willie saw a note in a different color of pen, perhaps written after the normal black-inked pen had run out, or before she bought the black-ink pen.

The note stood out because of one word. *Warehouse.*

This was the memory that Geneva had been worrying for the last several months. *Warehouse.*

Willie read the notes around it and found other words that made no sense to her.

Garlon and Crossbow.

She would have to look these up. Crossbow? English crossbow was credited with increasing the firepower of the English army by many times. What did that have to do with warehouse, or with Geneva's fears? and what was Garlon? Maybe some sort of French weapon.

Willie decided to borrow the book. She lifted the next book, intending to pull it out somewhat so that she could replace this one appropriately when the time came.

And then, she realized that the next book was not a book, but a box made to look like a book. She set it on the nearby desk and opened it.

Out fell receipts – rental receipts for equipment belonging to Larson Lumber, the first was a backhoe rented to a company called *International Relocation Services*.

"We Care for your Precious Objects."

Another receipt was for a building in Seattle, rented to *Hiltown Moving*. And a receipt for *Pauls Trucking*. Several others were stacked neatly in the box, as Geneva would do.

Willie knew Geneva no longer worked for Larson Lumber.

So, it was possible these had merely been forgotten when Geneva quit.

Quit, but not retired, after forty-some years. That didn't make any sense.

But Geneva had not been making sense for months.

Puzzled, Willie decided to borrow this book as well. She pulled other books into the space, so that these would not be missed if the wrong people came into this apartment.

Next, she studied the desk, but found only neat rows of pens and a stack of paper. She went to the coat closet, reached back inside and found the key to her apartment hanging exactly where Geneva had once asked her to hang it. She pocketed it.

A few minutes later she had watered Geneva's flowerpots and carried the watering can back to her room. In her other hand, she carried the top few sheets of paper from the stack.

Once in her room, she pulled out a drawing pencil and ran the side of the lead over the paper. Nothing showed up. She held it up to the light. Still nothing.

So much for what you learn about detective work from television, she thought.

Of course, it was possible Geneva had also known this trick and what she'd left on the stack was the second or third sheet below.

Willie sat on her bed and tried to imagine what Geneva had been trying to tell her. It had always been difficult to know how much had been memory, and how much a real worry from the present.

She glanced at the Elie Wiesel book and realized that the most continuous thread in their conversations had been warehouses of children.

Children waiting for trains to extermination camps.

Had those who threatened Geneva heard her talking this way and known that she knew something no one else should know?

So, who had heard her ramblings and accusations?

Nearly everyone in the dining room. But there was no way to know what the conversations meant to those who heard.

Willie's phone rang. When she answered, the voice at the other end was soft.

"Mrs. Stamps, Leneld here."

Glyn came into the room. She waved him to quiet. "I'm here, Leneld," she said.

"I followed the guy who lives above the pharmacy, you know, the guy Arwain was following. I lost him among the grocery warehouses and other buildings that back on the railroad."

"Are you whispering because you think he's near?"

"He must be, but I can't see him."

"Leave your phone on. Put it in your shirt pocket and lean against a building to protect your back and then don't move."

She heard him fumbling the phone into his pocket. She waited, holding a finger up to keep Glyn quiet.

After a minute, she heard a voice, far away from Leneld's phone.

"Who are you and what you doing here?"

"I'm Jane Fonda and I don't want my dad to know I smoke."

"Very funny."

"Yeah. Well, my mom is just as much a dictator about smoking as anybody I know, so I come here."

"But you're not smoking."

"Need a light," Leneld said.

"A green light? Or white," the voice asked. "Marlboroughs'll kill my horse and he's got arthritis. Green smokes would help his knees."

Willie shook her head, thinking, *Stop smart-mouthing. Just get out of there.*

The voice said, "Too bad for you, I don't use either. Just move on away from here," the voice had gotten a lot closer.

"You out for a walk? or you the security for the railroads?" Leneld asked.

"I own this building, and you're trespassing."

"Okay. Guess I'll have a smoke with someone else."

"Git going."

Willie heard moving cloth. The next time she heard the voice, it seemed farther away.

"I see you around here again, I'm calling the police." Leneld hollered back. "I'm gone."

Willie waited while he kept moving. She didn't dare say anything in case others were around who might hear the voice in his pocket.

After a few moments, Leneld whispered. "Got pen and paper?"

She answered, "I do."

"199 SE 2nd Avenue"

She heard traffic and loud brakes. "Get out of there."

"Catching the bus right now."

She waited, listening to the sounds of greeting the bus driver, the rustle of his shirt as he moved and, she thought, as he sat down. Then his voice came back on, close up. "I'm safe."

"Would you recognize the guy that accosted you?"

"Yes. Tall, next to no hair, strong, but cushy."

"Cushy?"

"Hasn't used his strength in a long time."

"Ahhh. Cushy. Good word. You should take up writing, Leneld."

"Think I will. Next week at the carcel, the prison."

"The guys there accepted you."

"See you soon, in the band's carcel in Holly Hill basement." She laughed. "Good night."

CHAPTER TWENTY-THREE

After Grandma described the phone call and Glyn took in the information about where Leneld was when he called, Glyn and Grandma Willie went over what they knew.

Glyn said, "We need help, especially for Rosaria and her friend Liza. We have no clues about them, only the LeapFrog bus."

"And the boyfriend," Grandma said. "This Chuck person.

Police know who he is, but they haven't found him yet."

"They know him? Why?"

She said, "Captain Reese says they've had him in their sights as a drug dealer, but this seems beyond drugs."

"Or an extension," Glyn said, " – a related business."

Grandma Willie glanced at him, biting her lips. After a moment, she said, "How is Violeta doing?"

"I think she's going to her school track work outs, and getting her homework done, but she's trying hard to have a stiff upper lip."

"Scary stuff. Is she safe at the track? On the way home?"

"Her dad picks her up from everywhere. His boss has told him to be where she is and come to work in between. The whole crew is worried for her."

"What does Mr. Aguirre do for a living?"

"He's part of a crew that works on tree farms. They plant, they harvest, they clear land and fertilize it. That sort of stuff."

Grandma Willie glanced up at him. "Do they own their own equipment? That's expensive machinery."

"Gee, I don't know. Never thought about that."

Grandma Willie stood up and shoved her walker toward her desk. "I want to show you something."

She pulled out a box that looked like a book, but opened on a pile of receipts.

* *

The receipts box pointed them at a company, but they weren't sure where that took them.

Grandma Willie said, "Geneva was very logical until she stopped working, so let's figure that something made her quit without waiting for retirement. She seems to have cut off all ties with Larson Lumber. I don't get it. She hasn't even tapped into her 401k, which she could do without contacting the company. And she has no pension, no company health coverage."

"So," Glyn said, "maybe something went down there that made her feel unsafe – like get-out-now. And maybe she feared any contact with her retirement and 401k would get back to the company, showing her home here at the retirement center."

"There may be more clues in her apartment, but the only one we have now is this box of receipts."

"Was she the bookkeeper?" Glyn asked.

"She was the secretary to the chief financial officer."

"Let's go through these, then, and see if there is some kind of pattern."

Twenty minutes later, Glyn said, "There are machine rentals – that's about a third of what they do.

"What kind of machines?" Grandma Willie asked. "Backhoes, ditch diggers, something called a Krummy, and personnel transport."

"Personnel transport. What's that?"

"Probably executive talk for ritzy cars," Glyn said. "What's a Krummy?"

Grandma Willie said, "Woods talk for a basic van. It becomes crummy by jouncing over unpaved roads all day, every day."

"Oh, a long Jeep in forest green," Glyn guessed. "Maybe the Jones Family Tree Farms need a Krummy."

"Your mom is about to buy one."

"Pretty much." Glyn said.

"What else is in that box?"

"The Larson Lumber Company has three times more personnel transport vehicles than Krummies."

"In that stack of receipts? I saw Cross-bow."

"Yes," Glyn said.

"Cross-bow, something called Garlon and Ketalar."

"That sounds like chemicals Grandpa Jones, dad's dad, and the family use on the tree farm," Glyn said.

Grandma Willie sat there a moment and then said, "Hand me your cell phone, please."

Glyn handed it over and showed Grandma Willie how to turn it on. Then she stopped and asked. "Can you look up things on this phone, like on a computer?"

"Sure. Here's the internet icon."

She clicked on it and spoke as she spelled, "GARLON".

Studying the screen she said, "Hmmm… a weed killer." She frowned. "Triclopyr."

Then she spelled out Cross Bow.

"Ahh…tripclopyr and 2,4-D …hormonal plant growth regulator. Wow! The Crossbow is now illegal for forestry use. Why are they selling that stuff?"

Glyn asked, "But the Garlon is legal for forestry use, right?"

"Right."

Glyn said, "What about that other stuff? That . . .?"

"Ketalar?"

Glyn grabbed his school backpack and hauled out his tablet computer. "Ketalar with a K?"

"Yes."

After several punches at the keyboard he said, "Ketamine, sold as Ketalar is a medication mainly used for starting and maintaining anesthesia. Induces a trance-like feeling while providing pain relief, sedation and memory loss."

Grandma Willie stood up and stared out the window to the east. "What does a lumber company need with Ketalar?"

"Get this, Grandma, it's on the list of World Health Organizations Essential Medicines, the most effective and safe medicines needed in the health system."

She turned and stared at him. "Who are Larsons selling it to?"

Glyn went back to the receipts. "The biggest shipment seems to go to Elmore's Veterinary hospital."

She frowned. "I don't think lumber companies have animals – not since the donkey was replaced by the steam engine."

"Injured loggers? Need sedation?" Glyn suggested. "Lumber company's not a hospital, nor that far from medical help. And that's a lot of Ketalar."

Gryf asked, "Why would a lumber company be the source of Ketalar, and why sell to a Vet hospital?"

"Good question."

" Something's backwards here," he said. "Let's get Captain Reese."

*   *

An hour later, Captain Reese and Officer Seneca had Glyn, Grandma Willie, Leneld and Violeta pouring over photos of possible people – people who may have had anything to do with either Trace, Rosaria or Liza Cramer.

At the same time, Reese asked for a warrant to search the books of Elmore's Veterinary Hospital.

In the perp photos, Leneld held up his photo album. "Here's the guy Arwain followed from the high school to the pharmacy on Grand."

Officer Seneca came over, saw who it was and said, "Man, you gotta tell her not to get into this stuff."

Leneld threw up his hands. "I don't tell that one 'not to' anything."

Seneca glanced at Leneld and said, "I thought she was your girl."

"Arwain? She …" and then he stopped, not sure how or whether to let Seneca in on the joke of the other day. "That Arwain is somethin', but she is presently under the sole ownership of Arwain Jones."

Seneca blanched, took the number and name off the photo, and said in a low voice. "You got any sway with her?"

"Her Grandma, maybe. Her mama, maybe. Nobody else I know tells Arwain what to do."

"This guy she followed – we think he's killed over nothing. Suspicion of being laughed at, that's enough for him to whip out a gun."

Leneld whipped out his phone. "Here's her phone number. Text her. She's probably in class at U of P during this hour."

Officer Seneca took the number into his cell, fumed a moment, started and then erased two text messages, and then strode over to Grandma Willie.

A moment later, Willie nodded and said, "I will text her."

CHAPTER TWENTY-FOUR

After class at the University of Portland, two young women sat in the student lounge under a purple and gold banner advertising the Pilots Women's soccer team. Arwain Jones pulled her dark hair into a ponytail, wrapped a band around it and let it smack her back.

Claudia watched this maneuver, flipped at her boycut red hair and said, "Don't you know a girl can run a lot faster without that old-fashioned weight of hair? The stuff is strictly a nuisance."

"True. Is it clogging your sinks or something? Am I a nuisance?

Claudia leaned back against a squeaky chair frame. "Don't sweat it, Arn. I'm totally fine with you staying in my apartment. The help with food and rent is great, and we can study together."

"And I give you someone to beat in soccer scrimmages."

"I always win," Claudia rightly pointed out. "You're too intent on finding the pass, and I know you from second grade. Gotta learn to pass with your other foot, girl."

"Plus, I've been skipping workouts to find this girl. You'd think there'd have been some clue."

"I wish," Claudia said. "You should hear my friend, Javier, on the guy's team. He's starting a help group – tell girls and boys, especially our DACA students and students from other countries, how to watch out for each other, so they won't get taken off the streets by ICE or any other gang."

"He's got a good idea, but how about after they're missing?" Arwain said, "Isn't there a better way to find missing people?

Shouldn't the police be interviewing more people at the bus stations, or talk to more bus drivers? Look for a pattern among the missing?"

Claudia's eyes narrowed at Arwain. "I know Javier would recommend doing stuff where you aren't alone, and where you have a plan how to get away."

"What are you saying? We shouldn't do anything?"

"I'm saying if you take that on, you're liable to talk to the wrong guy and set off a hunt for yourself. You could maybe sit in the bus station and check out what goes on, or take the bus yourself and see what might happen, but don't do stuff like that by yourself."

"Want to do it with me?"

"Sure, but what bus station? Where did this Rosaria get on?

And where did her friend Liza get on the bus to Newberg?"

"I think Rosaria got on in the LeapFrog Bus station down near the Portland railway station."

"I use that system. It's a transfer here and a transfer there . . . don't think the LeapFrog Bus goes direct to Newberg." Claudia said, pulling out her phone. She poked around and then said, "Yeah, there actually is a transfer. She probably took the number 44 bus to the Tigard Transfer Center, and then the number 5 bus. In between, you have to walk from one LeapFrog Bus stop to another, about a four-minute walk."

"Geez," Arwain said. "I wonder if my dad knows about the transfer and the walk. They could have disappeared anywhere along in there."

She hauled out her phone and dialed Dad. Luckily, he seemed to have kept his phone nearby. She could hear Rosaria's dad in the background. It sounded like they were in a car.

"Papa, does Mr. Aguirre know that the bus ride to Newberg and George Fox University involved a transfer that includes a short walk in Tigard from one part of the station to another four minutes away?"

"We're on Bluetooth" Dad said. "He heard your question." Arwain heard the two dads conferring. Mr. Aguirre said,

"No. Didn't know that. Where's the transfer?"

"Can you get online and plug in her start point and her destination, you'll see along the way where she had to change busses."

"Damn!" Dad said. "So, it was never going to be a straight- on, straight-off ride."

"No. Claudia and I are looking at the schedule online."

"Okay," Dad said. "We've got more questioning to do and more leg work. Thanks for the heads up."

After they hung up, Arwain saw the text from her Grandma Willie. "Guy you followed the other day has gun and has used it when he feels laughed at, or for nothing. Stay away."

Arwain texted back. "Going nowhere near him."

*   *

After texting Arwain to stay away from the gun- toting- short-fuse guy, Grandma Willie and the band plowed through more police ID photos and found three people they knew from Trace's life.

They corroborated Reese's identification of Small Pants, identifying his photo. He was well-known as a drug dealer and importer named Heinrich Strauss.

Toward the end of a long hunt, Jon found photos of Heinrich's skinny confederates. Officer Seneca whispered to Captain Reese.

"They IDed Franz Coron and Billy Bevit."

"Dagnab it!" Reese said. "We should have guessed." Seneca looked at Reese with his eyebrows raised. "What?" Reese said.

"Dagnab it? That's a new cuss word," Seneca said. "Yeah, and you're liable to hear some more new ones if Willie doesn't learn to lay low and let us do the work we were hired to do. "

CHAPTER TWENTY-FIVE

Back in her Holly Hill rooms, Willie sat in one of her pink side chairs and fanned herself. Glyn slumped into the other.

"How's Geneva?" he asked.

"Vague, but afraid. And she seems to have reason for fear. I want you to look at what I found in her room besides the box of receipts."

"The Ketalar has to be a clue," Glyn said, "but Captain Reese says the judge won't give him a warrant for the Vet hospital. Not enough to go on."

Willie said, "When I visited Geneva, she asked me to water her plants and emphasized that I read her books. I thought it was odd, until I found the receipt box we looked through."

Glyn moved over to the sofa next to the box of receipts, fingering his way through them again.

Willie said, "Right next to the book-box of receipts was Geneva's favorite book."

She put the Elie Wiesel book down and opened it to the back page where the red note had the word, 'Warehouses'.

"You know she kept talking about warehouses as places to hide kids before they were taken to the work camps."

"Yes."

Willie opened the box. "Well, I think I've found a connection to now and to why she left her job so abruptly."

Glyn leaned over.

Willie went on. "From the police files, we've got names of drug sellers, but no locations."

"Sure," Glyn said.

"At least the police know who these yahoos are.

"Yes," Glyn said, "but we're not making any headway on Rosaria and Liza's whereabouts."

Willie took one of the receipts from Geneva's box, and studied the company names.

"International Relocation Services. Hiltown Storage and Transfer, Seattle Transfer," she read. "We need an untraceable phone."

Glyn stared at her and said, "You think like a thief." She eyed him over her reading glasses. "Well?"

He reached into his pocket and pulled out a burner phone. "You've got about ten minutes on this one."

She glanced at him over her glasses. "I'll ask later why you happen to have this."

He pulled out another. "This one's about used up. They're for band reviews. Calls and texts on Yelp and Band Stand. It's like creating seed money in the tip jar."

"Hmmph." She said, but took the phone.

He could hear the answer at the other end. "Larson Lumber."

"I am calling for Hiltown Storage and Transfer. We'd like to rent a backhoe."

"What's the location this time?"

"Tigard." Grandma Willie gave the address of the Tigard Hotel."

"You'll need to rent the back-hoe and its trailer, Ms"

"I have a receipt here for the last time we rented a backhoe and there's no mention of a trailer."

"Oh yes. That was the time you needed it at International Relocation, their main storage area, remember. That's so close, we just delivered the back-hoe directly."

"Oh, yes. That makes sense. So, what is the cost of the trailer?"

"That will be a deposit of fifty dollars plus $200 a day for the rental of the back-hoe and $100 a day for the trailer. Or you could have us deliver and take away for $250 a day, so you don't have to store the trailer."

"Sounds reasonable," Grandma Willie said, fanning herself with the receipt. She then arranged for delivery two months away and rang off.

Glyn said, "Hiltown Storage is in for a surprise."

"By two months out we should have these children back with us. Look up International Relocations Services, and find the address of their main building."

Glyn fiddled with his computer. "Looks like 199 SE 2nd Avenue. Isn't that where …?"

"Yes. It is."

"Wait," Glyn said. "So Leneld followed the disappearing drug seller …"

Willie nodded, "and he was invited off the property by the strong but cushy owner."

Grandma Willie pushed aside one of her stacks of magazines and stared at a map of Portland.

"How close is that building?" She asked.

Glyn moved aside another pile that fell to the floor. He opened the map further to reveal the area near Willamette River. "Right here, near the skate park and the railroad."

Grandma Willie saw the fallen papers just as Glyn picked them up.

Grandma Willie reached for the stack, saying, "Oh dear. Don Corrigan dropped those after choir rehearsal. I picked them up and forgot to give them back to him."

Glyn read the letterhead on the top of the stack. "International Relocation Services".

They looked at each other in surprise, and then Grandma Willie said. "Let's look at the rest of those papers."

CHAPTER TWENTY-SIX

Nothing in the Corrigan mail envelopes was much help, but the idea that one piece of mail came from International Relocation Services made Grandma Willie want to know more about that company and whatever connection it had with Corrigan.

When she opened the letter, what she found was merely an ad for the services of the company.

"Grandma," Glyn said, "A post-it." He showed her where a small yellow paper had stuck to the back of the ad.

When they looked at both sides, all they saw was a large question mark and no words. They went back to the envelope and found no hint about what the question mark might mean.

"Maybe significant," Grandma Willie said.

"Maybe an office accident of no meaning at all," Glyn suggested.

"I think we need to check out this place," she said, pointing at the address on the envelope. "It keeps coming up, like a sore thumb, trying to get my attention."

They called Willie's neighbor, Henry Crick.

A half hour later, Glyn walked through the night-darkened dining room toward the back door, where he was to meet Henry.

Of course, Henry was up for an adventure. And if it involved his precious cab, he was happy to oblige. He loved to show his daughter that the cab was still useful, and so was he.

Glyn wasn't so sure they should be doing this, but Grandma had vetoed calling Captain Reese or Officer Sidney Oberon Seneca.

"They get involved in this scouting expedition and that evidence won't be usable. They don't have a warrant. Us? We're just being curious."

As he entered the kitchen, a shadow loomed before Glyn, a slight, short person, her head surrounded by curly hair.

"Violeta."

Her shadow answered. "I thought you were through with work."

He thought fast. "Gotta go meet the guys for band practice." No way did he want her in on this bad idea.

"I thought I saw your Grandma Willie headed toward the front door."

"Yeah. Church thing tonight for her." And Mr. Henry Crick?"

"I think he's her taxicab tonight."

"But his daughter is selling that cab tomorrow."

"I don't think Henry's signed off on that idea. Or maybe this is his last taxi fling."

"Grandma Willie and Henry?" she laughed.

"Not what I meant," he huffed, trying to edge toward the door, afraid Violeta would follow him, and afraid Henry would leave without him.

In the dark, against the blacklight of the dining room windows, Violeta's head tilted to one side. She whispered, "You in a hurry?"

"Guys are waiting."

"See you tomorrow," she whispered, touching his arm.

He couldn't help himself. He took her hand and pulled her to him. She came so smoothly and fit so perfectly, that he lowered his head and tested a kiss.

Her mouth was warm and soft. Her hands came up to hold his jaw as she moved her lips, touching his nose and then his mouth again.

"Be careful," she whispered.

That startled him. "Just the guys," he said.

"Okay." She straightened up, pulling away. "Don't take chances."

He stared at her shadow a moment. "I won't. Dad picking you up?"

"In a minute," she said.

"Good," he said, as he sidled out the door.

CHAPTER TWENTY-SEVEN

That same day, about two hours earlier, Claudia Ash and Arwain Jones had been sitting toward the front of the number forty-four Leap Frog Bus headed toward Tigard. Neither of them talked much, both thinking this was where Rosaria and Liza had once sat, a mere four days ago.

"Did you talk to Javier and the campus safety committee?" Arwain asked.

"Yes. They want us to call Javier Lucero as soon as we get to Newberg."

Arwain glanced at her friend and said, "Actually, Javier wants you to call, right?"

Claudia fidgeted. "Well, it was Javier that got on the phone when he heard what we planned."

"Hmph," Arwain said. "He got on the phone when he heard it was you calling."

"Why do you think that?"

"The guy clearly likes short red hair."

"Huh-uh! He's always teasing me about my hair."

"I rest my case," Arwain said, laughing.

Up front, the bus driver spent some time talking on his cell phone through his blue-tooth and earphone.

"I'm on time," he said to the phone. "In fact, I may have to idle in Tigard. Two to transfer, there. Then back to Portland."

Arwain figured he meant them. They had asked how to transfer to the Newberg bus.

Claudia glanced out the window at the cars passing them on Interstate 5. "Your dad drive an Outback?"

"Sure. Green. You see him?"

"You kidding? On this road, if it isn't a gray Prius, it's a green Outback."

"So true. Is there a place in the world where Prius comes in blue? Maybe yellow?"

"We're turning off into Tigard," Claudia said.

The bus driver glanced back toward them as he made the turn. The ear bud for his phone barely fit on his large and balding head.

Arwain checked her notes. "The map says the transit mall is right at the Pacific Highway. Our transfer should be close."

When the bus pulled close to the metal roof over the transit center, both girls stood. The bus driver turned in his seat which wasn't easy, given his size. He said, "Your bus to Newberg is around the other side of the block. Just get off and walk left, cross the street and wait on the other side at the back of that small building."

"Thank you," Arwain said, as they walked toward the front door.

He grunted "Sure," and twisted back into his seat, signaling someone outside and again talking into his phone. "When's the Newberg coming?"

Arwain waited to see what answer he got, but Claudia stepped off the bus and looked anxious that Arwain follow. Arwain knew her phone would tell her when the bus should arrive, so she just got off.

"What?" she asked Claudia.

Claudia pulled her away from the bus. "I don't like bus drivers who are that interested in being helpful."

"That's his job. He was asking about our bus arrival time.

But I didn't get to hear the answer."

"Let's get across this street and look it up. I think there's a restaurant on the other side of that wait area."

"You hungry?" Arwain asked.

"Famished."

"We've got to get the next bus and get home before Javier starts to worry."

"Javier is a worrier."

"Me, too," Arwain said. "So, let's get the bus and worry about eating when we get home.

They crossed Commercial Street, walking toward the Oregon Rifle Works and the Ballroom Dance Company.

They passed a parked blue and white truck from Hiltown Storage and Transfer.

Two men came out of the nearby building. The truck door opened from the inside. Arwain glanced into the empty interior just as a pair of arms surrounded her. She kicked back with her left foot and twisted to whack the man in his Adams apple, but he covered her mouth and swore.

"Damn bitch." Then he coughed hard as he threw her into the truck and jumped in after.

Arwain glanced up, saw out the window on the far side, and realized that the bus driver was smoking and watching the melee surrounding them.

Claudia landed near her. The truck door slammed shut and the truck pulled out.

"I've got two transfers," the bus driver had said into his phone. He had signaled these bastards to be here.

Arwain knew the truck turned right at the next corner, but by then, her hands had been tied. A man sat on her legs and another yanked a scarf over her eyes.

She tried to keep track of the turns, and was pretty certain they had turned north onto Pacific Highway, back toward Portland, but the needle in her upper arm made her throat hot and her thinking fuzzy.

"Claudia?"

"Here."

"I'm drugged. You?" Claudia didn't answer.

CHAPTER TWENTY-EIGHT

"Papá," Violeta said. "Please follow that cab. Grandma Willie and Glyn are doing something they don't want me to know about, so I think it's dangerous."

"I saw Glyn get into the cab," Mr. Aguirre said. "You call his papá and keep him informed about where we are. I will drive."

* *

Javier Lucero called Claudia's parents, but wasn't able to get either of them. He then tried Arwain's phone number, but reached her mom, Mrs. Jones.

"They went on a LeapFrog bus to Newberg?" Mrs. Jones couldn't understand.

"Testing this theory they had about where Rosaria and somebody named Liza had to change buses."

"They told you? Why?"

"Because I started this campus safety committee and they thought somebody ought to know what they were doing."

"Just not Mom, who would have said, 'No'."

"I guess that's what they thought. They didn't call me when they were supposed to have arrived at the first stop in Tigard Transit

Center off Pacific Highway. And by now, they should have arrived in Newberg, so I'm thinking something happened in Tigard."

"Or they forgot to call," Mrs. Jones guessed. "But I'm pretty sure Claudia wouldn't forget."

"Good friend?" Mrs. Jones asked. "Yes. Pretty good," Javier said.

"All right, Javier. I've got your number and I'm going to call around. See if I can roust the girls or figure out where they are."

"Good," Javier said. "Meanwhile, I'll watch for your call."

"Call me or I'll call you if we hear anything," Mrs. Jones said.

"Right," Javier said.

What he didn't say was that he was in his car and approaching the transit stop in Tigard, watching to see what happened as the busses came and went.

*   *

Near the warehouse area in Portland, Glyn pulled Grandma Willie's walker out of the trunk of a taxi.

Henry, the taxi driver took Willie's handbag for safe keeping and glanced at her. "You sure about this, Wilhalmena?"

"Just hover around that corner, Henry. We'll be back in a jiff."

"I'm giving you five minutes."

"Ten," she said. "I'm a shuffler, remember?"

"Yeah, yeah." Henry pulled his cab out into Second Avenue.

Henry liked Grandma Willie because she wrote checks to him whenever they used his taxi. He used the checks to put off his daughter who wanted to take his cab to the dump.

"Why is this a good idea?" Glyn asked Grandma Willie, glancing at 199 SE 2nd Avenue.

"Old lady is a good disguise. Attentive and not-so- argumentative grandson is almost as good."

"We're not going in, you promised."

"Captain Reese needs an excuse to get a warrant," she said, pushing down on the lock that kept her walker supportive. "Help me cross the street."

* *

Violeta and her father pulled up a half block behind Henry's cab and watched Glyn get Willie's walker out of the trunk.

"Now what?" Papá asked. "They're not going to the skate park."

Violeta shook her head. "I don't know, Poppy. Seems like I should follow."

He put a hand on her shoulder, not hard, but ready to hold her in the car. "You will not. I can't lose you, too."

"Papá, without Rosie, we are falling apart. They are looking for Rosie."

"We are not crumbling yet, mi amor."

He looked at his phone and said, "I can't get ahold of Glyn's dad or his mom, or Arwain. I don't get it. They've always answered my texts right away."

CHAPTER TWENTY-NINE

An hour after they were grabbed and drugged, Arwain woke. She felt groggy, but she knew she'd been dumped into a bigger truck. She could smell the wet metal and the mold even as she smelled the fumes of a vehicle and heard the bigger motor. It changed gears to drive slowly backwards down what seemed like a steep incline.

She figured, Our truck going down a driveway, maybe. She thought she heard no one else, but she waited.

Finally, she whispered. "Claudia?"

No one answered her. She tried to loosen the ties around her hands and twisted against the ties at her feet. Nothing seemed to move.

Fear settled on her. It cooled the sweat of her shirt and roiled in her stomach.

In a moment, she heard the truck door open, and boots, more than one pair. She closed her eyes, determined not let them know she was awake.

"Why pack them in here? Why not take them directly south?" a wheedling voice asked.

" 'Cause the boss says so."

"I'm taking the redhead. You get the pony-tail gal."

"Why her?" the first man's voice asked. "She bites and kicks."

"Not with the drugs in her and not with those ropes on. Get her feet," the second man said.

Someone grabbed her hands. A moment later, her feet were yanked up by the rope. Her body hung low between two carriers, bumping along the metal floor for excruciating minutes while her hands lost feeling and her ankles tore against the rope as they lowered her out of the truck.

She heard a large garage door roll up and then the men carried her through what sounded like a medium sized space.

Someone's hip bumped the safety bar on a door. They pulled her through, hitting her ribs against the door jamb.

"Damn," grunted the guy at her feet. "Why aren't girls lighter?"

"Likes 'em zaftig, I guess."

"Doesn't look so zaftig."

"Solid muscle. That kind likes to fight. Some guys think that's more fun."

"That other one don't fight."

"She hasn't had a chance, yet. I knocked her out, first thing," The man at her hands said.

Get it over with, Arwain wanted to scream, but she had to listen and not interact with these hooligans. She wanted to learn as much as they might let out to an inert body.

A moment later, her feet dropped. Her heels hit the floor hard, sending jagged messages to her brain. She clamped her mouth tight, not to cry out.

Keys rattled, then metal scrunched into a keyhole and screeched to turn.

"Stand back," ordered the voice that had dropped her feet. "Here's another friend for you."

"Stand back," the other voice holding her hands said. "Get any closer, I'll shoot your foot."

The man grabbed again at her ankle ropes. The men lifted her, wrenching her right shoulder.

They swung once and tossed her. Two things she noticed as she hit the new floor hard. One, there was no mattress where she landed. Two, she had landed in a smaller space. It didn't echo.

"Can't you untie them?"

Trace? Arwain thought. She knew that was a boy's voice, but she couldn't be sure she recognized it under the strain and fear it projected.

"You do it, buddy," foot man said. "It'll give you an excuse to play around."

"Yeah," the other guy said, "'cept this one bites, so play with the other one."

The doorway clanged shut, the key turned, and the boots marched away.

After they were completely gone, someone fell next to her on the floor and pulled at ropes on her wrists.

"Arwain? Glyn's sister?" the voice asked. "Ahhgh!"

He backed off. She opened her eyes. "Trace?" she whispered.

"Yes."

"Been looking for you," she whispered. "Really? You?"

"The whole band – a lot of people."

He stared at his hands. "That how they caught you? Looking for me?"

She nodded. "I'm sorry, Ar.."

"Got drugs?" she asked.

"Sweated em out. Rather have died."

"But you didn't," she said. "We're also searching for a couple of girls."

"I heard 'em bring in two girls four days ago, then they took 'em out."

"Shit."

Trace looked startled. Arwain realized she didn't much talk that way. "I mean damn. I mean…"

"You mean…"

She rolled over and saw Claudia out cold and dribbling spit on the floor. "Shit!" she said.

"She's breathing. I took off her ropes and she mumbled something."

"Good. Got a blanket?"

He stood and pulled a thin blanket from a cot and put it over Claudia.

Arwain watched the rise and fall of Claudia's rib cage, then asked Trace. "You hear any names in that other room?"

"I heard 'em call one of the girls Liza. Don't know the name of the other one."

Arwain came alert. "Did anybody say where they were taking them?"

" 'Off to the trade,' the guy said. She called him a shit hole pimp. She also called him Chuck and begged him to take her home."

"Like that's going to happen."

After a moment, Trace spoke again. "Are we dead?"

"Not yet. Get the ropes off my hands. But be careful. I think they messed up my shoulder."

Trace started working at the hemp, it seemed like a thread at a time, but she could feel them loosen. She looked at Claudia and realized he'd only gotten as far as her wrist ropes. Her ankles were still tied.

"How long were those other girls here?"

"Maybe two days."

"Damn."

CHAPTER THIRTY

Grandma Willie pushed her walker down a long driveway as if, even in the dark, she knew where she was headed.

Suddenly, lights turned on at the front of each storage shed. Glyn pulled Grandma Willie close to the wall of the third shed.

"Grandma, movement turns these lights on. And if we're seen, there's no outlet here. No escape."

"Look between these little storage buildings and see what's there besides weeds."

Glyn didn't want to turn on a flashlight and announce their location. So, he walked between buildings, right to left and finally whispered. "Here, we can get to the back."

* *

Javier Lucero fidgeted with the team list for soccer at University of Portland. He laid it near the membership list of the U of P safety committee, and started to dial the home number for Claudia Ash. Then he punched the red phone symbol on this phone to hang up.

He knew he had an accent. He knew Claudia's family . . . reputed to be pretty suspicious about Hispanics in America. He knew he would get no help if he dialed the number he wanted to dial. But Claudia's phone hadn't answered for over an hour. He had to have help.

So, he sent his fingers farther down the soccer list and dialed the number for Susan and Merlyn Jones. He hoped he'd found the right way to break his news. Arwain was in whatever had happened, just as much as his Claudia.

"Hello?"

Mrs. Jones, this is Javier Lucero." Silence. The pounding of his heart.

And then she said, "Javier from U of P? Soccer?"

"Yes, ma'am. I'm the one who called you earlier."

"Are you all right?"

His heart stopped its noise. Stopped cold.

"Mrs. Jones, I'm fine, but worried because Arwain and Claudia never arrived at George Fox."

"Let me get off and call the Papá. They are close there, to the Tigard Station."

Javier said, "I am in the Tigard Transit Station watching for them. What car?"

"Subaru, green, GBS 059."

"I saw it. Drove in. Waited. Drove out again five minutes ago."

"Stay."

"I'm staying. White Prius. Old, Grey. 9Q 56789."

"Talk to you soon."

CHAPTER THIRTY-ONE

Violeta and her father knocked on the window of Henry's taxi on Northeast 2nd Avenue in Portland.

He rolled the window down. "Hey Vi, what cha doin' out here?"

"My question exactly," Violeta said. "Do you think we should follow Mrs. Stamps into the driveway? She's not very fast."

Henry Crick opened his door. "Been thinking the same thing." He rolled out, cranked up his window and locked the door. "But I think we should stick to the back of these little storage places."

"Wait a minute," Mr. Aguirre said. "There's a truck turning into the driveway where she went."

"Hunker down this side of my cab," Henry whispered.

* *

Grandma Willie pushed her walker over at a fast clip. They slipped between two storage buildings just as car lights turned into the driveway.

"Whew," Grandma Willie whispered.

"That's a truck," Glyn whispered. "Lights at eye level for me."

They both hugged the wall with their backs. The truck drove by. After it passed, Grandma Willie started to push further back between the buildings.

Glyn said, "I want to know what that big truck is doing here. "Don't let them see you," Grandma hissed.

He whispered, "See what's back behind these sheds, and then meet me here."

She nodded and picked up her folded walker, trudging off between the two sheds toward the back. Glyn shook his head, thinking he might have to pick Grandma up out of the tall grass when her legs gave out.

He inched out into the driveway again, checking for any other trucks coming his way. Finding the way clear, he followed the truck, avoiding the little entry lights and hugging close to the sheds as he moved.

As he came to the last shed, he saw that the truck had backed down a steep driveway into the basement of a taller and older building. A lamp above the entry to the basement showed him that the asphalt on the drive shone smooth and un-pitted.

"The new digs by Larson Lumber's rentable backhoe," Glyn whispered to himself.

The door to the basement rolled up at that moment. Glyn backed into the shadows of a nearby pillar, listening to the two men who came out.

"Quit your whining," grumbled the smaller of the two men. The other held up his left hand. "She bit me. See the blood?"

"So, put a band aid on it."

"It went right in there. You can even see the shape of her upper teeth."

"Dream on it then," the tall guy said.

Glyn texted Grandma Willie. *One guy said some girl bit the driver. Means he's got girls. Hope it's Rosaria.*

Glyn then watched the men, collecting their descriptions. If some girl bit this guy, he probably deserved it, and Glyn wanted to be able to identify both of them later on.

He catalogued into his phone as they ambled to their truck.

Five foot three or so, my chest, barely. Black hair, stringy ponytail, boots with metal toes, Carhart pants and Filson red-black jacket. Dark eyebrows, one eyebrow turns up at the left outer corner. Light eyes, maybe blue or green.

Other guy. Taller, maybe five eleven, same work boots, blond, cleaner, eyes far apart and some dark color. No eyebrows that can be seen. Nose crooked, like boxer damage.

The guys swung into the truck, put it in gear and backed up the driveway toward the corner of Glyn's shed. Glyn rolled around the corner to the far side and stood still, glad of his dark clothes as the lights flashed on the wall across from him. The truck lights then turned to take the truck away.

He came out from behind the shed long enough to see that the license plate was missing, but the truck had a clear Chevrolet cross sign and a name on the back door: *Hiltown Storage and Transfer.*

"Dang," he whispered. "That's the company that rented the backhoe. What did that guy mean about teeth marks?"

Some girl had been fighting him. Rosaria.

He started to call Captain Reese. Just then, the truck stopped near the shed where he'd left Grandma Willie.

Glyn tensed. The truck began to back up. Had they seen her.

Seen him?

He stood behind the shed again and opened his phone, dialing the cell that Captain Reese had given Grandma Willie.

A sleepy voice answered. "Yeah?"

"Glyn Jones here. I think I've found where they hide the missing girls. Got a pen?"

"Yep. They close? That why you whisper?"

Glyn was thankful Reese understood the need to be brief and quiet.

"Yes," Glyn said. "199 SE 2nd Avenue. Come to the end of the driveway. Driveway recently dug down to a basement.

Bring help."

"Willie there?"

"Yes."

"Be right there. Stay hidden."

Glyn turned off the ring sounds, closed the phone and pocketed it, glancing around for any kind of weapon he might use.

At least, he thought, they don't seem to have spotted Grandma.

The truck didn't veer toward him, but went right down the driveway again, backwards.

Glyn realized his phone was his weapon. He opened it up and began filming the next activity,

The tall man got out of the driver's seat and called to the other side of the truck. "I'm not driving this package all the way to Chico. And this time, you get to carry the bitch."

"This is stupid," the short guy said. "We just dumped 'em in here, now he wants them out again?"

The door to the basement began its noisy rise as the two men stomped down the incline on opposite sides of the truck.

They ducked inside and disappeared.

Glyn ran back up the driveway to Grandma Willie's shed. "Gran, they have the girls, and they went back to get them again."

His grandmother came out of the grasses carrying her walker.

Glyn said, "You gotta stop Henry from coming in here because Cap Reese is coming with police cars."

Grandma turned left up toward Second Avenue, leaving her walker, and ran about as fast as he had ever seen anybody run on stubby legs and carrying sixty pounds of extra weight.

Over her shoulder, she rasped, "Stay out of sight. Disable the truck."

He stared around him, thinking, Disable? How? Then he grabbed up the walker and ran back to the truck, listened for the two men and heard no voices. He dropped the walker on its side in front of the front left tire and tried the door to the cab.

They hadn't left the keys inside. He ran to the back of the truck where the two doors had been left open and he climbed in, searching for anything he might use. Nothing appeared, except a pile of old blankets. He grabbed one, hopped out again and slid into the opening of the garage, found the switch that let the door down and pushed it. Inside the garage, he still didn't hear any voices, so when the door was closed, he dropped the blanket in the dark over the laser that allowed the door to go up and down.

He could at least slow them and maybe keep Rosaria inside the basement and garage until Reese arrived.

He pushed himself into a corner of the garage area, waiting.

He had nothing to fight off the two men, but he had surprise, and maybe a girl that bit and fought.

Minutes later, he heard the boots of one man and the slap of bare feet.

Out of the basement area, shuffled Trace, sweat running off his face, his curly hair sticking out in all directions. His hands were tied behind his back, and he bent over like a very sick man. The shorter man pushed Trace up the driveway with the end of a pipe.

Glyn thought to grab that pipe and swing it, but at that moment, the second man came out carrying a girl over his shoulders.

She clearly was out cold. Her short red hair bobbed as the man moved. Her head and her arms swung back and forth with each step the man took.

The short man pushed the button to open the garage. "What the hell?"

"Open the damned door," the taller guy said. "Won't go."

"Use the button."

"I'm using the fucking button."

CHAPTER THIRTY-TWO

Glyn pushed himself deeper in the shadows as the two men punched the button over and over again.

Trace glanced toward the blanket over the laser, but said nothing.

"Don't tell me we're gonna be stuck in here," short man said.

"Worked a minute ago. What could go wrong?"

"Battery?" short man asked.

They both looked up at the ceiling where the garage door opener hooked up.

"Get your clicker out and flick it," tall man said.

Short man fished in his pocket and said, "I left it in the truck.

By now, Trace was looking all around him, searching, Glyn thought, for the source of the blanket, the reprieve from being shoved into the truck and taken out of Portland.

Glyn listened for sirens, hoping Reese knew not to use them, but wanting to hear some help coming.

"What'd you do that for?" the tall man said, bending over and yanking the blanket off of the laser. "Don't you know nothing?"

"Do what?" the short man huffed. "Punch the door open."

"I did."

The tall man bellowed his disgust, punched the door button and then had to rebalance the girl on his shoulder. Her red hair shone in the garage lights.

The door rose. There were no police cars blocking the way.

"Get 'em in the truck," Tall man hollered.

The short man forced Trace up the step into the back of the truck.

The bigger man dumped the girl on the floor of the truck, letting her head hit the rhino-lining. He hissed, "You're driving the first two hours. I'm going back after the biter. Start the motor."

Now, Glyn thought, *I can take the one and wait for the other to come back weighed down with another girl.*

The bigger man shuffled slowly back into the basement. By the time he had disappeared, the shorter man had jumped into the cab.

Glyn heard the cab doors click locked.

Too late for an attack on him, but I can take the other one when he returns.

Glyn cast about for some weapon. but saw only stacks of papers and black bags of garbage. He lifted the bags. Nothing heavy in them. Might stuff one in the guy's face, but that will only startle him.

He'll drop the girl and come at me. Not good for her or me. "Glyn," Trace hissed. "Get us out of here."

"I'm gonna attack that guy when he gets back."

"He's got a gun."

"Quiet. I hear him."

"Phone?"

"Yep," Glyn said.

"Hang onto it. They took ours."

Glyn backed into the corner again, the black garbage bag in his grip. He checked that his phone was in his pocket, and waited.

Out into the lights of the little sheds, the tall man came with another body slung over his left shoulder. His right hand held a gun, aimed at the side of his victim.

"Best not try anything," the tall man said. "Can't go far and then I shoot you, Bitch."

The girl raised her head and stared back into the shadows, seemed to see Glyn. Her eyes widened. She raised her tied hands to warn him to stop.

He stopped, horrified.

Arwain! Tied and gagged.

The man threw her onto the truck bed, climbed in and yanked her by the hair farther back into the darkness. He climbed back down and strode to the truck cab, banged on it and yelled, "Use the fuckin' closer on the garage."

Glyn knew he had only a moment. He took the garbage bag with him, climbed up into the back of the truck and stuffed himself among the blankets and behind the garbage bag.

Trace sank to the floor between Glyn and the open truck door. When the tall man came back, the garage door started rolling shut. The man slammed the truck doors closed. Turned the safety handle to hold them in, and left the four of them in the dark.

As the tall man climbed into the cab up front, Glyn studied their situation. Curtains over the window between the truck bed and the cab, a definite plus.

He peeked behind the curtain and found the window closed.

Another point in their favor.

But the window could be opened from the inside, he knew, so not much of a safety for them in the truck bed. He fished in his shirt pocket and found a pen. Not much help, but he laid it in the sill of the cab window to make it harder to slide the window open. Thus, they couldn't quickly open it and the curtain would stay closed meanwhile.

They'd eventually break the pen, but it would take a couple of shoves. Time enough to hide again.

Maybe.

The truck started. Glyn felt a scrape. The truck lifted and then fell as it drove into what must have been Grandma Willie's walker. The two guys in front got out. The four in the back held still.

"Get behind the garbage bag," Trace whispered. So, Glyn hid again.

They heard the tall guy yelling at the shorter one. "What'd you leave all this metal here for, idiot? First the blanket, now this trash pile."

"Nothing to do with me," the other guy said. "Check the tire. Might a' cut it."

"Tire's fine. Get rolling."

They heard the two of them climb back into the cab and slam the doors. In seconds, the engine roared and the truck leapt forward.

All four of them rolled into the back door at the motion.

Glyn pulled them back into a safer space.

Trace rolled over and whispered. "I've got a knife can you untie us?"

"How'd you get a knife?"

"Stole it. Their kitchen."

Glyn glanced at the window. "Got anything I can jamb this window with?"

"No. Come on."

Glyn knelt next to Trace and glanced at Arwain. He took the knife and cut the rag from her mouth first. The knife wasn't very sharp, and it took some time to cut it.

As he sawed at the knot, he saw tears in her eyes.

He whispered. "I called the cops before he brought you all out. Reese and Seneca are on their way."

* *

Henry, Mr. Aguirre and Violeta stood between small sheds and saw Willie racing back toward them and toward the street.

The truck motor turned on and the lights caught her silhouette just as Violeta stepped out and pulled Willie into the space between sheds.

They heard metal crunch under the truck tires as Willie nearly fell on top of Violeta, gasping, "Glyn is back there. Henry can't come in the drive …"

"Henry Crick is here," Violeta said.

Papá Aguirre pushed both of them further back into the shadows and stood between them and the driveway. He pulled his phone out of his pocket.

Willie glanced around. "Don't dial Glyn's phone. They'll hear it."

"I'm dialing the police. What did you see?"

"Glyn texted they talked about a girl biting one of the drivers. I think they have put the girls in the basement of that building."

Papá Aguirre told Officer Seneca what Glyn had heard, and then he said to Willie and Henry. "Glyn already called them. They are on their way here. Stay put or you'll be in between police and the drivers."

CHAPTER THIRTY-THREE

His phone rattled, but didn't ring.

Trace whispered behind him. "Turn the sound off on that phone."

Glyn laid down the knife and fumbled out his phone to silence it. He saw that Reese had tried to text him.

Where are you?"

Glyn answered, "In white truck. In the truck bed. Hiltown Move and Storage. Heading south on 2nd Ave."

He finished getting the rag off of Arwain and then started on her hands.

"How about me," Trace hissed.

Glyn nodded toward the blond. "Gotta have her help with the other girl while I get you. No telling how long we have." He yanked at the ropes on Arwain's hands. "Who is she?" he whispered.

"My roommate, Claudia."

"Drugged?"

"More than me, I think."

He loosened the rope enough to get the dull knife under the first twist of the knot. "Keep your face back," he said.

As soon as the rope gave way, the knife just about left his grip.

Arwain's body jerked back. She stared up at him, both of them aware that he could have cut her.

"Here," he said, "use this on your legs and then get her."

She started sawing on her ankle bonds as he moved to Trace's hands.

"How the hell you find us?" Trace said. "Long story. Later."

He got Trace's ropes a strand or three at a time. They loosened, but wouldn't slip the knot. Agonizing moments later, Arwain handed him the knife and then she worked on the looser ropes that bound Claudia. All the while, she whispered to Claudia, trying to awaken her.

Glyn sawed away at Trace's wrist ropes. After a frustrating long time, Trace said, "Hold the knife steady and let me do the moving."

Trace moved his wrists back and forth across blade. It moved too much, so Glyn held it, blade point down and tight to the floor and one hand on the handle end. It stopped flexing.

Now Trace could get some power behind the blade. They could see progress.

When the threads finally gave, Glyn handed the knife to Trace and pulled out his phone.

He texted Reese. "All untied."

"Why you inside?" Reese texted.

"With Trace, Arwain, Claudia. All okay but Claudia drugged."

Reese texted back. "Following you. Willie and Henry follow us with Violeta and her dad. Describe driver."

"*Two men.*" He gave a brief description. "*Short guy drives. Heading south. Said to Chico, California.*"

"*Roadblock at empty field ahead. Hang onto something. May roll.*"

Glyn whispered to Trace and Arwain. "Police roadblock. We gotta grab side truck rails and hang on."

Arwain grabbed for the blanket pile and pulled the garbage bag toward the truck wall. "Help me hold Claudia," she said.

Trace whispered, "He'll swerve right off the road. Right side will be down first when it rolls."

Glyn didn't question him. Trace knew stuff.

They pulled blankets and soft garbage to act as a bumper between Claudia and the right side of the truck. All three of them grabbed the cargo hooks.

"Coats between face and truck," Glyn said, whipping off his own coat. Arwain pulled off Claudia's coat and made as thick a pillow for her as she could.

"Trace, your arm heals faster than face," Arwain said, so Trace pulled Claudia's limp arm up to shelter her face and then did the same for himself.

"Hope this shell doesn't collapse on us," Trace said. "Hook up so we don't fly into each other," Arwain whispered.

Glyn figured she was right. So, he hooked one leg around Trace's waist and let Trace latch his legs around Claudia, while Arwain grabbed his own waist with her legs.

Up front, the driver shouted. "Fucking damn."

CHAPTER THIRTY-FOUR

The truck jerked right, skidded and swerved. Glyn feared he wouldn't be able to hang on. The pressure on his fingers yanked right, then up and down as the truck rolled, but he hung on with his legs to Trace and felt Arwain's legs tighten around his waist.

"Protect your head," he yelled, plowing his head into his coat as the shell of the truck screeched and caved toward them.

The truck came to rest on the side where they were. Silence surrounded them.

"Arwain?" Glyn shouted. "Here. Trace is …"

"She fell away from me at the last moment," Trace yelled. "Got my legs around her, but she's turned and then fell away."

A sudden explosion ripped through the quiet.

"Get us out," Glyn yelled. Arwain and Trace joined him, screaming and banging on the truck sides.

Someone sent a shot through the cab toward the back where they lay.

"No guns!" Someone shouted. "Kids in back!"

Then the sound of metal prying metal. Light flooded in and hands pulled on legs.

"Seneca, get Claudia out. Drugged," Arwain shouted. "She's out," Officer Seneca said, "Trace, too. Can you crawl toward me?"

Glyn pulled on his sister's leg. "Quick before it blows."

She crawled, too, pulling at him as she went. He found his right leg unable to move and didn't know why.

"Seneca, Glyn's bleeding," she cried. "Help me get him out."

Officer Seneca had climbed in and pulled Glyn into his arms, shouting, "I've got him. Roll out, Arwain."

Glyn couldn't feel anything in his right leg, but the tug on his left was excruciating. In a moment, he was out into the light of a gray day and being carried well away from the truck.

"Run," Seneca shouted. "It's gonna blow."

In moments, the whole truck exploded. Metal flew past them. Officer Seneca jerked, tumbled to the ground and pulled Glyn and Arwain with him.

"Officer down," Arwain yelled. "Damned metal." She crawled around her brother to get to Seneca.

"Hold still, Seneca," she said. "Metal in your back. Don't move."

Glyn rolled over. Seneca's face looked white, but the officer gazed up at Arwain, and said, "Stop Glyn's bleeding."

Arwain turned to see Glyn, just as he blanked out.

*   *

Grandma Willie climbed out of Henry's car at the scene of the roll-over. Reese held her back while medics helped Glyn, who was unconscious, and Officer Seneca whose pain probably made him wish he were out.

Already in an ambulance and headed back into Portland, Claudia still had not regained consciousness.

On the ground far from the burning truck, and between Glyn and Officer Seneca, Arwain sat, interfering with everything the two medics tried to do.

Finally, the third medic said, "Miss, show me your medical degree, or stop talking."

"But…," she stuttered.

"Stop, so they can save both of them."

She stopped.

After a moment, Glyn's medic said to her, "You did a good job on the tourniquet. Saved his life."

CHAPTER THIRTY-FIVE

Javier watched the bus come into the Tigard transit center, watched passengers disembark and walk around the block and across the street to wait for the bus to Newberg. At this time of night, most of the passengers were broods of boys, coming back to Newberg from a night on the town, so fairly noisy and unruly. Two girls were with them.

Javier watched the bus driver watch the crowd and talk into his cell phone. Two big middle-aged men came out of a nearby building and headed for the crowd, but the bus driver shook his head and waved the guys away from the mob. Javier took a movie as the two nodded at the bus driver and retreated into the building. He took a close-up of each man and the driver, through the bus window.

Javier already had written the bus number in his notebook. Now he wrote a description of the bus driver and the two men, the building where they retreated and the exact time.

Then he took a photo of the boys and the two girls.

He waited. Nothing else happened before the bus pulled away, except that a van from Hiltown Moving and Storage pulled into the driveway, hesitated and then pulled back out. So, he took a photo of it as well.

After ten quiet minutes, the bus to Newberg pulled in and the whole crowd climbed aboard.

Javier called someone at his university and at George Fox University. They set in motion a police watch on this transfer point.

* *

Willie sat in Reese's car, exhausted and fretful. She saw a stretcher being loaded on the ambulance and tried to open the car door. It wouldn't budge.

"Child locks," Captain Reese said. "You need to quit and stay here. The medics are taking care of the kids."

Captain Reese felt rather than saw that Willie took her hand off the car door handle and leaned back for a moment. Then, she was on the alert again.

"Captain Reese," Willie said, "The van driver knows where he was going with our kids, and that's where we'll find Rosaria and Liza."

"He's in the second ambulance and not talking. The explosion sent him out into the field with a lot of damage to his body and a major whack on the head."

Willie said, "That driver may only have been in it for the first leg of the drive."

Reese asked, "And where was that?"

"Arwain heard him mention Chico. Well, you know that sleepy town was not the final destination, but it puts us on the way to the Central Valley." Willie said.

"And on into San Francisco. They could have been headed to Fresno, or Los Angeles, or . . ."

"Without the driver's information, even an educated guess, we've lost them."

Reese said, "You don't think I'm going to let him die, do you? I'm keeping him alive if at all possible."

Reese opened his door, "Be right back." He rolled out, leaving the front door closed and locked

As Reese strode toward the stretcher carrying Officer Seneca, Willie stood in the back seat, in-so-far as she could, stretched her stomach over the seat back, pulled her purse across the seat and used its hard corner to flip the child-door lock mechanism.

She was out before Reese got to Seneca. On her way to the low ground where her grandchildren sat, she heard Officer Seneca say, "That van driver is the key. Don't believe he didn't know the trip. Miss Jones says he was as much in the know as the dead guy."

CHAPTER THIRTY-SIX

Hours later, Grandma Willie sat next to Glyn's bed. Beside her, in the second bed, lay Trace. Trace's mother sat silent vigil while her son dreamed and thrashed, and then fell silent for interminable minutes.

On the other side of Glyn's bed, Willie's daughter, Susan, held his hand. Glyn's father paced the floor, fidgeting with his phone, with Glyn's toes and then, having paced to the head of the bed, watched the green lights on the monitor while he brushed fingers into Glyn's hair.

Susan said, "Mom, stop apologizing."

"If I hadn't taken him with me..."

"Then you'd never have known about Arwain and Claudia."

Grandma Willie nodded, but she thought about all the things she could have done differently... not letting Glyn go down that driveway, for one.

The truck driver, Aron Peterson, also lay in this hospital under guard. His tall buddy had not made it.

As Captain Reese put it, "The guard is at that bedroom door to keep Peterson in and all others out. They gotta know he knows stuff we want to know."

Willie had glanced at him.

He smiled. "Repetition is a literary device if you use it well," he said, quoting her. "Otherwise, it's literary laziness."

All that she used to teach these officers about writing, and she'd never really understood the horrors they had to write about.

*   *

Arwain sat in the hallway and regretted many things. Her brother, Glyn, lay in bed, his body trying to build strength and use the transfusion of A negative blood that came from his father. Trace lay in another bed in the same room, trying to rid his body of several drugs, some self-administered, others put into him by his kidnappers.

Mr. and Mrs. Ash, Claudia's family, sat in another room, watching for Claudia's body to rid itself of the anesthetic Ketalar. By the time the ambulance got to the hospital, Claudia's lungs were in respiratory trouble, a sign, the doctor had explained, that Claudia was allergic to the anesthetic. The doctors had hooked her up to oxygen, a heart monitor and a drip of some kind that Arwain hadn't understood at the time.

Across the hall from Claudia, Officer Seneca lay in a bed, shrapnel out, but a deep wound in his back. He tossed so much with worry that the nurse had to restrain him into sleeping on his stomach. His dreams made him cry out.

Arwain sat in the waiting room between the three rooms, listening for anything going on in either room, but not willing to commit to visiting Officer Seneca.

Yet, every time she heard him cry out, she jumped and then sank back into the sofa.

Next to Arwain, Violeta Aguirre and her mother and father hovered. Javier Lucero, from their university safety committee sat in a chair near the door to Claudia's room.

Arwain knew Javier stayed out of Claudia's room only because he feared her family wouldn't welcome him.

"You think they want to find some brown fellow loves their daughter?" he asked.

Arwain cocked her head to one side. "Does Claudia even know that?"

Javier pushed his shoes back and forth on the carpet. "Haven't found the time ..."

"You mean the courage?"

He looked at Arwain. "Well, that too."

Suddenly, Violeta looked up. "Don't waste any more time.

When she comes out of this, you better be honest." Javier nodded.

Arwain stood up and said, "Javier, come with me. Until later, you are our friend from the safety committee. Let them get to know you, first."

So, they went to Claudia's room. Up to that point, Arwain's visits to Claudia's room included "How could you," stares from Mr. Ash, Claudia's father and Mrs. Jenkins, her grandmother.

But Claudia's mother asked it out loud.

"Why did you two go on this fools' errand? She's never been that foolish before."

Arwain nodded, "Yes, Mrs. Ash. I should have told her no, when she offered to come."

Grandma stared at Javier, "Did you think this was a good idea?"

Before he could answer, Arwain said, "Javier would have told us not to do it, so we didn't tell him."

"Very smart young man," Grandma said. Then she glanced around. "Where is that Doctor Gabriel?"

Mr. Ash said, "Mother, she can't be here on demand. She has other patients."

Grandma flapped her hand at him. "This girl took her on a dangerous search. Why is she not also unconscious?"

Javier stood up and moved toward Claudia's feet. Arwain stood next to him so whatever gesture he made would seem to come from both of them.

Javier said, "Mrs. Ash, Arwain had the same drug in her, just less of it."

"Stupid to even be there," Grandma said.

"Mother," Mr. Ash began, but Arwain interrupted. "Yes, it seems stupid now." She reached out and touched Claudia's toes through the sheets and blankets, a gesture she felt Javier wanted to make, so she did it for both of them.

Arwain kept talking. "Neither of us thought it would be more than a bus ride – just as the girl we hoped to trace probably thought it was simply a ride to a new college life."

Finally, Claudia's mother asked, "Who were you tracing?"

"Her name is Rosaria Aguirre. She disappeared on her way to George Fox University in Newberg. We decided to take the same bus and see places where she might have gotten off – where she might have been kidnapped."

Claudia's dad suddenly spoke. "Well, you found it." The grandmother huffed, "Why aren't you drugged?"

"I was drugged, too, but I think they used more on her, or used the same container and had less left over for me."

The doctor moved into the room. She was a slender woman with jet dark hair and tired eyes. She looked like she ought to be relieved of some of the five patients that had been brought to her in the middle of the night.

"Good morning," she said, showing a slight trace of a Spanish accent. "I am Doctor Yolanda Gabriel. I am glad you are all together because I've been seeing very good signs for Claudia in my last two visits during the night."

Claudia's dad gestured toward his inert daughter. "How is this a good sign?"

"Her heart has slowed to a reasonable rate. Her blood pressure is down, close to normal. And her breathing is almost entirely on her own, although we'll leave the tubes in until she awakens."

Claudia's grandmother said, "Why is she not awake and this girl is up walking around."

Doctor Gabriel spoke to Arwain. "Your guess may be true. You had a lot less of the Ketalar than Claudia, but you had some. I told Nurse Tanner I wanted you checked every hour as well."

Arwain glanced toward her. "Mrs. Tanner has been checking me. About fifteen minutes ago. And Trace?"

"Your friend Trace is holding his own," Doctor Gabriel said. "Glyn, that's your brother, yes?"

"Yes."

"Your brother had none of the drug, but lost a lot of blood because of the gash on his leg. He's sleeping, but your grandmother should go home."

Arwain nodded, "But she won't. She feels guilty."

The doctor nodded. "I know. I'm hoping your taxi friend, Henry, is it? I'm hoping he can get her to go, but I want you still here to check on."

Arwain said, "I think if I stay here to look over everyone, then maybe Grandma will go home."

*   *

Later that morning, Captain Reese described the scene at the truck to Susan, Merlyn and Willie.

"Arwain tied off Glyn's leg and kept yelling for help for Seneca while she held the tourniquet tight. Quite a daughter you've got there."

But then, of course, Captain Reese took Willie aside. "What the hell did you intend to do?"

"Find you a reason for a warrant," she huffed at him, a lot more defensive than she wanted to sound.

"Well, you got a lot more than you bargained for." She nodded, subdued.

"But we got three kids back," he said.

She shook her head, "But not Rosaria and Liza."

"Not yet, but we've got a witness who knows where they were taking Arwain and Claudia."

She looked up.

He went on. "A witness who may live, but not if we send him to jail, because he'll be a dead man in there."

CHAPTER THIRTY-SEVEN

Officer Seneca awoke to find Arwain Jones hovering in the doorway to his room. From the way her curls stuck to her cheek, he guessed she'd had a rough night. He smiled at her.

"Glyn?" he asked.

"Still sleeping, but safe. Claudia has awakened for a few moments. Trace is ranting in his sleep but has good vitals. Grandma won't go home, and you had major veins and nerves severed."

"Good vitals," he said. "You've been learning doc talk."

She glanced at the ceiling and then at the monitor above his head. "Too much doc talk, in truth."

"And how are you?"

"They put some Ketalar in me, but not enough."

"Ketalar? What's that?"

"Anesthesia."

"Oh yeah. My vet used it when Shep broke his leg."

"Shep? Don't tell me he's a sheep dog. A German shepherd?"

"Nothing so fancy. A mongrel I found at the Humane Society. Face like a mischief monkey."

She actually took a step into his room. And she smiled. "How's Shep's leg now?"

Uh-oh, he thought, then blurted, "What day is it?"

That stopped her. She had to look at her watch. "I . . .I think it's Wednesday."

He twisted around, looking at the bedside table. "I don't suppose my phone is in sight."

She came fully into the room. "Bet it's in your clothes locker here." She opened the door. "Pants pocket?"

"Briefcase," he said.

She found it. As soon as he had it turned on, he dialed his sister.

She picked up on the third ring. Probably hunting under books on her desk. He wished his back would stop hammering at him. Sister found her phone.

"Yo, Puck. Can you get my key and go feed Shep? I'm in the hospital."

There was huffing at her end. "Now you tell me? What hospital? What's wrong? What's…?"

"Pookah, I need you to take care of Shep before you call anybody. He's been alone for two days as far as I can figure out. I just woke up."

"Shep can go potty all he wants if you don't come out with it. What hospital?"

Officer Seneca looked up at Arwain. "What hospital are we?"

"Emanuel. Northeast Portland." She stepped out and then back in. "You're in room 348. Ask at visitor information."

Seneca gave Puck directions for the dog and then finally said, "Thanks. He's probably going nutso."

His little phone felt like an ingot of hot iron. The pain of holding any weight shot from his back to his arm.

When he hung up, Arwain said, "I'm not asking about Puck."

"Little sister. Troublemaker. It's a …"

"Look, Sidney Oberon, I said I didn't want to know."

"Okay, Arwain Titania. Can I get something for this pain?"

"Be right back." She swiveled on her left foot, which he now realized wore only a sock, and hiked herself out his door.

He lay on his side, feeling ever greater stabs in his back, but still, he smiled. That girl was everything her grandmother had hinted. He wished to be done with this case and out of this hospital, taking her out to dinner.

He admitted to himself how relieved he'd been when he pried open that van door and found her safe.

*   *

"We get that the van was headed to Chico, California," Captain Reese said to Willie. "But no doubt that was just a rest stop on the way to Sacramento or San Francisco. We've got officers in all those bigger cities watching for white vans with that logo. Hiltown Moving and Storage."

"They're going over film from the streets?"

"And other records," Reese said.

"The driver, Peterson, he isn't helping?"

"Scared out of his wits. Watched enough television to know what a sieve a hospital can be."

"May I talk to him?" she asked.

"Not on your life. And it's your life I'm thinking of, not our liability. Forget the sweet old lady act. Stay away from these buzzards."

She said, "What about Hiltown Moving?"

"Being audited, and under surveillance."

"And the Ketalar?" she asked.

"Willie, you are done. Gave me enough of a heart attack to find you at that storage place."

"My guys …" she started. "Your gangster-writers?"

"My gentlemen suggested follow the drug source."

"And they are correct. We are trying to see where Ketalar is besides hospitals."

"You know, a hospital pharmacy could also be the source," she said.

"True. But you are to stop helping me."

"I help Rosaria and Liza. The longer they are in the claws of Hiltown Moving, the worse their lives."

"If you think you know something, you call me. No haring off to prove it first."

Willie merely looked at him. He leaned down into her face. "I know you heard me."

"I heard you," she said.

*   *

That afternoon, Henry Crick sat in his taxi and spoke to Willie and the dog in her arms. He groused at her. "Whose damned dog is that?"

"My friend, Vivian."

He frowned, one hand on the puppy's head. "You're going to allow them to give this dog drugs?

"I plead poverty and promise to come back with the money." Henry turned off the engine. "I'm coming in with you."

"Thank you," she said, lifted the basket for the little guy.

Until today, she hadn't much use for little yarkers like this. Several of her friends felt it necessary to carry something cuddly, but she'd always thought they could do better with a stuffed toy – less demanding and quieter.

However, this little guy was quiet. He sat in the basket and shivered as if everything around him were a fearsome monster. He made her feel protective.

She was pretty certain this trembling little fluff accounted for Henry Crick's wish to come into the veterinarian's lair. It had nothing to do with taking care of Wilhalmena Stamps.

The bell over the door was expected. What surprised Willie was the lack of pets and their owners. Elmore's was the biggest veterinarian in the northeast section of town, so she had assumed a full waiting room.

Possibly, she thought, 10 a.m. was early in the day for pet owners with jobs. But what about retirees? She'd assumed that at least fifty percent of retired people were like her friend Vivian. They needed something to hug. It seemed that way in Holly Hill.

A young man came to the front desk, looking as if he'd been up all night.

"Yeah?" he said.

Willie ignored his lack of training in customer service and moved straight to her problem. "Our Chewbacca has been tossing his cookies," Willie said.

"Yeah? That's what they do," the young man said.

She persisted, "I think he's eaten something poisonous."

He gazed at her. "Dogs are always eating things they shouldn't. Let's get the doc out here to take a look."

As the young man walked slowly into some back room, Willie glanced at Henry.

"Maybe he loves cats," Henry said.

"Or snakes." Willie glanced around the room. The vet had no dog scale, such as she used to see back in her doggy days when Susan and her brothers were children. The wall had two photos of dogs and three of cats, all of them crooked, possibly moved by doggy investigations.

The bell over the door rang again. A man in a suit walked in without a pet.

The young man returned to the front without a doctor. He said, "Yo?" to the newcomer.

The man in the suit glanced toward Willie, Henry and Chewbacca and then said, "I'm just here to pick up my prescription."

The young man reached down below the counter and brought up a package. "Mr. Martin," he said, handing over the package. Mr. Martin took the package and didn't even reach in a pocket for money or plastic. He walked out the door.

Willie said, "What about the vet?"

The young man looked at her blankly. "Oh yeah. He'll be here."

In a moment, a door from the back slammed and then the swinging door to the back of the shop swung out, letting in a man in a lab jacket. Willie noted the pens in his pocket and the name tag.

"Doctor Vanly," she said, "My Chewbacca has been throwing up."

The doctor smiled and said, "Well, let's take a look at this little fellow."

His smile and his interest made her dismiss the awkwardness of the young assistant and put a little more trust in this place.

She put the basket on the countertop.

Chewbacca's little face peaked out from under his overly-enthusiastic eyebrows. The two canine teeth of his underbite stuck straight up beyond his lip, making him look as if he had just eaten cake and was trying to hide the evidence.

"Aren't you a cute little fellow?" the doctor said as he lifted him up."

He started carrying Chewy to a side room, and spoke over his shoulder. "Come on in. Let's figure what's bothering him."

On the steel table, Chewy couldn't get a purchase, so stopped trying, sat down and barked once.

Doctor Vanly felt Chewy all over, which made the little dog growl, but he didn't snap.

Willie looked around the room. Advertisements for Super Healthy products partially covered paint on smooth walls. One Certificate for an Interstate Business Association hung next to Doctor Vanly's Veterinarian's license.

Out in the main room, she heard the doorbell ring again. A man's voice said, "You got the stuff?"

"Sure. You got cash?" the young assistant said.

Henry nudged Willie. She realized the doctor had been asking her a question.

"Oh, sorry. Nice dog and cat photos," she said lamely. "What has Chewy been eating?"

"My friend has been buying something she calls Extra Natural dog food." She didn't want to end up having to turn down Super Healthy. Extra Natural sounded good enough.

Doctor Vanly frowned. "That's not a brand I've heard of."

"Well," Willie said, listening to the exchange of money in the next room. "Well, maybe she said Super Natural. I'm not remembering exactly."

The man in the next room left.

"Doctor Vanly," Willie said. "How well do you know your young reception fellow?"

"Hired him three months ago. Why?"

"Ahh…" Willie said. "You know he's a little … shall we say, he's rude."

The good doctor stiffened. "I can't find anything wrong with Chewy, here. If he is eating only what your friend buys," and here the doctor glanced at Willie's short round self, "and only dog food, he should be all right. Cakes and cookies are not good for dogs."

Willie felt herself stiffen, but then the doorbell rang a third time. She stopped to hear the exchange in the next room.

Henry took over. "Our friend, who is Chewy's regular feeder, may have taken him into the park a few times. You never know what a dog might find in a park."

"That's true. Are you all the caretakers of the same dog?"

"Retirement home," Henry said. "People share pets in a retirement home."

"I see. Well, make sure that Chewy doesn't find things in the park. Since he's probably on a leash, that shouldn't be too hard."

Willie came back from her listening venture and said, "What do we owe you for the exam and the advice?"

"That will be sixty dollars."

Willie hauled a fold of twenty dollar bills out of her purse, handed them to the doctor and said. "Thank you very much for your help."

Doctor Vanly said, "Please take care of this at the front desk." He scratched something on a pad and handed it to her.

"Oh. All right," Willie said, looking at it.

Exam. Feed only food appropriate for dogs. No chocolate.

At the front desk, she handed her money to the young man, along with the doctor's bill. The young man said nothing to her, stamped the bill paid and opened a register to insert the bills.

The doctor retired to the back of the building, where they could hear a chorus of meows and barking until the door shut behind him.

Just then, another customer came in, hovered in the background and waited until Willie backed off the counter.

She fumbled with her purse and with Chewy's leash. Henry stepped up and took Chewy from her. She glanced at Henry and said, "I need to straighten the contents of this bag again.

The new person said, "Do you have my dog's medicine?"

"Yes, we do." The young man reached under the counter and handed over a package. The new visitor handed him some bills, and the young man put the bills in something under the counter.

Willie finished her fishing expedition in her purse and again took Chewy into her arms. "Well, we are done here, Henry."

Henry nodded, and they walked out the door just as the new visitor opened it.

Willie hustled herself into Henry's taxi. As she buckled in, Henry said, "I know. Follow that man."

"Yes, thank you."

Henry waited until the man had climbed into a car halfway down the block. Then his engine rattled to life.

He said, "Willie, write down license HMS 122, white Chevrolet."

Willie wrote and then said, "When we're done following, we should take this vehicle to the garage. Something needs adjusting."

"I believe my muffler suffered from some shooting metal during the van roll-over," he said. "He's turning left on MLK."

"I thought so."

"Okay," Henry said, "Where do you think he's going?" Willie said, "He'll hesitate at the Hiltown Moving and Storage on Second Avenue, but he'll go back around and on to the offices above the pharmacy on MLK."

"And you are so sure because…?"

"Each transaction that took place this morning, except one, happened without dog or cat, and happened without any money going into the till."

"Except your money, which the doctor billed."

"Right. And when the fellow we're following goes upstairs in that Grand Avenue Pharmacy building, we call Captain Reese and give him this location and the veterinarian offices to put on a watch."

"And then…?"

"And then we get your taxi fixed and filled up, because I think we're going on a road trip."

"There he goes. Right into the driveway at the Storage joint."

"Maybe he hasn't been told about yesterday's fiasco," Willie said.

"That was three days ago, Willie. We've all been at the hospital, remember?" Henry turned the corner and parked where he could see the driveway to the storage space.

"Dang. Those girls are lost to us. Poor Geneva."

"Willie," Henry said, looking into his rearview mirror,

"What does all this have to do with Geneva Oppenheim?"

"I have to show you her notes. She suspected… more, she knew and quit working because she was afraid they knew she knew. I believe this kidnapping business is what got her acting oddly."

"How did she know?"

"She was secretary to the finance officer of one of the companies involved."

"So, explain the road trip," Henry said, flexing his mirror to cover more of the storage buildings.

"Road trip. Captain Reese has covered all the big cities in California, but we know they were headed to Chico."

"He's coming out." Henry started his motor. "Wow. That's some hurry he's in. Straight down Second."

Willie said, "Let's head back to Grand Avenue and wait for him at a corner, if you can."

"Still think he's headed for the pharmacy building?"

"Yes. Angry that he wasn't told and went into the building to meet police."

"Why didn't they hold him?"

"Hear the sirens?"

They both fell silent as they listened. Henry pulled over again at Taylor and Grand Avenue, where four lanes hustled north.

"He's gonna try to lose them," Henry said. "And we don't want to be on the street when he careens up Grand Avenue."

"Okay, we sit tight," Willie said.

The sirens faded into the southern distance. They sat in silence, each one petting the small dog between them. Finally, Henry said, "We're not getting out and following anybody.

You got that?"

"I don't think we're going to get the chance. Sirens have stopped. They probably got him."

About two minutes of silence went by. Henry said, "I think you're right…oh hell. Here he comes."

Willie glanced in the makeup mirror on her side. "License HMS whatever, and white."

Henry turned the corner onto Grand. He signaled and scooted into the right lane two cars behind the white Chev. In a couple of blocks, he turned right, following the Chev as it hunted for parking. They slowed for a stop sign, watching the fellow pull into a parking spot half a block behind them.

Willie tried the passenger door. "Let me out."

"Nope," Henry said. He turned on his flashers. I'm stopped here, just follow him with your eyes. If you're right, the pharmacy building is one block behind us, and you'll be able to see him enter it."

Willie fumed, but sat tight, fiddling with mirrors since she couldn't turn around far enough. Cars came up behind them, got frustrated and went around on the left.

"I got him in my side mirror," Henry said. "Is he?"

"Just as you predicted. Side door to the upper floors. Let's see what lights go on up there. Oh, there's already a light on the third floor, east corner."

They waited. Finally, Henry said, "Second floor lights, the whole floor, looks like."

"Good enough," Willie said and took out her phone to call Captain Reese.

CHAPTER THIRTY-EIGHT

Captain Rob Reese sat in the chair next to the bed of Officer Sidney O. Seneca when his phone began to buzz.

"Drat all heck," he said, looking at the phone screen. "Mrs. Stamps?" Sidney asked.

Reese nodded and spoke into the phone. "Wilhalmena Stamps, where are you?" He knew he better get that info first.

"Uh-huh," he said, and pulled a note pad from his hip pocket. "Uh-huh. So, then you… Is Henry Crick helping you do this stuff?"

He nodded a few times. Officer Sidney O. Seneca tried to turn over to see his Captain's face better, but the jagged pain in his back stopped him. Sweat broke out and ran down his neck.

Captain Reese handed him a tissue and nearly yelled into the phone. "You are to stay in the car. Oh, that's good. We've already got someone watching that place. Yes, since Arwain followed that skinny buzzard into it."

He listened a moment and then spoke. "Elmore's Vet on MLK. Okay. Why not the doc, too? Who's inventorying his Ketalar, after all?"

Officer Seneca watched Reese listen. At the moment the big question in his mind was the location of Mrs. Stamps' granddaughter.

If the granddaughter were anything like the brother and the grandmother then…"

"Where's Arwain?" he whispered. Reese didn't hear him.

So, he shouted, "Where's Arwain?"

Reese held the phone away from his ears. Sidney O heard loud and clear.

"She better be in school or I'll have her hide."

Sidney yelled, "Not snooping with you, eh?"

"Young man …"

Reese took over again. "Wilhalmena, how come it is okay for you to go hunting up trouble, but not Arwain? Is this ageism?"

"I take Glyn with me," she defended.

"Well, you got him in the hospital and if you keep on keeping on, you'll have Henry in the hospital, too. Put Henry on the phone."

Henry said, "We're on speaker phone."

"I don't care if we're on satellite TV. You stop aiding and abetting that woman before she gets you killed."

"Got her locked in my car."

"Yeah? I tried that myself. She escaped."

"Yes sir. I'll keep that in mind."

Reese said, "Bring her in to the station. She's got a class to teach this afternoon, and Leneld is chomping at the bit to accompany her."

*   *

At the prison, toward the end of the writing class, the fellows were reluctant to leave. Leneld didn't budge from his seat next to George Wilson as they puzzled out the route that a van might take to get rid of contraband – Grandma Willie hadn't said what kind of contraband, but the guys in the class had guessed it was the kidnapped kids.

"Damn," Alliteration Artimus had said, "We were hoping you had them rescued by now."

"Me too," Willie said, but she didn't mention the one van and the police tail and roadblock or the injuries. Leneld knew Glyn was getting better, but Seneca, the policeman who hauled Glyn and Claudia out of the truck had a nasty infection in his back. That had Willie very worried.

George said to Leneld, "They'll know the police are lookin' in the big cities, so they've got a place to stash them that's not obvious – some minor way station has become the main tank 'til they think it's blown over."

Leneld nodded. He didn't know what to tell George, so he left it. "Thanks," he said. "We'll keep that in mind."

"Naw," George said. "The police have blinders on, like all the time. Thinkin' they got the bad guys figured out. So, look at the by-ways."

Leneld nodded. "I think Mrs. Stamps has been wondering that same thing. Wanna talk to her?"

"Sure."

*   *

After the class, Leneld and Willie drove north to Portland and to Emanuel Hospital. The two of them worried about many people.

They knew that while they waited out Sidney Seneca's' infection, Merlyn and Susan Jones had joined Augusto and Camelia Aguirre on the road. The four were on their way to Chico, California. As soon as Captain Reese had assured Augusto Aguirre that they were looking in all the big cities, Augusto had tumbled to the same thought that George Wilson had given Leneld.

"The kidnappers have to know about the over-turned van," Mr. Aguirre had said to Merlyn. "They will have pulled all their Moving and Storage vans off the highway and stopped all traffic where it was."

Merlyn had agreed. "The best we know is that Chico was at least a stop."

Augusto whipped out his phone. "Gonna call Rosaria's god-father."

"Who's he?" Merlyn asked.

"Adalberto Mendez, Sheriff of Chico County. Remember, we lived there for a long time. I think we head there."

Camelia and Susan wouldn't let them go alone. Camelia's argument was the clearest. "As strangers, two couples are a lot less threatening than two thugs like you."

Merlyn had chuckled at being called a thug. Augusto said, "But Sheriff Mendez will vouch for us."

"Yeah," Camelia said. "Right after the local police shoot you for wearing that ugly shirt while being Mexican."

So, in about five minutes, the Aguirres and Joneses planned a trip together, and then Merlyn pulled his Ford Taurus out of the garage, and they'd piled four small suitcases in the back.

Willie had not been at all happy about their decision, but Merlyn and Susan told Willie she'd done enough by rescuing their son and daughter. Now she was to make sure Glyn did his physical therapy and stay the heck out of it until they figured out where the kidnappers had taken Rosaria and Liza.

Claudia's parents spent long hours in her room. Liza's parents were working with the police to figure out who the boyfriend really was, since Trace had heard Liza talking to a Chuck as if he were one of the kidnappers.

"Mom," Susan had said. "You have to make certain Glyn comes out of this whole. We're going to Chico."

So, Leneld and Willie had come to the hospital. They first checked on the guards outside driver Peterson's hospital room door. Then Leneld went to find Glyn in the physical therapy room.

Willie discovered her granddaughter alone in a waiting room.

"Arwain?"

Arwain tried to brighten up, but her smile was only mouth motion.

"What's the matter?" Willie asked. "Claudia is talking."

"That's good news. How is Sidney?"

Arwain looked away, but Willie could see the pucker of fear around her eyes.

"Not doing well, eh?" Willie said.

"He shouldn't have been there. I should have gotten out faster. I shouldn't have let Claudia come with me."

Willie sat down. "You had a good plan, and you two were together because that's safer. The kidnappers caused the situation by taking you. Then they used drugs they didn't understand. Finally, the reason Sidney got hurt is that Peterson tried to evade the roadblock."

Willie put her arm on Arwain's shoulder, and suddenly Arwain fell into her grandmother's arms, crying. "I wanted to help," she hiccupped. "I only wanted … wanted Violeta's family together again."

Willie decided not to tell her yet about Merlyn and Susan's trip. She had enough to worry about. So, she just rocked her and remembered when Arwain had been a little girl with scraped knees from scootering too fast.

After a few moments, Willie asked, "Tell me what's happening with Sidney."

New tears welled up as she said, "They're about to operate on him again."

*   *

An hour later, back in the hospital, Captain Reese hovered in the waiting room with Arwain and Glyn. Willie and Leneld sat next to Glyn's wheelchair, where his leg lay on a board, straight out from his hip.

They all awaited the outcome of a second operation on Sidney Seneca. The doctors had seen a hint of a small piece of shrapnel deeper inside Sidney's back. They believed that accounted for the sudden onset of an infection. Everyone in the room hoped they were right. Hospital-caused infections were very difficult to get rid of.

This hospital had a good record for following clean protocol –
also known as not sharing infections from patient to patient.

When Doctor Yolanda came out, she said, "The last piece of
shrapnel nicked his spinal cord before we got him under. We got it
out, but it did some damage, and he can't feel his feet.

We hope that aspect will clear up with a little time."

"His infection?" asked Captain Reese.

"It's responding to anti-biotic, but he's allergic to penicillin so we
had to use something not so powerful."

"Did he know about the penicillin?"

"Not 'til we tried it. He got a rash of welts all over his chest."

*   *

After the worry about Sidney, Willie looked around. "Where's
Violeta?"

Arwain said, "I haven't seen her this afternoon."

Willie had a sudden premonition. "We'd better find her. You look
in Glyn's room. I'll take the hospital cafeteria and the waiting lounges.
Call me when you find her."

*   *

Violeta stood in the eighth-floor hallway at Holly Hill Retirement
staring at her phone. Glyn had called.

"We're worried. Where are you?"

"No worries," she said. "I am working. Work is harder when you
are not here to help, so get well."

"And how do I say that in Spanish?"

"You say "Si, Senorita."

He laughed. "Oh, so that's how it is, eh?"

Minutes and sweet talk later, when she hung up the phone, she
reached into her pocket and brought out the key to Willie's apartment.
She was allowed to clean rooms now that she'd become a permanent

member of the staff. Willie's apartment needed a lot of cleaning since she hadn't stopped any of her magazines. Stuff was all over the large coffee table, and the book stacks had grown in Willie's and Glyn's rooms.

While she cleaned, Violeta searched for reasons to hope. As she organized the magazines by title, she realized that Willie had probably applied for every Readers' Digest contest possible and had kept copies of her applications folded into the magazines. Violeta began organizing the contest applications by date into a file folder. Many were long past their due date, but Violeta kept them so she could show Willie that those contests had ended without a win for the Stamps clan.

Violeta wondered if anyone had won. There were many entry dates. She'd never heard an announcement about winners. Flipping through a couple of magazines, she found no advertisement announcing winners there either.

Did anyone ever check to see if there were winners? Was anyone aware and following up to see if these contests were the real thing?

She came across an especially lumpy Readers' Digest, the most recent issue. In its middle, she found an envelope addressed to Wilhalmena Stamps. It was sealed, but she could tell Willie must have brought it up from the mailbox recently, but didn't realize it was inside the magazine.

She started to set it on the desk in the slot she had labeled 'to read' mail.

The envelope wouldn't fit in the already stuffed slot. It fell out and down to the floor.

In very small print on the back, she saw the return address was for Geneva Oppenheim.

Violeta knew it was Geneva's talk that had sent Willie and Glyn to the right warehouse.

She opened the letter and read the first line. "This is to warn you …"

So, she opened the note all the way. The handwriting seemed hurried and cramped.

This is to warn you, Willie. Doctor Sartan brought me back to get some clothes and while there, I saw someone I recognize. He was at the front desk acting like he wanted to visit someone living now in Holly Hill Retirement. I don't know his name, but he works with International Relocation Services, and with the ones who keep children in the tree farm chemical warehouse next to the train track. They know I know, and I think he really was there looking for me.

You must stop them.

Geneva

p.s. I'm sorry to have suspected you. I know you are not the cook. She was fat and ugly. Not you at all.

Violeta grabbed her cell phone, locked herself in Willie's apartment and dialed the number for Captain Reese.

*   *

Captain Reese was on his feet as soon as he heard what Violeta had found. "Get out of her apartment." He said. "Take the letter hidden in your cleaning supplies. Go to the kitchen and stay in the kitchen with other people. Talk to no one about this."

He rounded up his detectives and sent a crew off to International Relocation Services in the Convention Center and the Rose Quarter area near the east end of the Steel Bridge.

They moved on south toward the Burnside Bridge and the skate park, and the Hiltown Moving and Storage building. Two men went to Elmore's Vet Service.

They had warrants, supplied by Judge Jones who was not a relative of Glyn's. The Judge had supplied the warrant soon after hearing Willie and Henry's vet story from Captain Reese.

And now, with Geneva's letter, they had a chance to tie the kidnappings to the businesses.

Reese himself took three detectives and a plain car to the back of Holly Hill, where he knocked on the kitchen door.

Chef Judson answered. "She's here."

"Good," Reese said. When Violeta came out of the linen storage, Reese said, "You two must mention this to no one. Any word of this and you'll both be in danger."

Judson nodded.

Violeta asked, "Do you want the note?"

He reached out for it. "We're untangling the who is behind a mess of ownership shells, so talk to no one about this. Someone is afraid of Miss Oppenheim because of this information."

"Yes, sir." Violeta glanced at Judson. "We are the only ones who know."

"Yes. Are you willing to testify to how you found it?"

"Yes. I hope it will help get my sister back and find out who threatens Missus Oppenheim."

*   *

Merlyn drove into Chico, California, with Augusto Aguirre navigating. Camelia and Susan talked quietly in the back seat, tense, yet hopeful.

Augusto said, "Get off the freeway and find Sixth and Main.

Buses run from near there along Fifth. I remember planting near here and the buses all went out of those areas."

Merlyn wheeled his Ford off at the next exit. He found Main with little trouble.

"Looks like we're in a college town here."

"Yes," Camelia said. "I wanted the girls to go to Chico State, but our jobs got moved to tree farms farther north."

Susan leaned over Merlyn's shoulder. "There, see the bus pulling out?"

"I do."

"Let's pull over and get out to see what looks possible as a place to hide any Hiltown vans, and maybe any other transportation they might use to move the girls farther south."

Just before they opened the car doors, Camelia said, "We need to stay together as couples. You remember, Augusto, how many times you were stopped on the streets here when it was just you or you and another Piñero."

"Si, si, si," Augusto said. "I need my Camelia to keep me out of the police radar system. They are always hunting up those who don't belong."

Susan said, "I bet that happens in Portland, too."

"It does," he said.

Merlyn said, "Really? In Portland?"

Camelia laughed and said, "Did you just beam down from Jupiter?"

Merlyn chuckled. "Nope. Beamed out of my math books and my piano dream world."

Augusto glanced around, "Did you see that van come out of that garage? Same size as Hiltown's vans, but not the same color."

"Painted?" Camelia asked.

"Good paint job," Augusto said. "Not a fast cover-up."

"Okay," Susan said. "Let's go into this coffee shop and watch for other similar traffic." She pointed at a sign on a door window.

They discovered that the coffee shop actually was upstairs, and seemed to be run by a tall red-headed man who made them welcome right away.

Camelia asked him, "May we sit by the windows. We'd like to look out on the streets and take in the town."

"Sure," he said and wiped off a table for them. The two wives scooted in close to the windows.

The taller husbands could see over them to the slightly farther away streets.

"Looking for anything in particular?" the host asked. "Places for lots of people to stay for a day or two," Augusto said.

"And transportation for groups of six or more to other cities," Susan added.

"Ah," he said. "Let me introduce myself. I'm the Presbyterian chaplain at the local college. Name's Jim."

"Mucho gusto de conocerlo, Jim," Augusto said.

"El gusto es mio," he said. "And recently, I've had my eye on that garage across Fifth down there."

Camelia said, very carefully, "Thank you. We'll take a look."

He took their lunch order and went back to the kitchen. "That was weird," Merlyn said.

Augusto said, "You mean a chaplain running a lunch and coffee place."

"That, and him mentioning that same garage."

The four of them watched it for a time. Nothing came out or went into it. Then their lunch came. Augusto asked the host, "Isn't being a chaplain a full-time job?"

Jim hung his kitchen towel in his belt and said, "It is, and this shop is my church. Meet people where they are. Don't wait for them to come to an empty building."

"Good idea," Susan said, "But what interests you about the garage down there?"

"I'm thinking it would make a great apartment building for low-income housing," Jim said.

"But it's a garage."

"Part of the garage is for cars, part is offices."

"But," Augusto said, "We've been here for half an hour and not one vehicle has entered that garage. Is business that bad in this town?"

"Not until this last week," Jim said.

Susan scooted over in the booth and said, "Could you sit down with us? We have a story to tell you."

He folded his tall self into the booth, saying, "I thought you might."

*   *

Pastor Jim accompanied Augusto to the building they suspected. They walked all around it, noting that not one light was on inside the offices.

"A weekday at one in the afternoon," Augusto said. "How likely is that?"

Jim called a realtor friend.

"Yeah, that dump is empty. I got lots of clients looking for office space, but they cleared that place out four days ago. Said they had dangerous heating situation and it was going to take three months to make it right."

"I've seen no gas hook up here. What's the danger?" Jim asked.

"Nobody said. Businesses out on the street with no warning."

Off the phone, Augusto whispered at Jim, "Four days ago?"

"That about the time of the van roll over you mentioned?" Jim asked.

"Yes. Time to call the sheriff."

"I agree."

*   *

When Reese was gone with Geneva's letter, Violeta sat down, put her head in her arms and sobbed.

Judson came over close, took his apron off and put a hand on her arm.

"Gal," he said, "You been through Armageddon, and it ain't over yet. I been praying they find your Rosaria soon. Real soon."

At that moment, Leneld and the Ancient Nation crew came in the back door fresh from the hospital. She knew they'd been visiting Trace and Glynn. She glanced at them and whispered, "I didn't… I didn't want all these people hurt."

Leneld sat down next to her. "Glyn, he's getting better. We came to tell you. Claudia is awake from the Ketalar. Trace is sleeping normally and Sidney Seneca, his wound is starting to heal."

She looked up at him. "I . . ."

Leneld nodded. "I know. But we're going to find them. And none of us would have anything less than to be working at finding Liza and Rosaria."

Markus sat down too. "Can we take over your wait job for tonight?"

"Yeah," Judson said, "You go into the chapel and pray.

Your Mamá and Papá will be back soon. You'll see."

*   *

In Chico, California, Susan and Merlyn hunkered near the car, talking to Camelia and Augusto. Glyn's parents prepared to step around the chains that cut off the driveway to the building on Fifth. Each of them carried a couple of long towels, and a Mace canister supplied by the good pastor.

Pastor Jim and two of his college student waiters stood next to his Peugeot. Jim watched and held his cell phone at the ready. His share of towels and Mace were in his apron pockets which he had left on when he flipped the Closed sign on the restaurant. His two waiter-students understood the plan.

Each had a cell phone. One had the only rope they'd been able to find in the kitchen pantry. Everyone had the longest and strongest towels available to a well-stocked pub.

Camelia stood to the right side of their Ford Taurus.

Augusto sat in the driver's side outside the parking lot because Susan thought it safer for the Aguirres not to be trespassing.

Susan said, "Merl and me, we're just a benign couple who've lost our Subaru."

"Si, si, si," Camelia nodded. "Whereas we get caught in there, and we are obviously looking to steal something."

"What?" Merlyn asked.

"Merl," Susan said. "Join the real world. Read the newspapers."

"Oh. Yeah," he said. "That stuff. People making assumptions."

"Yes," Camelia said. "Learn to think strategically. Avoid the white man and his fears."

Merlyn chuckled. "I'm sorry. On behalf of the naïve and the fearful, I apologize."

"Thank you, my friend," Augusto said. "Let's do this thing and find our girls."

Susan noticed that Liza was now one of 'our girls' for Augusto. She pulled Merlyn with her toward the garage.

Once inside, they found no other vehicles, but they did see an exit onto Fifth Avenue. The whole place echoed with every footstep.

Susan bent down and picked up a lump of cloth.

She whispered, "Look, Merl. Camelia does this kind of embroidery."

He stared at what seemed to be a little purse of velvet with a flower on the front.

"A rose," Merl whispered.

Susan said, "They are here for sure."

He nodded. They started to descend the ramp, but heard an engine turn on in the lower level.

A rough voice shouted, "They're out cold and we gotta get going. You follow us closely."

Susan knew he meant the girls were out cold. She started to run down, but Merl yanked on Susan's arm.

"They're down there," Susan objected. "Use the plan! Get help."

She ran with him back up the ramp and hit the sidewalk waving at their confederates. Pastor Jim raised his phone just as a yellow van broke the wooden armature and roared out of the garage by the exit on Main Street. The van wheeled left down Fifth Avenue.

The pastor clicked his phone camera, then jumped in his car talking to an operator. They heard him yell, "Mendez, they're coming down Fifth."

He took off, following the yellow van. "A second van," Merl yelled.

Camelia leapt away from their car. Augusto swerved the car across the street, and then he rolled over to the right side and out the door Camelia had just vacated. The second yellow van shot out of the garage, turned the corner and plowed into the Taurus. Augusto jumped up on the sidewalk, yelled, "Get 'em," and ran to the driver's side van door.

Merl and Augusto opened each front door, pulling the driver and his confederate onto the street. A gun clattered to the street on the right side.

The guys were big, muscled and ready to fight.

"Yikes," Susan yelled, and landed on the driver's legs. As Augusto tied her guy's hands with his share of towels, she saw under the van, on the other side. Camelia whacked the sideman in the head with his own gun. Merl yanked a big towel around his wrists.

Other traffic on Main and Fifth screeched to a halt, avoiding the back of the van and what was left of the old Taurus.

Several drivers nearby got out. Susan called to them, "Help us. Kidnappers."

Augusto came up with the keys from the van driver. They opened the door to the back. The stench came out first, nearly gagging Susan.

"Girls," she yelled and climbed in. Camelia followed and they tested each girl's pulse.

"Erratic and slow, and now no pulse." Susan recognized the signs.

"All drugged like Claudia and Arwain."

"This one has stopped beating."

"Call an ambulance," Merl shouted. Then he saw that several cell phones were already up among the other citizens.

Camelia called. "We need two more to do CPR on these girls. Susan, and you, Mrs….?"

Susan reached down to help the third woman climb in. "Camelia will show you how."

Camelia called. "Gusto, get the first aid from the Taurus."

He was already handing them up to her. "Is she there?" he asked.

"No," Camelia said. "But very sick." She handed Susan and the other woman a face guard for each victim's mouth, and said, "Watch me."

Susan placed the mask over the girl nearest her and began pumping on her breastbone as Camelia did. The other woman seemed to know what she was doing already, so Susan glanced over at Camelia who pumped and counted to 20 and then blew into the mouth of the face guard three times.

She did the same. She saw the girl's chest rise, and went back to pumping, hoping to restart her heart.

She knew Camelia was concentrating on starting the heart of the girl she had. Susan prayed that someone was doing the same for Liza and Rosaria. She, too, concentrated on the small blond she hoped to save.

"Come on, Honey, Mama's here. Come back to us." Breathe. Breathe. Breathe.

Pump and cajole. Pump and pray.

Finally, Camelia's girl coughed and rolled onto her side.

Camelia soothed, "Si, Mi Amor, yes, keep breathing. You are with friends at last. Con amigos."

What seemed like minutes later, both Susan's blond and the little red head of the other woman began to breath and pump on their own.

Susan noticed that Merl and Augusto were helping the other cars back out of Fifth Avenue. "Make room for ambulances," they told the other drivers.

Soon, two ambulances barreled up Main Street, slowed and came onto the sidewalk to get around the traffic jam.

*   *

In his car, Pastor Jim kept talking to Sheriff Adalberto Mendez on his Bluetooth.

"We've got a roadblock ahead, Jim," Adalberto said. "Slow down. We've got this."

Jim slowed, backing off the yellow van, but he said, "Berto, up in Oregon, the roadblock caused a roll over."

"Yup. I know. We've got ambulances and helicopters hovering."

"Wish I'd told you my suspicions of that building."

"Yeah," Adalberto said. "Been looking for these vans for days. Got people entering the building right now."

"Good. May be more kids in there."

"Here he comes."

*   *

Jim pulled in, far behind the van. "Stay inside," he said to his student friends.

The van stopped. The sheriff bull horned "Everyone out of the van with your hands up."

Slowly, the driver's door opened. The driver stepped out, hands in the air.

"Passenger out," the sheriff said.

Out flew a handgun, then a rifle. Everyone outside tensed. The driver crouched, shouting, "Don't shoot. Don't shoot."

The sheriff announced, "Passenger step out and away from the van."

The second man stepped out, hands in the air. "Both of you, on the ground, arms out."

They lowered themselves slowly, stretched out and waited. The sheriff approached, reached into the van and pulled out the keys.

At the back door, the sheriff called out, "You men cuff those two and then let the medics in."

The sheriff opened the door and found one girl on top of another. Five girls in all. One he recognized.

"Oh, Rosie," he seemed to whine. Then he hollered "Get the medics over here quick." And he climbed in, cradling his goddaughter in his arms.

*   *

That same morning, in Holly Hill Retirement, the guys took Violeta's clean up shift, Leneld scanned the dining room. He knew this was a retirement home, but it surprised him to find African Americans growing old here, not just white folks. He watched as people got slowly up from their chairs, waited a moment and then started walking. That was how his grandma had become. "Creaky" she called it.

He liked what he saw, though. People enjoying each other, waiting for each other's slowness with a walker or a bum hip. Joking with each other as they moved out the door from the dining hall and into the hallway, the sitting room or on down to the library.

He noticed one man who didn't seem to have any friends, so he watched to see if any came up to him. There was something familiar about that short and roundish man, maybe like somebody Leneld had known in church, or the old version of a teacher he once had in school.

Judson came up beside him and seemed to notice who Leneld watched. "Alzheimers', it looks like. Bad way to end."

"Yeah, my grandpa had that," Leneld said. "Made my mom and grandma old, just making sure he didn't get lost."

"Did you know your grandpa?"

"When I was little. He could still play games. So, we had a fine time. Maybe remembering Grandpa's kind of blank stare, maybe that's why I recognize that guy."

"Yeah, the blank stare." Judson looked at Leneld and said, "What's with the rap group? I like the beats, but why the fast talk instead of a tune?"

Leneld smiled, "You ever see the movie My Fair Lady?"

"Sure. Chick flick."

"With music."

"Yeah, good music."

"You know that professor guy?" Leneld got a nod from Judson. "Professor, he was rapping whenever he had a song."

"Naw."

"Yep, had something to say, and said it in rhythm. That's rap."

"Oh. Okay. I'll listen more when you're down there."

"Boy, I hope we get back to it. This hunting for these girls and Trace, that's become scary."

"Sure has. Just working the sidelines, I've been scared for Violeta and her sister."

Leneld nodded. "Glyn's grandma shouldn't be doing this stuff."

"Yeah, should be retired," Judson said.

*   *

Working in the kitchen, or really just moving plates around in the sink, Violeta felt her fear rising again. Where was Rosie? And why couldn't she get ahold of Mamá and Papá?

Suddenly her phone rang. She didn't even dry her hands before she hauled it out of her pocket.

"Mamá?"

"We have her."

"Oh . . . oh!" Violeta sat hard on a stool. "What's that noise?"

"We are on a life-flight to Portland. Rosie has the Ketalar. Ten girls, so far . . ."

Violeta heard her mother crying amidst the whap-whap of a helicopter noise and the soothing sounds of her Papá.

"Where? When?"

"Chico. Adalberto sends his love. He pulled her from the van."

"Oh, Mamá. Oh, Mamá." Violeta could hardly believe. "Is Rosie . . ."

"The medics say she will be all right. She will be all right."

"I come to . . ."

"Emmanuel Hospital."

"I come."

"Come at eight this evening. That's when we will land."

A few moments later, Leneld wheeled Glyn into Holly Hill retirement center the back way, so Glyn could see Violeta in the kitchen. Judson saw what was about to happen and stepped out to let them have their moment.

She turned from the soapy sink, a big bright smile on her face.

"They have Rosie." She cried. "Flying from Chico to Emmanuel."

Glyn's laughter exploded from him. "Woah! How? "She will be okay. She will be safe! Oh, Glyn!"

Leneld said, "Good God! What a day. What great news." Glyn shouted. "Wahoo! So great!"

Violeta looked at Glyn, reaching to touch his hair, his shoulder, his arm. "You are home."

"Yeah," Glyn said softly.

Leneld watched Glyn duck his head in shy glee at her greeting. He tapped Glyn upside the head, saying "He means "I'm glad to see you."

Violeta brushed Leneld's comment away. "Lenny, I know what he means. He doesn't have to say it."

Not one of them noticed that Judson had left them alone, until Violeta turned around, she said, "Where'd that Judson go?"

"Out to check the potatoes," Leneld said. "And that's what I need to do."

After Glyn and Violeta watched him go, Violeta grabbed a towel, dried her hands and then put her hand on Glyn's slicked down wet hair. "I was so afraid for you all," she whispered.

He looked up, his eyes glistening. "I thought my sister might die. After the roll over, I thought I might never see you again."

She leaned down to hug him. "Mamá and Papá are flying back with Rosie. Your Mom and Dad are driving back from Chico. They all thought the police shouldn't skip the clue about Chico."

"I know," he leaned into her. "I tried to talk them out of it, but they just knew something. Your Papá used to work there, no?"

"Si, I was born there. So was Rosaria."

"I'm sorry all of this has happened, Honey," Glyn said, and then realized what he had said.

Violeta remained silent, breathing into his hair. At last, she said, "I found something. Captain Reese said I shouldn't tell anyone, but I tell you to keep you safe."

He looked up at her. "What?"

*   *

Soon after Violeta described Geneva's letter to Glyn, Leneld realized his friend needed to get back in bed, but Glyn didn't want Violeta alone.

"You come up to the rooms with us," Glyn said.

She shook her head, "I need to find your Grandma Willie and tell her about the note.

"Where the heck is she now?" Glyn asked. Leneld said, "Ask Henry. He's her wheels."

Violeta said, "Can Leneld take you and me to Emmanuel when they land at eight this evening? I will finish getting serving dishes ready for dinner and then come up, maybe Willie will return by then."

Leneld pushed Glyn's wheelchair to the elevators. As they passed the mailbox alcove, Leneld saw that same man on a telephone. He looked again. Something more than vacant stare made the man seem familiar, but he couldn't place the reason.

"Did you see that guy on his cell phone?" he whispered to Glyn.

"Who do you mean?"

Leneld turned the wheelchair, but by that time, the man must have walked back toward the Gift Shop or the dining room, so Leneld said, "Well he's gone now. Just feel I should know him."

Once in the elevator with other residents, Leneld pushed the button for the eighth floor.

*   *

After Captain Reese saw the note that Violeta had found, Captain Reese called Willie's phone.

When he asked, she said she was watering the plants in Geneva's apartment. She didn't mention that she snooped while there.

He read the note to her.

"Well," Willie said, "I'm glad she knew I wasn't the cook. But I should have been listening more carefully to what she said."

"This means that someone with access to apartments in Holly Hill knows what Geneva knows. They might know she tried to tell you, too. So, you be careful."

"I am careful," she said, "and I'll call you if I recognize who that might be."

As soon as Reese hung up, Willie moved carefully through the books and papers in Geneva's room. She knew Reese thought his men had searched this place, but Willie felt certain they'd missed something important.

She moved each book out, rifled its pages and then put it back exactly where it had been.

It was the books on the Holocaust that broke Willie's heart. She should have understood what Geneva tried to tell her about the warehouse and the train. She shouldn't have assumed so easily that Geneva's mind was slipping entirely back into those times.

Yes, Geneva had been shocked to find that warehouses near railroad tracks were used to store the kidnapped children. And the shock had made it hard for her to stay in the present.

But Willie knew Geneva before the shock, and she should have trusted that her friend had discovered something.

After the books, Willie discovered a small file box that Geneva had hidden in one of many shoe boxes on her shoe rack.

Moments later, she had found the evidence that had sent Geneva from her job.

A receipt for concrete work under the building on second included a note to install cages and hooks for chains strong enough to contain "feral dogs".

The dogs … Geneva had often mentioned dogs as guards at Mittlebau-Dora.

And under that receipt, deeds that showed International Relocation Services owned the building at second and several other buildings up and down the coast. In a fold of several badly xeroxed papers, Willie discovered that Hiltown Transfer and Storage and Larson Lumber were also owned by International Relocation Services, also known as IRS. All of these deeds and ownership papers were signed by Donald Corrigan CEO of IRS, and Christopher Rylant, Chairman of the Board.

So, Willie realized, Geneva, in her position as secretary at Larson Lumber had never met the CEO or the board chair of International Relocation. She wouldn't have known that Corrigan and Rylant were waiting to see what she knew.

That first dinner where Geneva accused her of being the cook, she had also let loose with her accusations about the uses of the warehouse near the railroad. Her agitation and her loud fear had brought on the threats.

Willie was glad Geneva trusted Doctor Sartan and no one else knew where she had gone.

And Corrigan was no Alzheimer's patient. Willie lifted the phone to call Captain Reese.

*   *

Twenty minutes after getting the dinner set-up prepared, Violeta stood in the eighth-floor hall, getting ready to visit Glyn in Willie's apartment and then go to Emmanuel Hospital for the family reunion.

As the last of the residents went into their rooms to get ready for dinner, Old Mr. Corrigan came up beside her.

"I need to get into my room, Miss. Could you unlock it for me? I think I left my key on the library table."

"Certainly, Mr. Corrigan. You are in room eight?"

"No, right here in fourteen."

"Oh no, sir," she said, remembering his forgetfulness. "I am certain you are in room eight."

"Young lady," he said, expanding his arms and blocking her path, "Don't pretend you don't know me. I have been in room fourteen for two months now."

Violeta knew this was Geneva Oppenheim's room. She backed up toward the room where Willie and Glyn lived.

Mr. Corrigan followed her closely. "I know you have the key to my room," he said. You must give it to me now or I will complain to the manager."

"Then you will have to complain, Mr. Corrigan. Fourteen is not your room."

She turned around in the hall, intending to walk quickly away from this man, who seemed ever more out of control. By now, she was beyond Glyn's room and so was the man who followed her.

As she turned to check his pursuit, he pulled a small gun from his pocket. "You will give me the key, Miss."

She stopped walking away and faced him. "Mr. Corrigan remember that you forget sometimes. It is very frustrating."

She backed a little and continued talking, understanding that this was not forgetfulness, and he was not what he had seemed for so long. Now she had to get to the metal fire door at the end of the hall. From behind that door, she could safely call Captain Reese.

Corrigan followed.

She said, "I will be glad to open eight for you."

As she backed up, a door behind Mr. Corrigan silently opened and a wheelchair poked out into the hall.

Now, she feared for Glyn and had to keep this man facing this way and following her.

She decided to pretend he wasn't really threatening her, and that she thought he suffered an Alzheimer's moment.

"Mr. Corrigan, do you remember Mrs. Kleiner's little dog that is so cute?"

He stopped. "Why?"

"She lives next door to you, remember?" Violeta tried to keep her gaze on Mr. Corrigan as Glyn and his chair rolled quietly toward them.

Behind Glyn, Leneld came out into the hall.

And beyond them, so did Grandma Willie, from room fourteen – Geneva's room.

Facing Violeta, Mr. Corrigan seemed unaware of the others. "Not putting up with your stalling, get down to that room." He waved the gun and started to turn back toward room fourteen.

At that moment, Glyn rammed Corrigan's legs with the wheelchair and his board-stiff leg.

"Gahhh!" Glyn shouted and doubled over his leg.

Corrigan fell to the floor, but got off one shot that ricocheted off a metal door jamb and into Leneld's leg. Glyn backed and roared his wheels into Corrigan's chest. Violeta's foot came down on the gun hand. A second shot slammed into the wall outside Mrs. Kleiner's room. Inside, her dog barked.

As the dog noise grew frantic, Violeta leaned all her weight on Corrigan's gun wrist. Leneld reached over, grabbed the gun. and took it from Mr. Corrigan's now-paralyzed hand.

Mrs. Kleiner opened her door and stared in horror at the young black man outside her apartment.

Violeta yelled, "Missus. Please call the police. Mr. Corrigan has shot Leneld."

The door slammed shut.

Leneld put the gun on the ground away from Corrigan, saying "Dang. She won't believe that story."

Violeta hauled out her cell phone. "But Captain Reese will believe it."

At that moment, the elevator door opened. Mr. Corrigan's nephew, Mr. Rylant, stepped out.

He turned toward the melee in the hall, aiming his gun at Glyn and Violeta.

Grandma Willie lifted her walker. He heard her motion and started to turn.

Violeta screamed, "I'll shoot you."

He turned back in her direction, just as Willie beaned him.

His collapse was slow. The look on his face completely confused.

"Never under-estimate the aged," she said as she hit him once more. He dropped flat.

Leneld limped closer and took another look at Mr. Rylant.

His eyes grew wide. "I know you." He turned to Glyn to explain.

But Glyn shook his head. "Don't." And then he spoke in rap rhythm to Leneld.

"Little communicatin' Not guess our cogitatin'"

Leneld snorted. He grabbed at his bleeding leg. Even in pain, he glanced at Violeta, answering Glyn in rhythm.

"That tyco's tough. Keep her on your side,

Cause she'll go far and…"

Violeta interrupted the rapping, "Sit down, Len. 'fore you fall down. Captain Reese is on his way."

She kept her foot on Corrigan's arm. Corrigan panted, "You got this all wrong. I'm trying to get to my room. You can't just …"

Glyn said, "Give it up, Corrigan."

Willie said, "Lenny, you'd best be rolling up those pants and stopping that bleeding."

Glyn whipped a handkerchief from his back pocket. "Mostly clean," he said, and handed it to Leneld.

Willie took the gun from Rylant's limp hand.

She said, "Glyn, keep that wheel over Corrigan's body, just so we can keep track of him till Reese arrives."

The doors at either end of the hall opened and police entered with guns drawn.

Reese bent over huffing and leaning on his knees.

Willie said, "You need more workouts, evidently."

He glared at her. "I need you to move to the second floor." She laughed, "Probably will. One day."

EPILOGUE

Eight months later, the Ancient Nation held a show at the Roseland Theater. They were such a success that two weeks after that, on a starry evening, the band re-opened in the larger venue at the Burnside Barns, where there was room for dancing and a stage big enough to contain Trace and Leneld's moves.

Lonny came to rehearsals direct from anger management classes, where he told the others, "I'm learning to put a cork in it, and breathe through my Irish nose."

Leneld laughed. "Glad to know that. Can you rap around cork?"

Lon laughed, and pretended to talk with cork in his mouth. "It's a hit," Leneld announced.

On the night of the second opening, as Willie and Henry arrived at the Burnside Barns, a cheer went up from all who knew the story of the hunt and the rescues.

Willie lifted her walker and did a brief dance. The crowd roared its approval.

Augusto and Camelia danced in a circle with their arms around their two daughters.

Susan and Merlyn danced over to Willie. Susan laughed, "Act your age, Mom."

"Glad to oblige," Willie said, and did another shimmy. In the crowd, acting as a "Big Band Bouncer", Artimus Alliteration was two months out of the "Federal Fun Fiesta at the Sheridan Summer

School" as he called it. He had a day job in the Holly Hill kitchen where he kept Chef Judson entertained with stories.

George Wilson also now enjoyed a new life outside the walls, helping encourage kids to exit their drug life. Willie and George Wilson had helped Artimus write his exit papers.

Artimus' parole officer had learned the word alliteration, and hoped Artimus had some other more saleable skills up his sleeves.

Artimus laughed at that request, saying. "Saleable Skills, indeed."

And then he had plunked down a 'Righteous Resume' of the skills Willie and George had unearthed from his long, life story.

Both Artimus and George had a letter of recommendation in their files thanking them for material help to the police and the families as they figured out how to locate missing people.

Small pants, AKA Heinrich Strauss, awaited trial on drug dealing, kidnapping and human trafficking. His skinny associates were in a jail drug rehab program that was new and very needed.

The three companies involved in the 'Relocation Services' were now shut down. The court had ordered that they first pay retirement, and all benefits to Geneva and other good workers who were caught in the process of closing the companies' underhanded secondary businesses. Geneva's 401K was vested, and now, she could access it without fear of those who were in jail.

Elmore's Vet was sold to a more businesslike veterinarian. Doctor Vanly now attended classes in better business practices, such as keeping track of what his colleagues did while he took care of the cute puppies. His receptionist Charles sat in a prison on a charge of selling drugs, and conspiracy to aid in the kidnapping and selling of humans. Charles was Chuck, the 'boy friend' who had abducted Liza and then met Rosaria in the Tigard bus station.

Out of the three buildings known to belong to Relocation, sixty-three girls and boys were rescued. Many needed long- term psychiatric and health care. This care was also part of the settlement with the companies.

But Officer Reese also learned about other young women and men who had been sold further down the chain. He and Detective Sidney O. Seneca worked with other police departments to investigate new businesses, and hunt for more victims of trafficking up and down the west coast.

Liza's acquaintance, Chuck turned out to be Rylant's son.

Father and son awaited trial in very separate jails.

Corrigan was unable to convince the judge of his Alzheimers diagnosis. His last effort to get at Geneva's papers, threatening Violeta with a gun, made a clear case against him.

Rosaria enrolled at George Fox with little fanfare. The school kept her name out of its warnings to students and parents about travel. She recovered with many long weekends at home with her sister and parents.

The van driver died of his injuries three weeks after rolling his vehicle, but the information he had provided meant the Leapfrog Bus company lost most of its drivers to prison. Its CEO sat in Sheridan prison. Leapfrog's name became synonymous with sleaze, and it, too, was ordered to pay for the recovery and support of its victims.

Once freed of fear for Felipe and Anita's Chevron family, Ancient Nation joined a fix-it-up weekend, filling bullet holes and repainting the station with Felipe, his family and friends.

Geneva Oppenheim returned to Holly Hill, and in court, was able to set out very clearly how she had discovered the plot against children. These days, she often spoke at schools about her experiences in Mittle-Bau Dora and her life as an orphaned survivor after the war.

Doctor Sartan accompanied her on the first few of these school days, but soon realized that Geneva was once again her bright and determined self.

Geneva and Willie returned to their friendship. Geneva came down to the rehearsals of the band but didn't want to be at the concerts with so many people. Crowds brought up too many memories.

The Ancient Nation families attended the Burnside Barn show, along with Captain Reese, Augusto, Camelia and Violeta and even Chef Judson.

Toward the evening's end, Sidney could be seen on crutches dancing in a circle around a laughing Arwain, while Claudia and Javier urged him on.

By closing time, the ticket office announced that Ancient Nations had sold out the Burnside Barns for the next six Fridays.

As the lights were about to go out in the Barns, Glyn and Violeta found Willie, asleep on a couch in one of the lounges. Henry sat nearby, smiling and reading a booklet about how to use the Square to take credit card payment from his taxi customers.

ACKNOWLEDGEMENTS

Thank you to the Truckers Against Trafficking for your efforts on behalf of stolen and trafficked human beings. Your trainings of other truckers for how to spot trafficking and how to involve the law in stopping it are a light in the deep darkness that is this evil trade.

Thank you to my family for inspiring the idea that old people and young – a grandmother and her grandchildren might work together to solve mysteries and create a safer world.

The characters herein, and their actions are fiction, but of course, they are based on the personalities, delights and foibles of people I know. So, readers who know me, start guessing . . . Maybe someone in here is partly you.

WORKING TO STOP HUMAN TRAFFICKING

Sheriff Mendez mentions that he has had calls from Truckers Against Trafficking. Here is a description of their work.

Truckers Against Trafficking (TAT) began in 2011. Between its beginning and December 2019, 2,496 calls to the hotline had been made about 663 incidences of human trafficking. 1,230 victims were involved. All 50 state trucking associations have now partnered with TAT and they are beginning work with the provinces of Canada.

Anyone can join in the fight against human trafficking. If you are in the United States and believe someone may be a victim of human trafficking, call the 24-hour National Human Trafficking Hotline at 1-888-373-7888 or report an emergency to law enforcement by calling 911.

Charity Navigator evaluates non-profits working against human trafficking. Here is a link to their work: https://www.charitynavigator. org/index.cfm. You can donate toward their mission or become a volunteer.

What you can do for yourself and your neighbors: Be alert and aware of what is happening around you. Keep yourself safe and be willing to call for help if you believe someone is being forced to work without freedom to leave their workplace or their job.

ABOUT THE AUTHOR

Rae Richen is author of adventures for adults and young adults, of romantic suspense and of the newest Glyn Jones and Grandma Willie mystery series. Join Rae Richen as we explore fear and power, greed and human need in short stories and novels, articles, interviews, and essays.

Using family relationships and the backdrop of historical events, Rae Richen writes to bring focus to the themes that drive our human race. The characters in these stories face a confusing world of hypocrisy with courageous honesty. The humor, friendships, and caring they bring to these situations help them forge new solutions to age-old problems.

Learn more about this author at www.raerichen.com or contact her at rae@raerichen.com .

ALSO BY RAE RICHEN

Uncharted Territory – a father-son adventure in the mountains and in learning to accept and love, in spite of the fragility of life.

Scapegoat: The Price of Freedom – a teen and his friends struggle with a culture of easy accusation during the McCarthy Anti-Communist era.

Scapegoat: The Hounded – after September 11, 2001, a grandfather and grandson work to create safety and freedom for friends falsely accused of treason.

In Concert – A novel of suspense and romance when a famous musician is stalked by a vicious man who wants to own her and her son. Visit www.raerichen.com/in-concert and read the first chapter for free.

Frozen Trust – a novel of espionage and romance within the United States during World War II. Visit www.raerichen.com/frozen-trust and read the first chapter for free.

Sentinels of Solitude – a novel of suspense and love during a murderous land grab in the lush Willamette Valley of Oregon.

A Fool's Gold, a novel of treachery and romance in the Rocky Mountains of Colorado during the mining fever of the 1880s.

Those Who Curse You – Inner city architect Sarah Rohann takes on four street kids as apprentices creating an extraordinary makeshift family. But when Kevin, the newest apprentice, mysteriously disappears, Sarah's world is shaken.

Visit www.raerichen.com/books for more information.

www.ingramcontent.com/pod-product-compliance
Lightning Source LLC
Chambersburg PA
CBHW061527210726
48287CB00006B/1864